CORPSE DIPLOMATIQUE

"Like [a] top vacation on [the] Riviera—good!"
—*Saturday Review of Literature*

Other Delano Ames Mysteries from
Perennial Library:

CORPSE
DIPLOMATIQUE

DELANO
AMES

PERENNIAL LIBRARY
Harper & Row, Publishers
New York, Cambridge, Philadelphia, San Francisco
London, Mexico City, São Paulo, Sydney

The characters in this novel are entirely imaginary and have no relation to any living person

A hardcover edition of this book was originally published in England by Hodder & Staughton. It is here reprinted by arrangement.

CORPSE DIPLOMATIQUE. Copyright 1950 by Delano Ames. All rights reserved. Printed in the United States of America. No part of this book may be used or reproduced in any manner whatsoever without written permission except in the case of brief quotations embodied in critical articles and reviews. For information address Harper & Row, Publishers, Inc., 10 East 53rd Street, New York, N.Y. 10022. Published simultaneously in Canada by Fitzhenry & Whiteside Limited, Toronto.

First PERENNIAL LIBRARY edition published 1983.

Library of Congress Cataloging in Publication Data

Ames, Delano, 1906–
    Corpse diplomatique.

    (Perennial library ; P637)
    I. Title.
PR6001.M54C6 1983   813'.54   82-48239
ISBN 0-06-080637-0 (pbk.)

83 84 85 86 10 9 8 7 6 5 4 3 2 1

To
KATE

Chapter

I

DAGOBERT HAD IN MIND A LONELY VILLAGE PERCHED ON a rocky hillside in the Basses-Alpes where we could study Provençal, so we went to the Hotel Negresco on the Promenade des Anglais.

In this way we got our names in the *Riviera-Gazette* among recent arrivals in Nice. We were listed with the King of Sweden, Mrs. Stuyvesant Reinlander III of Philadelphia and someone called S.A.Bao U. I wasn't dressed for it, but it was pleasant while it lasted.

" It's the only place I could think of," Dagobert apologised as he put his mackintosh and hobnailed boots in the vast Louis Quinze wardrobe. " It's nice and central," he added.

" Yes, I noticed the police station around the corner. Still they won't present the bill for a week, probably."

" It's all local colour," he said cheerfully. " S.A.Bao U. will be useful when we visit Siam, or would it be Burma ? . . . I wonder what the inside of a French police station looks like."

" Dagobert," I asked suddenly, " did we buy return tickets ? "

He removed the belt from his corduroy trousers and shook out his grey flannel suit which had been rolled up in the rucksack.

" I suppose one changes for dinner," he said. " Well, in a way no. It seemed such a lot to spend all at once. You worry too much about essentials, Jane."

I didn't say " somebody has to," though the thought

did cross my mind. I live with Dagobert—in fact he is my husband—and I have learned that discussions beginning in this way never get anywhere. He simply agrees with you and a few minutes later you find you're talking excitedly about something else—such as going to Nice.

Only two nights ago I had embarked upon one of those practical conversations. We were having a quiet pint at the Freemasons' Arms, around the corner from us in Hampstead, when I made a passing allusion to a letter from one Bertram Jennings offering Dagobert a job in the advertising department of Delish-O-Vite.

Dagobert has managed to keep very busy since we were married. He has, for example, badly shaken the musical world with his brochure on Adam de la Halle. He has considerably complicated the accepted theory about the Mayan system of mathematical notation. Once he even made a guinea, for a receipe for dandelion soufflé in *Woman's Friend*.

But as he has never dabbled in steady work, I lightly touched upon the subject-matter of Bertram Jennings' letter, suggesting that a job might make an interesting diversion.

He was delighted to discuss it. Could he wear a bowler? He'd always wanted to wear a bowler. He even ordered a glass of Delish-O-Vite and experimented. With ice and a double rum it was quite drinkable.

" Bertram," he said, returning to his pint. " You're quite right, Jane. D'you know it's a scandalous thing, but there's not a decent English translation of Bertran de Born."

For a moment I thought it was delayed action from the Delish-O-Vite, but I saw the far-away look in his eye and stirred uncomfortably. Instead of talking about something else I foolishly said :

" Who is Bertran de Born ? "

He looked distressed at the question and glanced round for fear someone had heard me.

" Don't say things like that in the Freemason's Arms," he said. " The place is crawling with intelligentsia. It gives such a bad impression."

" Oh, you mean *the* Bertran de Born ! " I corrected myself. " The one we ran into in the Café Royal that time."

Dagobert ordered two more pints. " He died in 1215," he explained hastily. " He was a troubadour and one of the most important poets of the twelfth century. Dante praised him highly, and on the whole one must agree · with Dante. Don't you think ? " He brought the barmaid graciously into the conversation.

A horse called Dante had come in second in the three-thirty at Gatwick that afternoon and one topic led to another. But the damage had been done. Though I didn't quite know what was coming, I knew it wasn't going to be a job in the advertisement department of Delish-O-Vite. On the way home Dagobert said thoughtfully :

" The chief difficulty is that he wrote in Provençal."

" Isn't there a place called Provence ? With Aix in it ? "

I had recently studied an article in Vogue about Aix and its Casino and I felt I was sowing the seeds rather cunningly. I will never learn about Dagobert.

Twenty-four hours later we were on our way to a place called Tourette-en-Provence, which Baedeker describes as a *curieux spécimen* of ancient fortified village, with narrow, vaulted streets, picturesque, but " *d'aspect sordide et misérable.*" We had a tricky arrangement with the Bank Manager, rucksacks, a London Library copy of Bertran de Born and two (single) tickets as far as Nice.

Dagobert had also brought along my typewriter, feeling that I should be glad of some occupation while he

chatted with the local herdsmen in the language of
Bertran de Born. There was, he said, always a market
for books with such catchy titles as " Off the Beaten
Track in Haute-Provence." Or, if I preferred, I could
begin my novel—something earthy and full of primitive
passions with the Mistral running through it.

One would live simply, rising at dawn with the peasants,
living frugally on a handful of olives, a little goat's cheese
and cornmeal, wearing blue jeans and rope-soled sandals,
getting sun-tanned and healthy and spending practically
nothing. In brief, the prospect sounded thoroughly
depressing.

Reality, however, is never so grim as anticipation, and
when I had finished bathing in the deep marble pool of
our Second Empire bathroom I felt more able to face
the future. While I was standing in front of the tall
gilt mirrors wondering what to do about my one afternoon dress and hoping I shouldn't meet Mrs. S. Reinlander III, Dagobert came in and announced that the
bus for Tourette-en-Provence left at five-thirty the next
morning. He suggested a quiet evening with a stroll
along the Promenade and perhaps a modest aperitif in
one of the smaller cafés before dinner. He would wait
for me in the lobby below.

He was not in the lobby half an hour later when I
went down, but I had one of those minor adventures
which do so much to restore a woman's self-confidence.
I was drifting vaguely around trying to convey the impression that I lived here when a voice just behind me
murmured something I didn't quite catch.

Startled, I turned and said : " I beg your pardon."

A man in a leather arm-chair beside a potted palm was
contemplating me earnestly. It was a long, speculative
stare which so engrossed him that he forgot to stand up.

" I said," he explained with a hopeful smile, " *Mademoiselle est charmante.*"

I looked around for a moment and then, with a becoming blush, was forced to the conclusion he meant me. I smiled nervously, muttered " How nice of you," and fled. In one of the lobby mirrors I caught a glimpse of him. He had risen to his full height of about five feet two and was watching me with an air of indecision.

He was a man of about forty, dark, plumpish and slightly bald. He looked very smart in his blue and white *suéde* sandals, his faultless beige flannels and his pale blue neatly-waisted yachting jacket with the green orchid in the buttonhole. He was the kind of man I always find myself getting involved with at cocktail parties and literary gatherings. They tell me, generally in broken English, about their wives, show me pictures of their children and ask is it true that Englishmen do not understand about love ? If there is dancing I always have one as a partner. They come up to my shoulder, breathe heavily down my neck and do complicated steps which I can't follow. To be quite honest, I have a slight weakness for the type.

It would, however, have been too complicated had I turned up with an admirer in tow. I therefore swept with dignity through the first door I saw.

It led into the dining-room, where forty or fifty waiters stood guard over half that number of tables which gleamed with silver and shone with starched linen. Though no one had yet begun to dine, the head waiter took my precipitous entrance in his stride and welcomed me as though I'd been expected. I explained that I was looking for my husband.

" Mr. Brown," he said, " is taking an aperitif on the terrace. If madam will allow me to show her the way."

I followed him through further doors which led out on to the terrace, wondering how he knew Dagobert's name. I caught one shattering glimpse of the bill of fare in his hand ; the soup, I think, ran into four figures.

I found Dagobert sitting under a striped umbrella, sipping a *Noilly Prat*. He looked as though he owned the place. He stood up and held my chair for me. He was wearing a beret I'd forgotten he had. A copy of a French Communist newspaper was folded beside his saucer and he had bought a packet of Gauloises cigarettes. He gesticulated in a very Latin way as he asked the waiter to bring me a *Dubonnet*. He looked essentially, unmistakably English. I'd never noticed it before.

" One could be quite comfortable here," he said, handing me the salted almonds. " Or do you find the atmosphere uncongenial to work ? "

" I don't want to seem mean-spirited," I said, accepting the almonds, " but are these thrown in ? "

Properly he ignored the question. " We could probably persuade the management to provide a small table for your typewriter on our private balcony," he said. " If you feel the place really inspires you, I could doubtless take lessons in Provençal at the Universal School of Languages. How did you think of starting your novel ? "

" I haven't thought."

" You should," he said, sweeping the luxurious appointments of the terrace with an appreciative eye. " One has to pay for this sort of thing. Couldn't it begin right here with . . . let's see . . . with what ? "

He paused, frowning. I drank my *Dubonnet* and thought of other things. Dagobert is always thinking of ways for *me* to begin a novel. He has the mistaken impression that I am happier when occupied.

The sun was setting in the hills behind us somewhere and the bay had gone pink and blue; the water was so smooth and nebulous that you couldn't tell where it left off and the sky began. I continued to sip my *Dubonnet* and watch the frocks along the Promenade go by.

Gradually I became aware of a familiar face above the

shrubbery which divided the Negresco terrace from the pavement. It regarded me interrogatively. Where, the dark, reproachful eyes seemed to say, had I gone so suddenly ? My admirer had caught up with me again.

I looked away, feeling foolish, only to realise that he was now making his way towards the deserted table just beside our own. Dagobert, too, had noticed him. He came out of his brood suddenly.

" Say, for instance," he nodded towards the new-comer, " that man suddenly fell dead."

Dagobert does not always realise how far his voice carries. My friend stopped short in his tracks and looked acutely uncomfortable. I smiled at him vaguely, handed Dagobert the dish of olives and tried to change the subject. Meanwhile a waiter had installed him at the table beside us. He ordered black coffee and unfolded a newspaper.

" There is a knife in his back," Dagobert said.

I heard the newspaper beside me rustle. I hastily finished my *Dubonnet* and gathered up my handbag.

" There were," I said in a discreet whisper, " two or three restaurants near the railway station where they seemed to have meals for around two hundred francs."

" I rather thought a dozen oysters and the *Queues d'écrevisses à la Nantua.*"

" There's no reason why you shouldn't think of them."

" All right—half a dozen," he compromised, signalling for the waiter.

The waiter arrived and he ordered a *Pernod* and an *Amer Picon.* " You don't like the knife," he said. " I'm only trying to help."

" About dinner," I said.

" I have it ! His coffee's poisoned."

I didn't dare look, but I'm certain our neighbour suddenly spilled the coffee he had just raised to his lips. I heard his cup clatter back on to the saucer and a moment later he called the waiter and ordered a whisky and soda.

" You were mentioning the crayfish," Dagobert said. " The *Máitre d'Hotel* tells me he has a very decent *Bâtard-Montrachet* which would go nicely. Tentatively, I've ordered a bottle of 1933 *Charmes Chambertin* to follow, if that suits you."

" Would there be anything to eat with it ? " I asked, getting carried away in spite of native caution. A night and a day in a third-class French train with a stale ham sandwich and an orange lent the conversation an air of fantasy.

While Dagobert explained how he and the head waiter had reached friendly agreement on Capon *en pâte belle aurore* I forgot my admirer, though once I caught a glimpse of him stroking his butterfly moustache and studying me. He glanced at Dagobert, sighed and re-turned—with reluctance, I thought—to his newspaper.

" Is that man annoying you ? " Dagobert asked.

" On the contrary."

" I was afraid of that." Dagobert relaxed. " Then there's something the chef rather prides himself on. You take hearts of artichokes, marinade them in sour cream, rosemary, thyme and bay leaves, flank them with asparagus tips and drench the dish with Normandy butter."

" Do we have a pudding ? " I asked. " Or do we cut our losses there ? "

The *Pernod* and the *Amer Picon* had arrived and the waiter had thoughtfully brought a dish of potato chips. An almost full moon rose and hung like a Japanese lantern behind Cap Ferrat. Along the coast the lights went on one by one and the Corniche roads across the mountains towards Monte Carlo wore a string of luminous pearls.

" The setting would be good," Dagobert said, breaking

off to give his full attention to the Arab carpet-seller who was spreading out his wares at our feet.

For the next five minutes there was a violent argument. Dagobert talking in a mixture of French and Provençal, the Arab in English. I thought for a moment there were going to be blows, but it ended with an amical exchange of cigarettes and handshakes. The Arab was to call on us next time he was in Hampstead and Dagobert had two or three interesting addresses in the Kasbah in Tunis. We also now owned a small Oriental prayer rug.

" Of course it's obvious," Dagobert said as the Arab proceeded towards the next table. " He's not an Arab at all. It's a disguise. Suddenly from under his pile of carpets he whips out a gun— and bang ! "

I was covertly watching our neighbour while Dagobert spoke. A subtle change had come over him during the past few minutes. Either he had become discouraged, or in the gathering darkness my charms had waned. Truth forces me to confess that he had not glanced in my direction for ten minutes. I was feeling a little hurt by such inconstancy.

I saw that he was deep in his newspaper and that something in it absorbed his entire attention. It may have been a trick of the artificial light, but there were deep shadows under his eyes and the thin line of his moustache twitched occasionally. While he read he had absentmindedly pulled the green orchid in his buttonhole to shreds.

He came to only as Dagobert pronounced the word, " Bang." He leapt out of his seat. He relaxed again immediately, but as he gulped down his whisky his hands were shaking.

To my surprise Dagobert tactfully changed the subject. " There's a *marron soufflé*," he said, reverting to our standard topic, " or they have a thing which is made with whipped cream, crushed strawberries, pistachios and

walnuts soaked in brandy. It's frozen and they pour
kirsch over it."

" We'll need something with kirsch poured over it,"
I said.

" It's called *bombe* something or other."

I heard a sharp scraping sound behind me. Our neighbour had abruptly risen. He had gone so white I thought
he was ill. Without waiting to settle his bill he wove
rapidly through the tables towards the pavement. A
large new limousine of American make was parked in
front of the terrace. A uniformed chauffeur—a small
dark man with impassive features—held the door for
him. He got in and the car drove fifty yards down the
Promenade, stopping in front of the Bar d'Angleterre.

Dagobert had already recovered the newspaper he had
left behind him. " Sorry about the *bombe*," he said
briefly. " It was quite unconscious."

" Do you think we might go in and have it ? " I suggested.

He didn't answer ; he was rapidly skimming the page
that had so gripped my late admirer. I saw him start
slightly. Then, without a word, he handed the paper
across to me.

I know Dagobert's technique when he's trying to work
up my interest. Though it was true that our friend's
behaviour was eccentric, it was also true that Dagobert
was trying to make me start a book. He is ruthless on
these occasions and will seize on the most far-fetched
occurrence to rouse my suspicions, hoping they will turn
into a first chapter. The slight start, the grim expression
on his face as he handed me the paper were familiar.
Being human, however, I looked.

The first thing I saw was a picture of the Duchess of
Windsor watching a Battle of Flowers at Cannes. Beside
that there was something about the dock strike at Bor-
deaux—either it had just been settled or it had got worse

—my French frequently leads me into such uncertainties. I spelled out the item beneath that.

" Incidents mar Presidential Election in Santa Rica ? " I suggested. " Where is Santa Rica ? "

" Not that ! " he said impatiently. " The headline. . . . It's just south of Guatemala," he added in a more conciliatory tone. " Or is it north of Honduras ? There are some rather striking Mayan pyramids there. Let me read it to you."

I handed back the paper gratefully.

" Has Jean Potin returned to the Riviera ? " he translated. " Inspector Lucas of the Police Judiciaire believes this is quite probable and the Brigade Mobile of Nice has been alerted accordingly. Inspector Lucas points out that Jean Potin first met the woman he subsequently murdered in the lobby of a fashionable Nice hotel and that maniacs of Potin's type tend to repeat the pattern of their crimes. Potin, it is believed, has murdered more than one woman by the same method—that is by means of a home-made bomb left in a suitcase under her bed. Though no photograph of Potin is available, he is described as dark, slightly bald, small, running to fat, in his forties, with a taste for imported whisky, a passion for orchids and an unaccountable but fatal attraction for women."

" What time did you say our bus left for Tourette-en-Provence ? " I asked.

Dagobert looked around for the waiter. " Shall we have a drink here," he said, " or go along to the Bar d'Angleterre ? "

" Couldn't we do it after dinner ? " I asked, feeling weak in the knees and distinctly uninterested in food " I mean the Capon and the—er—*bombe* . . . will they keep ? Perhaps I should say that he made an attempt —that is, I think he did—to pick me up in the lobby."

" Splendid ! "

" Some husbands would react differently," I said. Then, suddenly suspicious, I added : " Let me have that newspaper again ! "

While he paid the bill I re-read the paragraph about Jean Potin. It was there all right.

" You don't, I suppose," Dagobert said as he over-tipped the waiter, " know who that man was who bolted without paying his bill ? "

The waiter shrugged indifferently. " Don Diego has an account with us," he said.

Dagobert's face fell. " Don Diego ? " he repeated.

" Don Diego Sebastiano. He's the Vice-Consul in Nice for Santa Rica."

Chapter

2

MY MOST VIVID MEMORY OF THAT NIGHT WAS THE PERFECT
dinner to which Dagobert had given so much thought.
Even in retrospect I like to recall it in detail: the oysters,
the crayfish in their creamy sauce oozing button mush-
rooms, the capon, golden and succulent, bursting with
truffles, the hearts of artichokes, firm and fragrant, the
subtle piquancy of the ice-pudding with its tang of kirsch
counter-balancing the too voluptuous suavity of the
frozen whipped cream.

It was a memorable meal. Of course we didn't have
it, but I like to think about it.

"One can eat at any time," Dagobert said as we
found a corner in the Bar d'Angleterre and ordered a
St. Raphael and a *Byrrh*.

"Yes," I said. "Do you remember we ate only
yesterday?"

"I shall need your co-operation."

"What are we trying to do exactly?"

"Find out what's eating Don Diego."

"Don't keep using the word eating!"

Something was, however, distinctly wrong with the
Vice-Consul for Santa Rica. Though we had installed
ourselves beside him, he had not even observed our
arrival. He was drinking whisky again and had bought
half a dozen newspapers in nearly as many languages.
He was studying the foreign news columns of *The Times*
and biting his fingernails.

"Bad news?" Dagobert asked in French.

Don Diego did not look up.

" *Epouvantable !* " he confirmed with a slight shudder.
" *C'est la fin !* "

" The end of what ? " Dagobert said, startled back into
English.

" Me, probably," Don Diego murmured, switching
mechanically into the same language.

The effort brought him with a start from *The Times*.
He recognised Dagobert without pleasure. He broke
into a slight sweat.

" Look," he pleaded, " my nerves aren't good."

" Yes. Why is that ? "

" I've never done anybody any harm. Not you, anyway," he corrected himself. " I don't even know who
you are. Couldn't we leave it like that ? "

" What are you drinking ? " Dagobert asked.

" Whisky."

Dagobert ordered it. " What's a place like Santa
Rica doing with a Vice-Consul in a place like Nice ? "

" What, indeed ? " Don Diego said gloomily.

" What do you do ? "

" I have a place in the Boulevard Victor Hugo. It
has the Santa Rican flag outside. It's open between
eleven and twelve on the first Thursday of every month.
During that hour I am always there. I open the newspapers to which I subscribe and read the comics. Once
a year I make out an official report : Exports to Santa
Rica, nil ; Imports from Santa Rica, nil ; Visas granted,
nil."

" The work sounds interesting," Dagobert nodded.

" If you needed a secretary," I smiled encouragingly,
remembering that I was supposed to co-operate.

He glanced at me with a flicker of interest, which died
down immediately. " Those days," he said, " are over."
He glanced at his wrist-watch that said eight o'clock.
and added : " Which reminds me . . ."

" Meeting someone ? "

He shrugged. " You know Suzette—at the Brooklyn Bar around the corner ? "

" No."

" Then you're the only man in Nice who doesn't," he sighed tolerantly, finishing off his whisky. " She can wait. She won't, but . . ." He broke off suddenly and an idea, obviously unpleasant, struck him. " How do I know she's not one of them ? "

" One of who ? "

He began to bite his fingernails again. " No, she's too dumb. But they'll probably watch the place."

" Who would watch the place ? "

" *They!* " Don Diego exploded irritably. " How do I know who ? If I did, would I be getting so goddam excited ? Madam," he rose suddenly and bowed with elaborate courtesy in my direction, " *je vous demande mille pardons.* You will please forgive me. Who you are I do not know. May I say that you are very charming and a pleasure to look at ? May I say that you remind me of the first woman I loved. It was at the State Ball when my uncle . . ." He broke off and crossed himself reverently. " Don Filippo Gonzales de la Torreda became President. I do not know her name. Her eyes were your eyes. But, madam, you have a husband who asks many questions—why, I do not know. You have a husband who suddenly says ' Bang ! ' A husband who speaks of knives, and poisoned coffee and of bombs. A husband who makes me very, very nervous."

He broke off to regard Dagobert more closely. His dark eyes were bleary and seemed to have trouble in focusing. I saw he was swaying slightly on his feet. He put a podgy, carefully-manicured hand on Dagobert's shoulder, partly in a sudden surge of affection, partly to steady himself.

" A husband whom I could perhaps learn to love like

a brother," he said, and collapsed back on to the stuffed leather seat.

I thought for a moment he had passed out, but he recovered instantly.

" Madam," he said, " it is a terrible thing to confess : I am intoxicated. I am by nature an abstemious man. I am a man who always has minded his own business. For six years I represent my country in Nice. I live discreetly and soberly. I do no harm. In fact I do nothing. To-day things begin to happen to me. I arrive home this morning and there have been telephone calls for me. Who ? No names left. Why is this ? I go to the café on the corner and think. I drink a whisky. I go home again. A man has called on me. No name. But he tells the concierge he is from Santa Rica. *There are no Santa Ricans in the south of France!* I drink a whisky. I go to luncheon at the Brooklyn Bar. I have *bouillabaisse*. I am half poisoned and am sick in the gentleman's toilet. I walk home. A big limousine comes on to the pavement and I am nearly run over. I drink a whisky. I walk along the Promenade des Anglais, where they are building a block of flats. A brick falls from the scaffolding and misses me by an inch. I drink a whisky. I see on the Negresco terrace a so charming young woman. I approach. Her husband points at me and says, ' That man suddenly falls dead ' ! "

He rose again, supporting himself against the edge of the table. He glanced around him with confidence, like an orator who is aware he is holding his audience. He was, as a matter of fact, holding his audience. Our entire corner of the café was watching with fascination.

" But I do *not* fall dead," he said, waving his left hand and swaying slightly. " That is where they are wrong. I defy them. I laugh in their face. I, Don Diego Sebastiano de la Torreda, Vice-Consul of the ancient republic of Santa Rica, I spit upon them ! "

He let go of the table with his remaining hand and called imperiously : " Garçon ! These are my friends. Their glasses are empty."

To the delight of the company he stumbled and fell flat across the table.   This time he really had passed out.

Dagobert and the waiter—neither of whom shared the general merriment—got him to the door.   While they were getting him into his car I glanced at *The Times'* account of the " incidents " which had marred yesterday's Santa Rican presidential election.

One of them was the assassination of the late President, Don Filippo Gonzales de la Torreda.

Chapter

3

" ONE THING ABOUT A SCENE LIKE THAT," DAGOBERT said as he came back. " It has a sobering effect which enables one to have another drink without ill effect. I thought a *Suze* and a *Cinzano*? " he added, looking round for the waiter.

" Would it be greedy if I had one of those rolls on the counter instead ? "

" If you're not afraid it will spoil your dinner," he said. " Do you think Don Diego will do ? "

" For what purpose ? "

" Chapter One of ' Off the Beaten Track in Haute-Provence '. "

" He's off the beaten track all right. No, on the whole I preferred Jean Potin with his fatal attraction for women."

" So did I," Dagobert confessed, " but we have to take these things as they come. . . . I should, of course, have taken him home, but Juan is very good at such jobs."

" Who's Juan ? "

" Juan Moro, his chauffeur—a pure Mayan Indian, by the way. Face cut out of stone, expressionless, faithful to the death—used to putting the young master to bed. Apparently he does it about once a week."

" Why do we always pick up unlikely drunks ? " I complained.

" Could it be the sort of places we frequent ? . . . If you're dead set against the *Suze* and the *Cinzano* we might as well go round to the Brooklyn Bar."

I rose philosophically. "They serve *bouillabaisse*," I recalled. "It may be poisoned, but at least it's food."

"It would be a shock," Dagobert said thoughtfully as we walked round the corner, "if Don Diego *really* had something to worry about."

"He has," I pointed out practically. "The rival political party in Santa Rica has seized power which means he's out of a job."

"And what a job!" Dagobert said enviously. "No, I mean if someone actually is out for his blood."

I knew what he meant, but I refused to argue on an empty stomach.

"What about ' The Man from Santa Rica ' ?" he said. "I was thinking about him as a potential assassin, but he'd also make a title."

"They might have eggs and bacon," I said.

"I've got it! *Corpse Diplomatique*. Do you spell corps and corpse differently ?"

"No, Dagobert," I said gently. "No."

"Somehow I thought you did," he sighed.

"In many ways I'm looking forward to Tourette-en-Provence."

"Tourette ?" he repeated, recalling the word with an effort. "Yes, of course. The trouble is, Jane, that our drama all takes place in Santa Rica. It seems rather odd coming to the south of France in order to write about a Central American revolution. I've always wanted to see those Mayan pyramids. Mathematically they pose several interesting questions."

"We've already had Mayan mathematics," I reminded him shortly.

"True." He shrugged. "We'd feel awful mugs if we never saw Don Diego again."

I agreed mechanically, though I felt I could easily support that hardship.

We found the Brooklyn Bar all too readily. It was

only a stone's throw from the Premenade des Anglais and its name was outlined in red neon lighting. It was, as Don Diego had suggested, being watched, though not, as far as I could see, by mysterious Santa Ricans.

The American Mediterranean Fleet was in and two very tough-looking Shore Police were leaning casually in the door. From inside came the blare of a wireless and when you entered and got used to the cigarette smoke you could almost see across the room. I clung to Dagobert while we fought our way towards a corner table which had just been vacated, due to the timely arrest of its two former occupants.

" It's cosy," Dagobert shouted as we wedged ourselves in.

" Yes," I shouted back, remembering as though in a vision the vast, cool dining-room of the Negresco.

" I wonder which one is Suzette ? " he yelled.

" Yes, *crêpes suzette*, by all means," I yelled back, no longer caring.

The Brooklyn Bar was long and narrow—at least it was narrow—and at a rough estimate it must have contained the full complement of a medium-sized cruiser. There were also about a dozen young women present, mostly jammed up against the bar, and fighting for—among other things—breathing space.

A young man with a pleasant grin and shrewd brown eyes slouched up to our table and said, " Howdy, folks ? "

He was dressed in a battle jacket and khaki trousers from the pockets of which he never removed his hands.

" I'm Joe," he explained simply, " and I own this joint. I haven't seen you around before, have I ? English ? "

We admitted it.

" I like Limeys," he said. " Always have, for some reason. Now what can I do you for ? " Without removing his hands from his pockets he nudged Dagobert, in case he'd missed it.

" Which one's Suzette ? " Dagobert asked.

Joe glanced at me and then at Dagobert with a faintly worried expression. Without the disarming smile his face was hard and business-like. He was good-looking in a loutish way. His teeth were regular and white and his skin was bronzed by the sun. He was squat in shape and indolent in movement, but he gave an impression of health and vitality.

" Suzette ? " he repeated doubtfully.

" I'd like to meet her—if it could be arranged."

" Yeah—it could be arranged," he said, now avoiding my eye. He spoke out of the corner of his mouth. " Say, why don't you come back later ? "

" You mean without me ? " I suggested gaily.

He grinned. " I guess that's about what I meant," he shrugged good-naturedly. "No—joking aside—what's a nice young guy like. . . . I don't think I got your name."

" Brown."

" Brown, with a nice young wife . . . are you the wife ? "

" I am."

" There you are," he said. " Just like I was saying. No, you don't want to get mixed up with that kind of stuff. I don't like to see it—not in my bar. Say, how long are you stopping in Nice ? "

" What kind of stuff ? " Dagobert asked, not unnaturally interested.

Joe looked pained at the question. For the first time he removed a hand from his pocket. " *You* know," he drawled, jerking a thumb over his shoulder. " That's Suzette over there—the little red-head, and boy ! as far as I'm concerned you can have it ! "

Suzette was at the table opposite, sitting with one leg negligently over the knees of a Marine sergeant who had gone to sleep. She was small and shapely and had flaming red hair which fell in a page-boy bob around her shoulders. She wore cream satin slacks, high-heeled gold slippers and a knitted emerald green sweater. She looked bored and rather cross. There was a bad-tempered pout on her heavily-smeared lips and her small, sharp eyes were vicious.

It struck me that probably no one had offered her any dinner.

" Do you want it ? " Joe grunted.

Dagobert nodded. " I hate to be the only man in Nice who doesn't know her," he explained to me.

Joe made a sound which was half whistle, half hiss. Suzette glanced up like a dog aroused by a familiar call. Her face became animated suddenly and she looked quite seductive. She removed her leg from the Marine's knees and joined us. She snuggled up to Joe kittenishly and rubbed her cheek against his arm. Whether it was a professional gesture or affection, I couldn't tell. In either case, it left Joe unmoved. He released himself from her entwining arm with an air of distaste.

" These people want to meet you—for some reason," he said.

She gave me a brief, contemptuous stare and then studied Dagobert, who had risen, from head to foot.

" Limey ? " she said.

Joe nodded. " Yeah."

" Okay, okay," she cooed forgivingly. " He's kinda cute, at that." She sidled up to Dagobert, stroking the lapels of his flannel jacket. " You wanna dance, honey boy ? "

" I was just going to suggest it,". Dagobert said, looking silly.

He glanced at me desperately, but I refused to come to his rescue. It was not until ten or fifteen minutes later that I began to wonder if I'd been meant to.

Joe, clicking his tongue with disapproval, watched them disappear into the scrum. " I still don't get it." He shook his head. " The more I see of human nature in this place, the less I understand it."

" Do you know Don Diego Sebastiano ? " I asked.

" Sure I know him," Joe answered briefly. " Shall I get you something to drink ? "

" I thought I saw some food going past a minute ago."

" Anything you like," he said. " Steak and chips ? Ham and eggs ? Chicken and waffles ? Hamburger and fried onions ? Just like home."

" I'll have that," I said dreamily. " And a glass of iced water."

" See you later," he drawled pleasantly, slouching off to greet a young woman who had come in a few minutes ago and had ventured only a step or two inside the door.

I had noticed her when she first entered and wondered what she was doing here. From her clothes I was certain she was American. The small hat on the back of her head, the seersucker suit and the white buckskin loafers were almost uniform this season with the more earnest sort of young American tourist. She looked about seventeen and was painfully shy.

She had arrived while Suzette was pawing Joe and I had noticed her otherwise expressionless face go white with distaste. Since then she had kept her eyes lowered, holding her thin body taut and distant from the milling crowd of sailors around her. Not one of them had tried to speak to her.

She thawed slightly as Joe greeted her with his easy good humour and spoke to him timidly. In the racket I couldn't hear her voice. She opened her handbag and rustled among its contents. Joe walked out into the street with her and a moment later returned by himself.

I, meanwhile, had been less successful in keeping myself to myself. The Marine sergeant at the table opposite had suddenly come to life, searched in vain for Suzette, and spotted me instead. He made his way unsteadily across the intervening space and said :

" How about it, babe ? "

" How about what ? "

" How about a bit of *parlez-voo*. *Voulez-voo* . . . jeeze, this language ! You know."

" I'm afraid I don't."

" Sure you do. You a friend of Suzette ? I mean doing anything, huh ? "

" Yes, I'm waiting for my husband and for something to eat. Chiefly the latter."

" Come again," he said, looking puzzled.

A waiter, sent by Joe, arrived at that moment with a plate. On the plate I recognised a very stale ham sandwich and an orange.

" Joe says to tell you," he apologised, " that the Marines have eaten us right out and will this do ? "

" Wozzat about the Marines ? " my new friend demanded belligerently.

I fell upon the food without argument. It was the best ham sandwich and orange I had seen since—I think—Lyons. Dagobert rejoined me just as I'd finished the sandwich and was wondering how to get another. He looked hot, but pleased with himself.

" I've found out some fascinating things," he whispered as he slipped in beside me.

" Who is this guy ? " demanded the Marine whom I had temporarily forgotten.

He had wedged himself in on the other s'de of me and dropped off to sleep again. I introduced him. His name was, I believe, Buckshot, and he came from Columbus, Ohio. He shook hands very formally with Dagobert, and when he learned that we had once motored through Columbus, Ohio, he shook hands all over again with both of us. There were two other Marines somewhere around, also from Columbus, Ohio, whom he'd very much like us to meet.

While he went to find them I said to Dagobert: "What fascinating things ? "

" About Don Diego."

" Oh," I said.   " If that bus for Tourette-en-Provence leaves at five-thirty in the morning . . ."

" Suzette doesn't think we shall see him again either."

" No, Dagobert."   I shook my head.   " It sounds very sinister the way you put it, but have you noticed what's just come in ? "

He followed my glance.   The Vice-Consul of Santa Rica stood in the door, looking sober, self-possessed and clear-eyed.   He had obviously had a bath, a shave, changed his clothes and stuck a fresh orchid in his button-hole.   He saw us and bowed politely.

Before we had recovered from our admiration for his recuperative powers, Buckshot was back again, accompanied by the two Marines from Columbus, Ohio.   They looked about sixteen years old.

The events of the next few minutes—like those of the remainder of that evening—remain slightly confused in my mind.   We were shaking hands all round when Buck-shot suddenly saw Don Diego Sebastiano.   The sight recalled unpleasant associations to his mind.   He had, it seemed, been in the Brooklyn Bar at luncheon and, as he said, " doing all right with that cute little red-head " when Don Diego arrived.   There had been un-pleasantness, in the course of which Suzette had had her jumper torn and Buckshot had been removed by the Shore Police.   He had been brooding over the incident ever since and now I saw his jaw harden.

" I'm gonna get that dago ! " he said.

His two companions had been in other ports with their fellow townsman.   They grabbed him just as he lurched into action, aided by Dagobert and a watchful Joe.   We found ourselves a moment later outside the Brooklyn Bar, piling into a taxi, watched by the imperturbable Juan at the wheel of the large limousine bearing the plate C.D. I don't quite know what Dagobert and I were doing there, but apparently we were about to see the town. At the moment it seemed an excellent plan.

I remember Joe shoving a handful of business cards at Dagobert and asking us to come back again to-morrow, Something to do with Black Market financial transactions, I think. I remember Dagobert seemed to be very excited about it. Joe explained that he gave better rates than any other reputable banker in Nice for dollars, pounds, escudos, rubles, "anything you got." International—that's what the Brooklyn was.

"Why, only this morning," he said, "I had a guy in here changing Santa Rican pesos."

Chapter

4

I AM A LITTLE HAZY ABOUT THE CHRONOLOGY OF THE
rest of that evening. Here and there fragmentary impressions remain, but whether we went to Juan-les-Pins
after we went to Monte Carlo or whether it was the other
way around, I'm not sure. We seemed to meet a lot of
interesting people of various nationalities, and sometimes our group changed in constitution. At one period
there were half a dozen sailors—French, I think—with
us ; I remember this because someone tried to tell them
the joke about *matelots* and *matelas*, and they couldn't
grasp it.

At other times we rubbed shoulders with high society ;
I distinctly remember evening dresses and dinner jackets
somewhere, and dancing with a Danish count who knew
Mrs. Reinlander and told me about bacon exports. As
a compatriot I met during the course of the evening
succinctly put it : " It isn't much like Huddersfield, is
it ? " We agreed that it made a nice change.

Buckshot and his two marines were charming, and
remained with us until the end. Within an hour Dagobert had practically joined the American Marines, the
alternative being that they desert and come to Tourette-
en-Provence with us.

They were very sympathetic and helpful about my
novel—all were great readers and recommended plenty
of blood and action. Buckshot was convinced that the
answer lay in having someone strangle Don Diego Sebastiano, and volunteered to do it himself. His companions

inclined towards the opinion that Joe should be the
victim. He had done them dirt in the matter of a
certain fifty bucks they'd changed with him. In one
bistro our story confidence became so animated we were
asked to leave.

That was on the way to Monte Carlo. We liked the
flood-lit flower beds outside the Casino, but inside we
found the atmosphere depressing. Neither Dagobert nor
Buckshot felt really at home in the cathedral-like gloom
of the *Salons Privés* where the slightest sound above a
whisper attracted a battery of disapproving eyes. They
left after a modest flutter which didn't affect the bank
much one way or another, while the two Marines and I
remained for a while.

I was spellbound by the solemnity of the scene.
Around such green baize tables I could picture such
haggard faces signing historic documents. Whenever the
little ivory ball settled with a click in its groove I felt
my heart stop beating, as though something of epoch-
making importance had happened. It was most awe-
inspiring. In my *naïveté* I had always somehow imagined
that roulette at Monte Carlo was a kind of game.

Most of the serious players were women of about
eighty in home-made hats who took notes of every
number as it turned up, and then made complicated
mathematical computations.

But one I noticed especially because she was only
about fifty, and she gambled with a kind of fevered
insouciance which gave you the impression that she was
enjoying herself. She was dressed in a pre-war black
lace evening gown and her fat fingers, flashing with
diamonds, looked as though they spent most of the time
in dish-water. In one turn of the wheel she won five
thousand francs, and she broke all the rules by emitting
a small squeal of delight and turning round to talk
volubly in French to the man behind her.

I had been certain her companion was English until he answered her in French as fluent as her own. He was younger than she, and apparently from a different social class. He was tall and very handsome in a distinguished, rather old-fashioned way. I immediately thought of ex-cavalry officer.

It is odd how vividly he struck me then. I think it was because, as he removed his eye-glass, I saw that he had a black eye—an incongruous touch. I watched them leave the tables and go towards the adjoining dining-room, where a moment later she was almost up to her elbows in a dish of *moules à la marinière*. She was sucking each mussel shell with a relish that made her escort wince, and my own mouth water.

I found Dagobert and Buckshot having a riotous time with the fruit machines in the Casino lobby. Dagobert had won eleven francs and they were debating whether to continue with the luck running their way or to break off and invest their winnings towards a drink. I remembered that we had kept the taxi waiting. We all bought coloured picture post cards of the Casino and addressed them to friends in Columbus, Ohio.

We found Nice—that is to say, it was the taxi-driver actually who found Nice again—what I mean is, we found it strangely quiet. Even the Brooklyn Bar had turned out its neon sign. We discovered a café on the old port, however, and held a conference on the subject of what to do next. The café had the fascinating name of the Cave de Bacchus and Dagobert had a long conversation with the owner in Provençal, that is, he was almost sure it was Provençal.

It was in the Cave de Bacchus, after I had rejected a proposition to go moonlight bathing, that Dagobert unhappily introduced our companions to the game he had just invented.

The principle was the same as thinking of poets starting with A. Someone says " Matthew Arnold," then the next player says, " Auden," the next " Alfred Austin," and so on, until someone fails. When the A's are exhausted you begin on Blake, Browning and George Barker.

Dagobert's game was equally simple. You ordered drinks starting with A. Player Number One had Anisette. The man on the right ordered, say, Absinthe, then Avocat, then Arrack, and so forth until no one could remember any more beginning with A. The loser had to have a glass of beer. Then you passed on to Benedictine, Brandy, Burgundy, etc., etc.

In a place like the Cave de Bacchus which prided itself on its stock the game had great educational scope, and Buckshot and his two shipmates took to it—if I may use a most inappropriate metaphor—like ducks to water. We had arrived at such esoteric things as Fernet Branca and Framboise when the management suggested that the Cotton Club was still open.

I rather think we lost Buckshot and the other two somewhere between the Cave de Bacchus and the Cotton Club. The Cotton Club had an indirect but important bearing on our immediate future because it was there we met Iris Makepeace.

When I first saw her she was dancing with a man who reminded me of the film actor Jean Gabin and whose name turned out to be Dieudonné Dompierre. They danced together—the cliché is unavoidable—as though they were made for each other. Her fair, smooth head came up to his shoulder and when she rested her cheek there she kept her eyes half closed. He gripped her hand hard and there was a set grim look on his face.

When the music stopped they released each other and stood without clapping, without expression, dazed, unaware of their surroundings, vaguely miserable. He murmured something monosyllabic in her ear, and she shook her head quickly ; she had gone deathly pale.

I retired to repair the ravages of the past few hours, and while I was sitting pessimistically in front of the mirror in the cloakroom she burst in behind me. She was laughing wildly, but when she saw me she made an effort to control herself.

" Sorry ; I didn't know anyone was here."

Her voice was attractive, like the rest of her, soft, pretty, with something uncertain about it which warned me to clear out as quickly as possible. I recognised the symptoms. Before I could escape she had begun to cry.

I said awkwardly, " Is there anything I can do ? "

" Yes ! " she said unexpectedly. " Turn me over your knee and give me a good thrashing."

" Do you need one ? "

" Dieudonné ! " she said. " Dieudonné . . . it means God-given, doesn't it ? That's what God, at this particular juncture, chose to give me ! " Disconcertingly she began to laugh again.

I edged towards the door. " My husband . . ." I murmured, unable to think of any better exit line.

"Is he the tall, nice-looking one ? " she said. "With sandy hair and the quizzical smile ? "

"It might be," I admitted. "Though I'd hate to say it to his face."

She had moistened her forefinger and was smoothing her eyebrows. " Have you been here all evening ? "

" Just arrived," I said, reflecting that Dagobert had made a greater impression than I had.

" I thought I hadn't seen him before," she nodded. "I—I haven't been in a very observant mood to-night." She slumped down on to the chair I had vacated and buried her face in her hands. " Oh, Lord ! Dear Lord ! " she whispered. " What shall I do ? "

Feeling the question was not addressed to me, I turned the door handle. She continued in a smothered sob :

"Don't ever let him go to the ends of the earth ! Or if you do—for God's sake *go with him.*"

"I'll keep that in mind," I nodded uncomfortably, wondering what we were talking about. "Who? Where?"

"Your husband."

"Oh."

"To places—like Central America."

There was a stool beside the door and I sat down on it abruptly.

"What kind of places in Central America?"

Even before she answered I knew what she was going to say. Our conversation had from the beginning been so implausible that this final touch of absurdity seemed almost inevitable.

"Like Santa Rica," she said.

She pushed the hair out of her face and stared at me appealingly. "Please," she added brokenly, "would you mind not talking about it?"

"I'd love not talking about it," I said fervently.

"One mustn't spoil the evening, must one?" she said brightly. "Not the *last* evening. That wouldn't be fair ! One comes to night clubs to dance and be gay and drink champagne."

She dabbed powder on her face as she spoke and her mouth quivered in a smile. Here eyes were an attractive light brown flecked with gold, slightly tragic at the moment. For some reason I suddenly suspected that they were watching their own effect in the mirror as she spoke. This gave the forced gaiety a faintly theatrical effect, and made me wonder if she might not be unconsciously putting on an act—not, of course, that dramatising your emotions means they aren't genuine.

"I love Nice, don't you?" she went on in a burst of

animation. " Where are you staying ? We're staying
. . . I'm staying at the Pension Victoria, which is frightfully reasonable—if that sort of thing interests you—
and bang on the Promenade. It's rather a find. That
is if you're looking for a place."

I suddenly remembered that Dagobert had discussed
with the proprietor a room over the Cave de Bacchus
with an arresting view of the cranes with which they
unloaded coal, and I made a mental note of the Pension
Victoria.

" You know the Brooklyn Bar—that dreadful place,"
she explained. " The Victoria's just round the corner.
It's my first time on the Riviera. We always went to
Switzerland. I adore it. It's been the grandest holiday
I've ever had. I "—the golden brown eyes filled with
tears—" I wouldn't have missed it for all the world."

We didn't stay long at the Cotton Club. Dance music
always makes Dagobert unhappy, and I'd had enough
unhappiness for the moment. Besides, we both suddenly
realised we had mislaid the Marines. We ran them to
earth near the railway station. They were drinking beer
thoughtfully and trying to remember drinks starting
with Z.

We got back to the Negresco about fifteen minutes
after the bus for Tourette-en-Provence had gone.

Chapter

5

IT IS FRIGHTENING HOW ADAPTABLE ONE IS. AFTER A
week of the Pension Victoria the chief difference between
life in Nice and in Hampstead was that we were on
the twenty-two bus route instead of the twenty-four.
The weather and Mrs. Andrioli's cooking were better, of
course, and we heard more English spoken, but we immediately settled down into a routine not unlike that at
home.

I like routine, and with Dagobert I lead a quiet, regular
life often for days at a time. We would ring for breakfast
at about nine, and if we were feeling energetic have it on
the balcony overlooking Cap d'Antibes and the buses
going to Cannes. I would read yesterday's Continental
Daily Mail while Dagobert did his Universal School Exer-
cises in Provençal. At eleven-thirty we'd go swimming
and return in time for luncheon. After that a short siesta,
tea and a stroll down the Promenade. Then an aperitif
somewhere and dinner, with coffee in the drawing-room,
from which we were generally driven to bed or to the
Municipal Casino by fellow guests who had beaten us
to the chairs which commanded the wireless.

In between times I kept beginning my novel, and
Dagobert got on with his studies and research—I think
it was into perfumery that first week.

He wasn't very helpful about my novel, in spite of
what he persisted in calling the " fascinating potenti-
alities " of our first night in Nice. He had, I think,
secretly been hoping for something appalling to happen

to Don Diego Sebastiano, but since Don Diego was still very much the man about town—we saw him occasionally on the Negresco terrace, or lunching with Suzette in the Brooklyn Bar, plainly in the best of spirits—Dagobert's interest had died down. Apparently, Don Diego had not even been relieved of his job at the Santa Rican Consulate. According to Joe, this seemed to worry Don Diego almost more than his first certainty that he would get the sack.

The book I kept beginning was called *Rue—With a Difference*, a title from, of course, "Hamlet," which seemed to suggest a theme, though gazing from my window over the Promenade I couldn't quite think what theme. I have a naïve theory about writing books. The theory is that you have only to look about, take a sympathetic and imaginative interest in the people around you, describe them as well as you can and record simply and honestly what they do and say.

This system means you have to move before the book's published, but it engenders realism. You lose friends, but you gain verisimilitude.

Introducing people is a more tricky business. In *Rue—With a Difference* I never got beyond Elinor Duffield.

Elinor Duffield was an American in her forties who was re-visiting the Riviera for the first time since nineteen twenty-seven. She had brought her daughter Sophie with her. Sophie was now about the same age as Elinor had been then, and I think Elinor's idea was that Sophie should enjoy the same kind of things that Elinor herself had enjoyed at Sophie's age.

The interesting thing was that Sophie refused to enjoy them. Elinor organised excursions to Grasse and the Gorges du Loup. She knew what hotels were fashionable and who was in them. She introduced Sophie to aquatic ski-ing at Cap d'Antibes, to clay pigeon shooting at Monte Carlo, to the dress shows at Cannes and to every available young man she could find.

Sophie accompanied her dutifully and spent all her time reading back numbers of *Time, Life* and *The Reader's Digest*.

Rue—With a Difference was to be a study of the difficulty of re-living your own life through somebody else's. I started it with an inquiry (imaginative) into Elinor's life with her husband, a successful banker called Arthur, in Buffalo, New York, and what it was that had brought her so shortly after his death—and with such a firm determination to be cheerful—back to Nice again.

That was before I had re-titled the thing with Dagobert's suggested *Corpse Diplomatique* and made an effort to re-capture my scattered memories of our first evening in Nice. By doing this I find I have already inadvertently introduced most of the people that matter. Well, perhaps not quite inadvertently. Naturally I've eliminated here and there and dwelt, not altogether by accident, on impressions which were faint at the time.

For instance, the shy young American girl who came into the Brooklyn Bar—as it happened to change a traveller's cheque with Joe Orsini—was actually Sophie Duffield.

The woman in the rusty black evening dress who won five thousand francs at the Casino in Monte Carlo and promptly transformed her winnings into *Moules à la marinière* was Mrs. Andrioli, who owned and managed the Victoria Pension. She was plump, practical and good natured.

Her escort on that evening, the ex-cavalry officer type, was also a fellow pensionnaire. In fact he had lived in the same room at the Victoria Pension—with an interval in the Bermudas during the German occupation—for over twenty years. He had lived in the Victoria Pension

even before Mrs. Andrioli bought it, coming, as it were,
with the place. His name was Major Hugh de Courcy
Arkwright. He was one of the most charming men I
have ever met and one of the most sympathetic. He
spoke French so perfectly that he actually taught
that language as well as English at the local Universal
School.

He occupied Room Twelve, next to ours, and, to introduce a note of scandal at this point, I was almost certain
that I heard feminine laughter in that room a night or
two after our arrival.

Of course, Iris Makepeace was one of our fellow guests,
and so was Dieudonné Dompierre. The "We're staying . . ." hastily corrected into "I'm staying" clearly
included Dieudonné, though their rooms were on different
floors.

Elinor Duffield explained to me one day how Santa
Rica had cropped up during that unlikely dialogue in
the women's cloakroom at the Cotton Club. Henry
Makepeace, Iris's husband, a geologist who worked for
the Standard Oil Company, was at the moment stationed
in Santa Rica. "He's supposed to be getting leave at
any moment," Elinor added, not with satisfaction, but
with regret. Elinor was incurably romantic.

Dieudonné we saw little of. Though he spoke English
reasonably well, he seemed shy of the company in the
drawing-room. He was also, with one thing and another,
very busy. The other thing was music. He was a
composer and one often heard the sound of the piano
Mrs. Andrioli had allowed him to install in his bedroom.

Apart from the above six people, there was a sprinkling
of Swiss, Belgians and Scandinavians whom I never really
got straight. I felt that the six were enough to go ahead
with, especially if I added—as Dagobert insisted—the
personnel of the Brooklyn Bar and the Santa Rican

Consulate. Unfortunately, Buckshot and his friends re-embarked the next day, and, except for post cards from Algiers and Barcelona, they disappeared from our lives.

But Joe, Suzette, Don Diego and Juan Moro brought my cast up to ten, which I felt was as many as I could deal with.

Then one evening there were only nine.

Chapter

6

I MUST HAVE MISSED SEEING MURDER COMMITTED BY about thirty seconds.

I was alone in the room, which was on the fourth floor of the building, sitting at the table beside the window musing about my characters, making aimless notes on the typewriter and hoping that Dagobert would come in so I could give up the pretence of work.

It was not quite five-thirty and I had just extracted the final watery dregs from the teapot Mrs. Andrioli had brought to me an hour ago. I opened the French window and walked out on to our small balcony in search of inspiration and to escape the cigarette smoke which is apt to hover in clouds over my typewriter when I'm stuck.

I searched the Promenade across the street hopefully for Dagobert. There had been a shower a few minutes previously and there were relatively few people walking, though under the awnings of the cafés below me the tables were crowded.

Our room was a corner room and by craning my head around the edge of the balcony I could see the narrow Rue Ravel which contained the Brooklyn Bar. I couldn't see the bar itself; though it was only a few hundred feet off the Promenade, it was on the wrong side for me to get a view of it. I noticed the sleek Packard with the C.D. plate parked opposite and wondered if Don Diego were paying court to Suzette.

From the floor below came the sound of the piano.
I recognised the famous *chaconne* from the unaccompanied violin sonata ; we have the Menuhin records of
it at home.   It sounded almost as heavenly on the piano.
Dieudonné Dompierre played Bach exquisitely.

Our balcony was divided from Major Arkwright's by
iron spikes and his windows were closed. I thought
I heard someone moving in his room—probably the maid,
though it seemed an odd hour to do the room—for Major
Arkwright usually didn't return from the Universal
School until after five-thirty.

I was turning reluctantly away when I caught sight
of a familiar figure coming leisurely along the Promenade.
He was dressed in immaculate green linen trousers, a
collarless orange sports jacket and a panama hat with
a silk band, patriotically gay with the red, white and
mauve of Santa Rica. He was appraising the women
he passed with that professional eye which had once
made my own heart flutter. I reflected philosophically
on the fickleness of Central American diplomats and
closed the window. I walked across to the dressing-
table, where Dagobert had arranged twelve scent bottles
to represent what he called " a chromatic scale of frag-
rance." I will say about his latest hobby that it kept
me in scent, though I had to fight against his tendency
to use the stuff himself. I thought I smelled something
burning somewhere and wondered where I'd put my last
cigarette.

I can't say that the noise actually startled me. I
thought it was a car back-firing somewhere, though the
sound had a high, whining quality which wasn't quite
right. It brought me back to the window again before
I'd located the smell of burning.

At the spot where I had last seen Don Diego Sebastiano
de la Torreda a knot of people had gathered, a knot
rapidly becoming a crowd. Gendarmes had leapt off

bicycles and were excitedly waving batons. A blue van, marked *Police Secours,* careened along the Promenade and swerved into the kerb.

I heard voices, a woman's urgent scream above them all, crying, "*A l'assassin! A l'assassin!*" I remember being struck by how theatrical the phrase sounded. Oddly enough, I also remembered the Bach *chaconne* continuing without interruption.

On the balcony diagonally beneath mine Sophie Duffield had appeared. She had evidently been lying down and was wearing a striped towelling bathrobe. She saw me and started.

"Where's Mother?" she called a little disconnectedly. "What's happened?"

I shook my head to indicate ignorance. I was clinging to the railings as though the balcony was swaying. I released my grip and came into the room again. I sat down wondering if I were going to be ill. It would be a shock, Dagobert had once said, if Don Diego *really* had something to worry about. I knew suddenly what the word "shock" meant. I felt cold and my stomach kept turning over.

Dagobert arrived a few minutes later. He was looking nearly as sick as I was.

"I saw—from the balcony," I said. "Is he . . . have they . . . ?"

"It was a rifle probably. They may be able to calculate where it was fired from. Perhaps a passing taxi, perhaps a window. The assassin missed—by about six inches."

I breathed slightly. "I saw Don Diego a moment before the shot."

"He stopped suddenly to stare at something in a bathing suit. The bullet shaved him. But it got the poor devil just beyond."

"How, how awful!"

Dagobert nodded and slumped down on the edge of the bed. He ran a hand through his hair. It was shaking.

"He was shot through the temple and died instantly," he said. "It was Major Hugh Arkwright."

Chapter

7

WHEN IT COMES DOWN TO IT NEITHER DAGOBERT NOR
I will ever make criminal investigators. We take a keen
and—we think—intelligent interest in crime, and it
frequently creeps into our conversation. Crime, according to one of Dagobert's many and varying theories on
the subject, is merely human behaviour over-simplified.
That's why it makes holiday reading. Robbery, rape,
murder are obvious manifestations, he says, of instincts
which most of us confuse and entangle with a thousand
other complex urges, checks and emotions. They are
the name of action, sicklied o'er (happily) by the pale
cast of thought. It sounds all right over coffee and
liqueurs.

But if an actual crime is committed, as it were, on our
doorstep, we slam the door and quickly think about
something else.

Did I tell Dagobert that I'd heard someone scrabbling
in Major Arkwright's room a moment before he was
shot ? Oh, no. Did I pause to wonder about the answer
to Sophie Duffield's question—where, indeed, *was* her
mother ? Did I even glance again towards the limousine
waiting opposite the Brooklyn Bar ?

No, oh, no. We both escaped from the Pension as
soon as we could and spent the evening quietly by ourselves in Menton. We talked about Bertran de Born
and discussed going to Tourette-en-Provence after all.

We were, of course, more upset over Hugh Arkwright's
death than we cared to admit. We both liked him.

We had played bridge with him and he had been most helpful to me with the names of agaves, Barbary figs and other unfamiliar local vegetation. Dagobert had walked home with him from the Universal School once or twice and found him informative on the perfume industry at Grasse.

We liked what he outwardly represented : the pre-war retired army officer, living simply but not ungraciously on (we supposed) a small pension, well informed, but without intellectual pretensions, socially useless except as an example of good manners, an embodiment of a certain code of behaviour which my mother comfortably calls that of a " gentleman."

One always thought of Hugh de Courcy Arkwright as a kind of museum piece. And yet he was only forty-five and by no means without masculine attraction. Iris said he devastated her, though sometimes I thought Iris devastated rather easily. Both Duffields, mother and daughter, would perk up whenever he entered the dining-room. Elinor's animation would double and even Sophie's expressionless face would occasionally colour as she murmured " Good evening " and concentrated again on her soup-plate. As for Mrs. Andrioli, she blatantly spoiled Major Arkwright, scolded him when he was late for meals and invariably reserved the best of everything for him.

All of this made the conviction which later took root in Dagobert's mind the more unlikely.

But that first night when we dined at Menton and rediscovered our interest in Tourette-en-Provence all that seemed unquestionable was that an innocent man had met a meaningless death which had been intended for another. We both shied away from the whole business and, like sensible people, left the clearing up to the police.

It was two days later before Dagobert recovered his normal and sometimes outrageous buoyancy. He had come, he said, to an unshakable conclusion. His conclusion was—he first enunciated it very casually in the drawing-room after dinner when everybody was there and someone had referred to the tragic accident—his conclusion was : " There are no such things as *accidents*."

It might, at this point, be less confusing to give the facts. Afterwards we can go into Dagobert's distortion of them. The former were at that moment harder to come by than the latter. Our sources of information were two : the local newspapers and Joe Orsini.

Attempted assassination—especially of foreigners with diplomatic passports resulting in the death of innocent tourists—is not a subject which newspapers in popular resorts care to play up. For news of the unknown killer who had shot at Don Diego you had to search at the bottom of columns about International Tennis tournaments, film festivals and the storms which were ravaging rival resorts on the Atlantic coast.

Nevertheless, at Dagobert's behest, I began searching *Nice-Matin* and *Espoir* and making a scrapbook of relevant cuttings. It didn't solve the mystery, but it took my mind off *Rue—With a Difference*.

Joe was a little more helpful. He had a friend who worked at the Prefecture de Police and he liked to convey the impression that there was little about the affair he didn't know.

Between the papers and Joe we gathered that this was the situation : the shot had been fired at precisely five-thirty from a carbine of the kind issued to American army officers in place of revolvers during the war. These carbines were extremely accurate within a range of the two or three hundred yards from which it was known that the shot had been fired. Such rifles were not uncommon, and being small and light, were easily concealed. In any event, the one from which the bullet had been fired had not been found.

The direction from which the bullet had been fired
had also been roughly determined. Dagobert tried to
explain it to me. Standing where Major Arkwright had
stood when he'd been hit, you swept an arc of about
twenty degrees, starting with the Pension Victoria, crossing the Rue Ravel and ending up at the Milk Bar a few
yards down the Promenade. Then you glanced up at
an angle of twenty degrees and took in everything between
that elevation and the street level. It sounded very
scientific.

All it meant, however, was that Major Arkwright had
not been shot by anyone in a boat or an aeroplane over-
head, or by anyone on the Promenade itself. It meant
he had been shot by someone from a window of the
Pension Victoria, the travel agency on the opposite
corner, the offices over the Milk Bar, or from any spot
beneath one of these, including three pavement cafés.
It also meant he could have been shot from the Rue
Ravel at least as far away as the Brooklyn Bar, or from
any vehicle parked or passing at the time. This narrowed
the assassin down to about five or six hundred people, all
of whom must have heard the shot, but not one of whom
—including me—could say precisely where it came from.

All of this was in *Nice-Matin* the next morning, plus
the information that Commissaire Morel of the Sécurité
Nationale and the Santa Rican Minister, Don Geronimo
de la Torreda (another uncle of Don Diego's) had arrived
from Paris by plane.

The afternoon paper carried a brief communiqué from
the Santa Rican Consulate which said that the attempt
on Don Diego's life had no political significance, but was
believed to be the act of a madman. It added that the
Consulate would be open for business as usual. Joe
told us in confidence that Don Diego had demanded
police protection and had locked himself inside his flat
in a bad state of jitters.

What was actually going on behind the scenes—according to Joe's friend at the Prefecture—was a round-up of every Santa Rican in France. The trouble was there were only a few dozen, chiefly in Paris, and their whereabouts at the time of the attempted assassination was known. Apart from Juan Moro and Don Diego himself, none of them was anywhere near Nice. It was true that a Santa Rican called Pedro Garcia had disembarked about ten days ago from a tramp steamer called the *Carrabia*, which had put in at Villefranche, three miles along the coast. It was probably this Pedro Garcia who had so agitated Don Diego by calling and leaving no name. He had been ashore that day. In any case, Garcia had re-embarked the next day and at the time of the shooting he was somewhere on the high seas.

Dagobert marked my dossier at this point with an asterisk, and added the comment : " A man *from* Santa Rica is not the same thing as *a* Santa Rican." But he didn't seem very thrilled with the distinction.

Commissaire Morel of the Sécurité Nationale was apparently as discouraged by the business as Dagobert was. He was toying with the theory that it was a *crime passionnel* of some sort. " These Frogs," Joe explained to us, " always figure it like that. A dame's got to be in it or it's not a crime."

It was, however, all too true that Don Diego had not spent the last six years in Nice only reading the comics. Before Suzette had taken possession of his affections his reputation as a heart-breaker had extended from Monte Carlo to Cannes, and even more recently during stormy intervals with Suzette he had been known on occasions to console himself. There were probably several husbands—according to Joe, several dozen husbands—around who would have enjoyed taking a pot-shot at the Vice-Consul for Santa Rica.

Commissaire Morel preferred not to dig too deeply into

Don Diego's amatory past. His inquiry was necessarily of a delicate sort, requiring diplomacy. Though it would certainly be awkward if the representative of a friendly foreign power were to be assassinated on French territory, it would also be awkward to expose his private life to newspaper publicity.

He arrested Suzette informally and on a different charge, but released her after a few hours of cross-examination. Joe's friend heard him say off the record that if it had been the other way round, if Don Diego had tried to murder Suzette the thing would make sense.

"What were the fascinating things Suzette told you that evening about Don Diego ? " I suddenly remembered to ask Dagobert.

He shook his head. " I've clean forgotten," he confessed. " I'll go round this evening while Don Diego's still in retirement and check up."

I continued to type my dossier. The political situation in Santa Rica (I wrote, changing the subject) remains obscure.

Fortunately, Joe had it at his fingertips.

Santa Rica, we gathered, had for the past six years been more or less the private property of the de la Torreda family. The head of the family, Don Filippo, Santa Rica's late president who had been assassinated in last week's elections, had eleven brothers and a vast number of nephews, legitimate and illegitimate, who made themselves as comfortable as the resources of the country would allow. Don Geronimo, the artistic member of the family, had been given the Paris Ministry. The Consulate at Nice had been " created " for Don Diego, who liked the South of France and whom it was thought desirable to remove as far as possible from Santa Rica for the same reason—outraged husbands—which was now giving Commissaire Morel such a headache.

The de la Torreda family kept on the best of terms

with the United Fruit Company who handled the entire banana crop and owned the mineral rights. It had therefore been thought safe to hold a presidential election, just to show the rest of the world the solidarity of the Santa Rican people with their government. Bull fights, free beer and carnivals had been provided.

Carelessly an opposition had been allowed to grow up during the last few months, a left wing movement calling itself the Popular Front. Its leader had been educated at Harvard and Oxford and he talked loosely about "new deals," "health insurance" and other revolutionary things.

He had been overwhelmingly elected.

When Don Filippo demanded fresh elections, this time more carefully supervised, an enthusiastic member of the successful Popular Front had shot him. It was at this point that novelty crept into Santa Rican politics. The newly-elected president promptly arrested the assassin, had him legally tried and hanged. He issued an amnesty for his late opponents, and announced that those relatives and friends of the de la Torreda family who were pulling their weight would not be automatically removed from their jobs.

Up to the moment there had been no suggestion that either Don Geronimo be relieved of the Paris ministry, nor that the Nice Consulate be abolished. Joe told us that Don Geronimo and Don Diego spent half their time closetted at the Consulate trying to think of things to justify their existence. Don Diego was already editing a lengthy report on "Agricultural Products of the Côte d'Azur, Suitable for Exploitation in Santa Rica," and he had in mind an advertising campaign designed to lure tourists away from the Riviera to Santa Rica, "the Côte d'Azur of Central America."

The recent Santa Rican elections had not, therefore, been "the end" of Don Diego as he had naturally feared

that evening in the Bar d'Angleterre. Unless, of course,
there was an unidentified fellow countryman of his still
at large who hadn't heard yet of the new president's
amnesty !

We approached the problem from another angle, namely
that of Don Diego's movements on the fatal Wednesday
afternoon. Here, too, Joe was invaluable. Don Diego
had lunched luxuriously by himself at the Ruhl and driven
home afterwards for a siesta. He had dismissed Juan
Moro and the car and told him to be at the Brooklyn
Bar from five o'clock onwards. Juan was still waiting
at five-thirty when the shot was fired. Don Diego had
meanwhile had his nap, taken a bath, changed his clothes
and strolled along the Promenade, from which he was
driven into the Scotch Tea House by the shower. There
he ate a peach melba, drank a bottle of lemonade, and
told the waitress that all women were cruel. The waitress
was apparently no exception to this general rule, and
when the shower was over Don Diego issued forth again.
He tried, without success, to pick up two or three women
on the Promenade and finally decided to run as usual
back to Suzette.

"He can't help it," Joe told us wonderingly. "A
guy like that, too. It would be pathetic if he didn't
deserve it."

The point was that there was no particular reason why
Don Diego should have been on the Promenade opposite
the Rue Ravel at precisely five-thirty. His movements
were never (like those of Major Arkwright) regular.

When the shot was fired he was, as Dagobert had
already told me, gazing at "something in a bathing
suit," trying possibly to forget Suzette. The bullet
which had killed Major Arkwright had missed him by
inches. He had nearly fainted with fright and clung
to the gendarmes, forgetting even Suzette in his haste
to get himself safely to the nearest police station. Juan

Moro had waited imperturbably in the car outside the Brooklyn Bar until after ten that night, when Joe told him to go home. Juan had driven off without a word.

That was the end of my dossier. I had worked hard on it and I felt hurt when Dagobert, after going through it before dinner that evening, tossed it absentmindedly into the waste-paper basket, though, of course, no harm was done as I fished it out again later. He was in one of his restless moods.

" Everybody's worrying about who tried to assassinate Don Diego," he said, rather unnecessarily, I felt. But I nodded patiently.

" That's right."

" I like the Santa Rican bits," he conceded. " It's a pity we can't use them."

" Why can't we ? "

" Because no one tried to kill Don Diego. Someone simply *succeeded in murdering Hugh Arkwright.*"

Chapter

8

As I have said, this was two days later and
Dagobert had regained his normal high spirits.
But there was a kind of specious plausibility about
the remark which made me feel uncomfortable.
Murder may not have been the right word, but it
was indubitable that someone *had* succeeded in killing
Major Arkwright.

"You have, of course, a good reason for saying that,"
I said.

He shook his head blandly. "No—but it's an idea,
isn't it ? "

"It is not ! " I said sharply. "Don't say things like
that. . . . It's—it's probably libellous, as well as being
bad for my nerves."

"We can look round the Pension for some reasons,"
he suggested hopefully. "Who, for instance, was rifling
Arkwright's room a moment before he was shot ? Why
did Iris Makepeace pay her bill that same evening, pack
her luggage, even take it to the station, then suddenly
change her mind and come back? Why did Sophie
Duffield, who was taking a series of fifteen French lessons
from him at the Universal suddenly break off in the middle
of the course about a week before he died ? Why was her
mother having a bath at the time ? There wasn't any
hot water. . . . You see, the sort of questions we can
ask people ? "

"I see them," I nodded grimly. "We'll be the life

and soul of the Pension if we go round asking them.
Have you already been doing so ? "

He evaded the question. I realised I hadn't seen him
all the afternoon. " The ordinary key doesn't unlock
Arkwright's door," he said, " though it's clearly labelled
Number Twelve and hung up with the others outside the
office."

" How do you know ? "

" I tried it yesterday. Mrs. Andrioli gave me a very
dirty look when I explained I thought it was our room,
especially as you were making a row on the typewriter
in here."

" There are probably other good pensions in Nice,"
I said. " I'll look around to-morrow."

" That spiked arrangement on the balcony is most
awkward."

" It's meant to be," I pointed out. " It's supposed
to keep people in this room from prying about in the
next."

He nodded. " It very nearly broke my neck. And
even after I'd negotiated it at great risk to life and
limb the French windows were locked. I didn't like
to break them in."

" That was remarkably restrained of you."

" Yes," he agreed. " Dompierre suddenly appeared on
the balcony below and rather cramped my style. But the
shutters were open."

" And you saw ? Dagobert ! " I gave up my pretence of indifference. " If all this is leading anywhere,
please tell me."

" Probably it isn't," he admitted. " There was a wire
waste-paper basket like the one in this room The
contents had been burned and it contained nothing but
ashes. Possibly that explains the burning smell you
thought you smelled that afternoon."

" The maid ? " I suggested.

" Mrs. Andrioli did Arkwright's room that afternoon. Do you remember she brought you tea ? It was the maid's afternoon off. Of course it may be Mrs. Andrioli's method of emptying waste-paper baskets, but it seems rather slapdash."

I sat down and re-lighted my cigarette, which had gone out. " Yes . . . ? " I said.

" We have just time for one before dinner. Shall we go around the corner ? "

" Yes," I said.

We found a table outside the Méditerranée. Dagobert ordered a *Cap Corse* for me and a *Berger* for himself.

" I'll be glad when we run out of names," he said. " Gin will taste good again. Where were we ? Oh, yes, clues. Not a very good one, but something to go on with."

" Why should anybody possibly want to kill a man like Major Arkwright ? "

" Jealousy ? Revenge ? Money ? " he suggested. " By the way, Arkwright left no will and he had no money. He wasn't a Major in any recognised army and he had no pension."

" How did he live ? Oh, yes—the Universal School of Languages."

" You know how much language teachers earn. The Pension Victoria charges one thousand francs a day. Shall we assume he wasn't murdered for his money ? "

" I don't mind assuming that he wasn't murdered at all," I said.

He measured water cautiously into his *Berger*, watching the greenish liquid cloud and turn white. I imagined he was thinking about Hugh Arkwright, but when I asked him he said he was wondering why drinks with anis in them went milky.

" Speaking of money," he added uncomfortably, " I

forgot to mention it, but I lent Arkwright a fiver the
other day. We were coming back from school together
and he hadn't his wallet with him."

" What's a fiver ? " I said carelessly. " We probably
have another one."

" I've been thinking about that fiver," he continued.
" It may have been an investment, sort of. We'd been
talking of this and that, the weather, politics, was this
our first visit to Nice, had I an uncle called Tancred
Brown, who used to have a hand loom in Cagnes-sur-mer,
were you any relation to the Hamishes who live near
Porlock in Somerset. I said yes, and also admitted
Uncle Tancred—he now does pottery in Portofino, by
the way."

" You seem to have the most diverting conversations,"
I prompted, wondering what, if anything, this was leading
up to.

He agreed. " It was only yesterday that I began to
wonder how he could possibly know your maiden name
was Hamish."

" How did he know ? Of course—the hotel registration
slips."

Dagobert shook his head. " I filled them out Mr. and
Mrs. D. Brown. Our passports, however, are in our top
bureau drawer. We must do something some day about
passports, by the way. They give the uninformed a
totally false impression of glamour."

I suddenly realised what he meant. We had never
got around to having a single passport. I still use my
old one in my maiden name of Jane Hamish. If Hugh
Arkwright knew my name was Hamish he must have
seen my passport, and if he had seen my passport he
must have assumed we were not married.

" In the nicest possible way," Dagobert frowned, " he
let me realise he knew this. Then ten minutes later he
borrowed a fiver from me. What it is to have a carefree

conscience! I was probably being blackmailed without even knowing it."

The thought cheered him up immensely. I wondered how many other people in the Pension had seen my passport.

"More interesting," Dagobert pointed out, "is to wonder how many other fivers Arkwright borrowed from fellow guests. Or if he ' borrowed ' so many from someone that the simplest solution was to shoot him."

"The simplest solution," I said, before he grew too enthusiastic, " is that someone trying to assassinate Don Diego merely killed Major Arkwright by mistake."

He looked injured. "Are you on my side or on Commissaire Morel's ? " he complained. " He has all the fun rounding up Santa Ricans, delving into Don Diego's disreputable past and issuing statements to the press while all that's left over for me is some rather unpromising snooping into waste-paper baskets. He gets his choice of theories while I have to take the remains that nobody's interested in. He gets his picture in the newspaper while I get nasty looks from Mrs. Andrioli. He rides around in a luxurious police car while I stand up all the way to Villefranche in the bus. He is honoured, well paid, while I rip my trousers on iron spikes and get touched for fivers. Why do I do all this ? Why do I sacrifice the first holiday I've had in weeks, neglect Bertran de Born, dance with women who call me " honey boy ' ? For your sake, Jane. Because I'm trying to help you in your literary career. Because—shall we have a drink ?—I think the beginning of *Rue—With a Difference* is lousy."

I hadn't been listening very carefully to all this. I know when Dagobert holds forth at length that he is worried. Where other people go silent he becomes

voluble. I said quietly : " Are we making up a book ?
Or are we trying to find out who killed Hugh Arkwright ? "

He relaxed. The smile—which Iris had called quizzical
—was gone.

" I don't know . . ." he muttered anxiously. " I just
don't know."

Chapter

9

IT WAS IN THE SITTING-ROOM AFTER DINNER THAT NIGHT when Dagobert observed that " there were no such things as accidents."

The remark was followed by a general and slightly awkward silence. Mrs. Andrioli, who had just brought in coffee, put the tray down with an unnecessary clatter which made Sophie, who was fussing with the wireless, jump. She spun round and mercifully abandoned her efforts to find the B.B.C. Light Programme.

" I don't want any coffee," she murmured. " Good night, everyone." She paused in the door to add perfunctorily : " Good night, Mother."

Elinor smiled at her brightly and promised to look in on her later. As a rule Elinor winced facetiously when Sophie called her " Mother." She insisted that her daughter call her Elinor, which Sophie normally did, though with reluctance.

" Yes, I think I see what you mean, Mr. Brown," Elinor said. " Accidents. Yes, I suppose what seem to us to be accidents are really part of a design which is too complex for ordinary mortals to grasp."

" Something along that line," Dagobert smiled indefinitely.

" In other words," Elinor persisted, " poor Major Arkwright had a kind of appointment with destiny. Like the man who went to Samarra. I think these things are so interesting. Would anyone like to play bridge ? "

She fixed Dieudonné Dompierre with her bright smile. He came to and, as he realised the question was addressed

to him, hastily took refuge in his drawing-room pretence
that he understood almost no Englilsh.

"Yes—I play for a while the piano—if you will please
excuse." He rose, abandoning his coffee and bowed diffidently to the company. As he passed Dagobert and me
beside the door he said : " Will you have brandy with me
in my room ? "

We nodded and followed him. Iris, who had been
cornered by a Swedish countess, watched our departure
enviously.

Dompierre's room was just beneath ours, a large,
pleasant room strewn with books, tennis raquets, bathing
suits and manuscript music. The counterpane had been
drawn up to conceal the unmade bed. As a semi-perma-
nent guest he had special rates with the management and
looked after himself.

The upright piano was against the wall next to the
French windows leading on to the narrow balcony. From
the stool you could see the spot on the Promenade where
Hugh Arkwright had been shot.

He did not apologise for the litter, but asked us to
sit down while he rummaged the wardrobe for glasses
and a bottle of Armagnac.

" If you can drink nescafé, I have an alcohol burner,"
he said as he filled the three minute glasses. " I
acquired the taste during the war when I was with the
American Army."

Dieudonné Dompierre was a pleasant-looking man in
a rugged, masculine way. Though he rarely smiled, his
face was extraordinarily mobile. He had a quick,
nervous way of frowning which had left ridges in his
low, powerful forehead. His deep-set eyes, though they
seldom stared at you, gave an impression that they
missed nothing.

He said, omitting the social preliminaries : " You meant
just now that Arkwright's death was not accidental."

" Yes," Dagobert said, trying not to look startled. " Yes, that's what I meant."

" Do you know who killed him ? "

" No. Do you ? "

Dompierre's forehead creased into a frown. He filled a battered saucepan at the wash-hand basin and put it on the alcohol burner. He seemed to be giving the question his consideration.

" No, I don't," he said finally. " But I am not particularly sorry he is dead."

Dagobert took his glass of brandy over to the piano, sat down on the adjustable stool and picked out with one finger what I recognised with an effort to be the theme of the Bach *chaconne* for unaccompanied violin.

" I thought," he said, " that Hugh de Courcy Arkwright was popular with one and all."

" Women liked him." The accent so pronounced in the public sitting-room was fainter. " He had that— what do you say ?—*milord* manner which flatters and reassures. I have been here since a year and I have scarcely talked with him. I cannot help you."

" Help me ? " Dagobert repeated, bewildered.

" Aren't you searching to find the murderer ? "

Dagobert finished his brandy. He had been unprepared for such plain speaking. " Well, yes, I suppose one is." He grinned. " Is it so obvious ? "

Dompierre shrugged. " You climb over railings into his room. You ask the concierge who is in the hotel at the time. You ask about if there are rifles. You scare Mrs. Andrioli."

" I do seem to have been busy," Dagobert said ruefully. " You can't help us. . . . May I inquire why you asked us to have a glass of brandy with you ? "

" Yes," he said, refilling Dagobert's glass. " Because I have a carbine like the one the papers say killed Arkwright."

Dagobert looked mildly surprised, but I realised the information had not startled him. He said, " Yes ? "

" This you knew already," Dompierre said. " Once I lent it to the concierge to shoot rabbits. Have you the intention to tell this to the police ? "

" No. I wasn't even going to tell Jane."

Dompierre looked ingenuously relieved. " I do not know whether you have ever experienced an *interrogatoire* by the French police," he said. " It is not like your polite English bobbies."

He brought me a cup of nescafé and lighted my cigarette. " This conversation is very boring," he apologised. " When Mrs. Makepeace comes perhaps please you will come to the Casino with us."

" Where is the gun ? " Dagobert asked.

" I don't know."

" You don't *know* ? "

Dompierre frowned. He cupped the lighted match in his hand to the cigarette butt in his own mouth and shook his head.

" Three or four days ago it was over there by the door in the cupboard. I looked for it this morning, but it was gone. I spoke to Mrs. Andrioli about this discreetly, and to-day she has been through every room in the hotel. She has not found it. It is not large, but it is too large to hide."

" Would it go in a suit-case ? "

" A long suit-case, yes," Dompierre nodded. " Mrs. Andrioli has also looked in such suit-cases. Nothing."

Dagobert exhaled cautiously as though he had forgotten to breathe for several minutes. He shifted slightly on the piano stool and glanced out of the window.

" You could," he said speculatively, " easily have shot Arkwright from this position. Then, realising that you were known to have a rifle, you could carry it out of the hotel in a suit-case at the first convenient opportunity.

and later report that it was missing. You could." He corrected himself amiably. " I mean, couldn't one ? "

" I know what you mean," Dompierre said briefly.

" However, you didn't," Dagobert suggested. " In the first place, you are the only one of us who has a really stylish alibi. You were playing the piano ; and Jane is certain you went right on playing the piano before, during and after the shot. D'you mind my talking like this, while I drink your brandy ? A purist might say it's none of my business."

" Please continue."

" The idea is, I take you completely into my confidence, blunder along . . ." He caught my eyes and winked, ". . . Think out loud. The way they do in those books where the sleuth gets pally and intimate with a trust-worthy character who turns out in the end to be the villain."

Dompierre smiled faintly. " I have read *Romans Policiers*."

" Then you know. In the second place, you had no motive."

Dompierre's faint smile vanished entirely. He turned to refill his own brandy glass.

" Arkwright," he said, " was blackmailing me."

" Oh," said Dagobert, nearly falling off the stool.

" Not for very much," Dompierre added. " I haven't got very much. But recently I have had three or four cheques from my music publishers in Paris. He watched the post and whenever this happened he " borrowed " a few thousand francs from me. I think he steamed open the envelopes because he always suggested a figure which was about ten per cent. of my cheque."

" You wouldn't, of course, like to say *why* he was blackmailing you ? "

" No ! " Dompierre's face darkened. " I would not."

The door opened and Iris Makepeace came in. I saw

Dieudonné glower disapprovingly at her for not knocking. In the public rooms of the Victoria Pension his manner towards Iris was always polite but reserved, an effect somewhat spoiled by her own behaviour. Iris was one of those women who radiate discretion, but still like the world to know that they are adored.

She gave Dieudonné a kind of open-secret smile of intimacy and sat down on the edge of his bed.

" I couldn't get away from the Countess," she explained. " Then the Duffield wanted us to take that dead-pan daughter of hers to the Casino. ' Poor Sophie seems to get so little fun out of life.' Poor Sophie ? The child's obviously suffering from arrested development—and likes it ! I told her we'd arranged to go with the Browns. You will come, won't you, Jane ? " she appealed.

" Unless you'd rather go by yourselves."

" Pierre thinks not," she said seriously. " Don't you, *chéri* ? I mean, in the circumstances—just at the moment, that is."

" What circumstances ? "

" With my husband arriving any moment," she explained with that candour which sometimes took my breath away—and, I fancy, Dompierre's, too.

" When is he coming ? " Dagobert asked curiously.

"According to Cook's, the *Scythia* docks at Marseilles to-night or early to-morrow morning. I suppose Henry will be on it. That was the plan." She smiled anxiously. " But it's been weeks since he wrote, which is so unlike him. . . . Two lumps, *chéri*," she broke off as Dompierre sullenly gave her coffee. " Have we finished the cherry brandy ? So unlike him—I'm terrified he may have gone down with malaria again or one of those other filthy things you get in places like Santa Rica, and has been afraid to write to me. It will be thrilling to see him ! Rather like being suddenly married to a tall, fair handsome stranger ! "

" Is Henry tall ? " Dagobert said.

" Well, not really," she admitted. " Just about right. But he's fair."

" And freckled ? " Dagobert asked.

We all stared at him. " Why did you ask that ? " Iris said. " Yes, as a matter of fact, he is."

" Part of my technical equipment for jolting people," Dagobert grinned sheepishly. " You have a photograph of him, haven't you ? "

" Yes," Iris nodded slowly. She eyed Dagobert doubtfully and continued with an effort to recapture her enthusiasm. " You'll all adore Henry. You, too, *chéri*." She smiled affectionately up at Dompierre, who had found the remains of the cherry brandy.

He winced, as he did every time she called him *chéri*, and said brusquely, " Shall we go ? "

" It's so cosy here," she said, snuggling back against the pillows which were heaped up under the counterpane.

She sipped her cherry brandy, making little " umm " sounds of pleasure and closed her eyes. In the half-light she looked soft and kittenish and content ; and about Sophie's age, although she was twenty-five.

" Mrs. Andrioli," she mused aloud, " has promised us Major Arkwright's room. It's a double, and Henry's bound to have a lot of luggage." She sat up abruptly, as though she had suddenly thought of something. " *Chéri*," she said, lowering her voice, " have you told them ? "

Dompierre nodded shortly, as though the subject were already closed. Iris's gold-flecked eyes widened as she glanced from Dagobert to me. " What do you think ? " she said.

" About . . ."

" About Major Arkwright blackmailing poor Pierre, who can't afford it, and all because . . ."

" No one is interested," Dompierre interrupted.

" Don't be silly, *chéri*," she laughed. " Jane and Dagobert won't be shocked. You're so old-fashioned. Why, even the Duffield smiles when you sneak around being so discreet. No. Major Arkwright was black-mailing Pierre because nearly two months ago, when I first came, we—we were rather naughty, weren't we, *chéri* ? "

Dompierre, looking blacker than ever, poured himself out a glass of brandy and swallowed it in a gulp. I sympathised with him. Iris continued, unaware of his feelings :

" We took the bus to a sweet little village in the mountains called Beuil and stayed the night ! " she said recklessly. " We registered as Monsieur et Madame. It was very silly, especially as Major Arkwright somehow found out all about it and actually got hold of the page with our signatures and Room Five after each! He didn't actually *say* he would show it to Henry, but we were afraid he *might*. So . . . what could one do ? "

" Shoot him," I suggested.

Iris laughed a little nervously and said : " Yes—wasn't that lucky ? " She broke off, appalled by what she had said. " I mean . . . you know what I mean."

" Did he try to blackmail you, too ? " Dagobert said.

" Oh, yes ! " she nodded. " He had, let's see, it must be ten or fifteen pounds out of me. I'd give *anything* rather than let Henry know, and I told him so. But he did it so nicely—it didn't seem at all like blackmail. You see, he gave me private lessons in French and then charged me five pounds an hour. He seemed almost embarrassed at taking the money. Afterwards he'd be so generous with it. Why, he even took me out to lunch a couple of times. That day we first met you two, for instance, and again only on Wednesday."

" On Wednesday ? You mean the day he was shot ? "

" So it was ! " Iris gasped. " And he was charming—never a word about Beuil. You couldn't help liking him, and he *was* attractive. Even that dull little Sophie was secretly smitten. . . . Oh, well," she ran the tip of her tongue round the empty liquor glass, which Dompierre did not re-fill, " perhaps it's just as well. As the Duffield says, an appointment with Destiny. By the way, where is Samarra ? The Italian Riviera ? " She noticed Dompierre fidgeting and stirred herself. " But you want to go, *chéri*, don't you ? You look *so* depressed. Don't look so depressed on our very last evening."

She took his hand and stroked it possessively. He snatched it away and looked savagely around for his hat.

" She has," I said to Dagobert later while we danced to the Casino Méditerranée's excellent Cuban band, " been using that ' our last evening ' line to my certain knowledge ever since that night over a week ago at the Cotton Club. You'd think it would begin to pall."

Dagobert nodded. " I think it has."

" Not," I said, " if you can judge by the look of dog-like devotion on his face at the moment. How does she get away with it ? Of course, I'm wildly envious."

" No, I think Iris is getting bored with it herself," Dagobert said.

" Women with reliable husbands in distant lands and fascinating young French composers madly in love with them on the spot," I said " do not get bored. They may get into emotional difficulties, they may get their hearts torn asunder, they may even get mildly black-mailed. But they do not get bored."

" And yet the whole time I danced with her," he said, " she talked of nothing else but Henry, and what fun it's going to be when he comes."

" It ought to be fun at that," I agreed, more cheerfully.

" Her idea at the moment," he said, " is a jolly and innocent threesome, with Henry and Dompierre both taking her out and dancing with her in turns. The two men will naturally be great friends, but sufficiently jealous of each other to keep them both on their toes."

" That's every woman's ambition," I sighed. " Quite impracticable. . . ."

He glanced at me sharply. " I get dreadful glimpses into feminine psychology living with you, Jane."

I changed the subject before we became more involved. " By the way," I said, " *have* you been exploring Iris's room at the Pension ? "

He shook his head, still brooding about other matters. " Then where did you see the photograph ? "

" What photograph ? " he asked absentmindedly.

" The one," I explained, " showing Henry's freckles."

" Oh. I—er—I merely thought he sounded like the sort who would have freckles. I say, that dance passed quickly, and, oddly enough, here we are at the bar ! "

Iris and Dompierre joined us, and when the music began again Iris immediately resigned Dompierre to me and danced off with Dagobert. I began to wonder if there really could be anything in Dagobert's unlikely theory that she was beginning to be bored with her lover : as though he had played his part in her emotional life and she had no further use for him.

Dompierre dutifully asked me to dance, but his heart was not in it. He kept pretending not to watch Iris and we tended to talk about the weather. He became genuinely animated only when the subject of Iris inevitably cropped up.

" She is really a very silly woman ! " he told me bitterly. " I shall be happy when this husband comes."

" Why did she pack up and leave the Pension the other day ? " I asked curiously.

His sensitive mouth twisted, as though the memory caused him pain. " It was my fault," he muttered. " We had a dispute. I told her to *fiche moi la paix*, to get the hell out. She cried. It is always my fault . . ."

We danced for a while in silence, but I knew he wanted to say more. Finally he said in a baffled tone :

" I don't understand English women. In France there is such a thing as a *mari complaisant*, but I've never heard of an *amant complaisant* ! "

" It's miles over my head," I confessed.

" She wants me to continue—just as before—after *he* comes." He added in an altered voice which made me suddenly feel sorry for him : " I cannot get on with my work."

I tried for a few minutes to encourage him to talk about his work, having read somewhere that that is the way for women to hold a man's interest. He spoke monosyllabically and kept glancing towards Iris and Dagobert.

" There is something," he said abruptly, " that I wished to say to you. That hotel in Beuil she talked about—that room Number Five. It is hard to explain. I spent that night walking. She would not unlock the door."

At about midnight I suggested going home—or else somewhere where there wasn't a Cuban band. Dagobert had danced solidly for more than two hours and I felt he'd done his duty .

Iris wouldn't hear of it. I was astonished to find Dagobert quite willing to go on dancing all night.

We very nearly did. It was past three when we came up in the lift. I noted sleepily that there was still a light in the sitting-room left on for us. Someone suggested turning it off, and I, stifling a yawn, turned to climb the remaining flight of stairs to our door.

My yawn froze into a kind of gape. A man had risen

as the sitting-room door opened. He was a man in his middle twenties, obviously English, with very fair hair and a face covered with freckles.

" Henry ! " gasped Iris, and threw herself dramatically into his arms.

Chapter

10

DAGOBERT HAD BOLTED HIS BREAKFAST, MUTTERED something about an early Universal lesson, dressed and gone before my eyes became sufficiently unstuck to note with horror that it was only half-past seven. Being fond of more than four hours' sleep, I pushed the breakfast tray aside, pulled the sheet over my head and went back to sleep again.

I awoke about ten to the sound of traffic in the Promenade outside, mingled with frightful discords from the piano in the room below. I ate the croissants Dagobert had left and rang optimistically and without result for fresh coffee. I dressed and decided to forage for myself. I found the maid and the kitchen-boy changing the single bed in Room Twelve next door for a double bed ; we were to have Iris and Henry Makepeace for neighbours. The Makepeaces had, I learned, gone off with a picnic for the day. I wished, listening to the horrid racket which continued from the piano, that they had taken Dieudonné Dompierre with them.

Mrs. Andrioli had gone to the funeral.

I went down to the deserted sitting-room and glanced through French illustrated magazines, resolving to do something constructive about my French. Through the glass doors which divided the sitting-room from the dining-room I saw the waiter re-arranging tables. The sun poured in, and through the open windows the air was sweet and balmy.

Hugh Arkwright's table, the small table in the corner

 ``` /g!!!


39...33aw 

from which he had kept a benevolent—and speculative?
—eye on the guests who had come and gone for twenty
years, had been removed, and a larger one, set for the
three Belgian women who had arrived yesterday, had
been put in its place. Already his single bed which
had not been moved for nearly a quarter of a century
had been dismantled. By this time doubtless he himself
had been quietly buried in a corner of the English church-
yard, attended to his last resting-place only by his land-
lady. A Consular telegram had notified his sole living
relative, a distant cousin in Australia whom he hadn't
seen since childhood. His clothes and few personal
belongings had been given by Mrs. Andrioli to a charit-
able institution. He had left no will and no money.

He had left, indeed, almost no trace behind of his
sojourn on earth; a pupil or two at the Universal who
might observe a new anonymous face across the *Premier
Livre*; a new, anonymous voice saying, "*C'est le crayon,
c'est la plume*"; a few transient pensionnaires who in the
evenings might have to find another fourth for bridge;
a newsvendor who wondered if the Monsieur Anglais to
whom he always sold a Continental *Daily Mail* had gone
home or taken his custom elsewhere.

He had also—I recalled with a start which brought me
from these morbid reflections—he had also left behind
him Dagobert, who was convinced that he was murdered!

The lift stopped outside—the Victoria Pension occu-
pied the third and fourth floors of the building—and the
hall door opened. Mrs. Andrioli, followed by the Duf-
fields, bustled in with a kind of well-that's-that air about
her; her oldest client had been safely buried and it was
time to think of menus for luncheon and repairs to the
plumbing in the fourth-floor-bathroom. But when she
removed her veil and neat black hat I saw that her nose
was red as though she had been crying.

Elinor and Sophie had gone to the funeral with her,
 ```

and I was a little surprised to notice that Elinor, too, had not remained dry-eyed. Only Sophie had evidently been unmoved, though she wore a dark frock with white collar and cuffs suitable for the occasion. They had bought a wreath, they told me. The Santa Rican Consulate had also sent one.

" You should have come with us," Elinor said. " It's so pathetic somehow to die without friends or relatives so far away from home.

" This was his home," Mrs. Andrioli reminded us practically. She rang the bell and ordered sweet biscuits and port. She poured out four glasses and asked to be excused while she changed. We heard her brisk footstep in the corridor as she went to Dompierre's room, knocked and told him not to play so loud. The piano immediately stopped. The ensuing silence was a relief.

" Poor Monsieur Dompierre," Elinor murmured sympathetically. " Though it's rather hard on the rest of us that he should take it so violently . . . They were rather sweet together, so bewildered and torn and in love."

" She has a *husband*, Mother ! " Sophie said.

Elinor smiled. " I suppose I was intolerant, too, at your age, Sophie," she said. " though I think I managed to have a better time. I wonder if the world *has* changed since my day ? "

It was the first time I'd ever heard Elinor Duffield admit even by implication that " her day " belonged to the past. The funeral of a man who was almost exactly her contemporary had probably shaken her.

" Judging from the behaviour of Mrs. Makepeace," Sophie said witheringly, " I'd say it hasn't changed a bit ! "

I'd never heard Sophie so bitter, nor, indeed, express any opinion of her own. She was stiff with distaste. Elinor glanced at me half apologetically.

" Do you think I am wrong, Jane," she said, " to treat

the child as though she were an adult ? She's nineteen . . ."

" Twenty-one," Sophie corrected mechanically.

". . . and when I was nineteen I had dozens of flirtations—in fact I was engaged to Arthur. We used to
read Scott Fitzgerald and drink bootleg gin out of hip
flasks and have necking parties and discuss what we
called the ' Facts of Life.' "

" I loathe the facts of life," Sophie echoed under her
breath.

" Perhaps we were a little wild and impulsive," she
continued, ignoring her daughter, " but at least we were
alive. When I was in Nice I don't think I ever went to
bed before dawn, and I was head over heels in love with
an Austrian count, an Italian professional footballer and
the local swimming instructor all at once. If Arthur
hadn't suddenly arrived from Buffalo and insisted on
getting married immediately, I don't know what would
have happened ! "

She broke off with a slight giggle, unaware of how
acutely she was embarrassing her daughter. And, to be
frank, I wondered if port at this hour of the day excited
her, and poured her out another glass.

" I hoped Sophie would have a good time, too," she
said. " I hoped we'd *both* have a good time. I know
how stupid it is for mothers to act as though their
daughters are only younger sisters—but . . . oh, well,
maybe it's been good for her French. I never bothered
about French. . . ." She sighed and sipped her port.
The momentary flush of colour had gone again from her
soft, plump face and she looked tired.

I said conversationally to Sophie : " You took French
lessons at the Universal for a while, didn't you ? "

Sophie had regained her normal party manners. She
nodded without bothering to speak.

" Did you enjoy them ? "

" They were all right."

" Didn't you have Major Arkwright ? "

She nodded again, as though bored with the subject.
" I must change a traveller's cheque, Mother—Elinor,"
she corrected herself.   " I'll be back in a few minutes."

" You changed one yesterday, *and* the day before,"
Elinor said.   " Why don't you change enough all at
once, so you don't have to keep going back ? "

" It's safer not to carry too much in cash," Sophie
explained from the door.   " Good-bye."   It was the first
cheerful sound she had produced.

Elinor glanced after her anxiously.   " I really ought
to go with her," she said, putting down her unfinished
port.

I began to say, " The Brooklyn Bar's only around the
corner," but she continued :

" The walk up to the American Express would do me
good," and it suddenly occurred to me that Elinor
Duffield might not know who her daughter's banker was.
Instead I said :

" I was specially interested in the Universal course
because I'm thinking of taking it myself.   Sophie didn't
finish it, did she ? "

Elinor shook her head vaguely.   " No, she didn't.   She
thought she wasn't getting enough out of it.   She loses
interest in things so quickly."

Mrs. Andrioli, who had done a quick change from her
Sunday black, had overheard this last remark.   There
was something very like malice in her black eyes.   She
tasted her port critically.

" You were very wise, I theenk," she said, smacking
her lips with satisfaction.

" In what way ? "

" Major Arkwright," she said, not without pride, " was
a *very* attractive man . . ."

Chapter

II

It was past eleven and as Dagobert hadn't come back from school, I decided to go swimming by myself. While I waited on the corner of the Rue Ravel to cross the Promenade, Joe and Sophie came out of the Brooklyn Bar and walked together towards me. Joe, bareheaded, his hands in his pockets, mouched along on the inside, kicking a stone along the pavement. Occasionally he would stop chewing gum to show his white teeth in a broad grin or to nod his head. Sophie talked to him shyly, but there was a tinge of colour in her usually colourless cheeks. It became a flush when she suddenly saw me. It was the second time to-day I had seen her almost showing emotion. She said " so long " to Joe, " Hi ! " to me, and hurried back to the Pension. Joe glanced after her with a shrug.

" That's a funny kid," he said to me. " Looks about fifteen and acts like about fifty. Do you know her old woman ? "

I reminded him that we lived in the same Pension.

" That's right," he nodded. " I guess somebody in the family's got to act like they were grown up. If Ma won't, then the kid's got to. Going swimming ? "

I said yes and he said he was, too. We crossed the Promenade and walked along the sea-wall. The pebble beach beneath us was thick with sun-bathers.

" She graduated from Buffalo High," Joe said. " Can you beat it ? "

" How do you mean ? "

"I once played football for old B.H.S. In fact I
was still there when I ran off and joined the army. Like
a sucker, I claimed I was nineteen. It's a small world."

"B.H.S. would be Buffalo High School," I suggested.
"So you're old school-mates, practically."

"Yeah," he grinned. "Though in my day they had
more zoom. Funny thing—a talk like that makes you
feel kinda homesick. Look at this place," he jerked an
appreciative thumb at the palm-fringed Promenade.
"It's got everything—climate, style, beauty. And then
you start missing Buffalo. It doesn't make sense." He
removed his hands from his pockets, leaned his elbows
against the iron railing with a sigh and gave his attention
to the bathers below.

He said abruptly: "Let's go along a few hundred
yards, where it isn't so crowded."

"I appreciate your delicacy," I said, "but this is one
of those situations a wife has to face squarely."

Just beneath us we had both simultaneously recognised
the body of Suzette—on further inspection she *was* wearing two bits of biege material which could be called a
bathing suit, and stretched beside her Dagobert. They
were eating *choux à la crème* and chocolate éclairs.

We climbed down the concrete steps and joined them.
They were talking animatedly in French, but broke off
when they saw us.

"Hi, Dagobert," Joe said.

Dagobert said, "Hi," and added, "We were just
talking about you. I thought you'd be asleep, Jane.
You know Mademoiselle Gosset. Will you have an
éclair?"

"I am not asleep," I said darkly, accepting the éclair
and shaking the hand which Suzette offered from her
recumbent position.

Joe retired to a cabin to change while I slipped out of
my dressing-gown. I felt over-clad in my one-piece navy

blue bathing suit from Harvey & Nichols. Suzette examined it in wonder, evidently taking it for some kind of fancy dress. After a moment's stare she put on her large sun-glasses and returned to the more interesting occupation of picking the scarlet varnish off her toe-nails.

" Suzette's been telling me about her interview with the police," Dagobert said, politely bringing me into the conversation.

" *Salauds !* " said Suzette dispassionately.

" They are unable to grasp why she refused Don Diego's offer of a flat in the suburbs with a maid of her own and thirty thousand francs a month spending money."

" *Salaud !* " she repeated, referring this time presumably to Don Diego himself.

" They infer from this that she doesn't like him," Dagobert explained. " And therefore it logically follows that she must have taken a pot-shot at him."

" If I knew to shoot Joe's gun maybe I do," Suzette nodded. " No, *sans blague,*" she looked up from her toe-nails, " Don Diego's okay. But for *sometimes.* Not for *all* times. He wants that I see no one except him. This would be like . . ." she searched for a word adequate to describe such slavery . . . " like being *married* ! "

" I see what you mean," I murmured.

" Maybe for you—maybe for some women—okay," she admitted tolerantly. " But I like to meet fellows, different guys, have some fun sometimes, *vous savez* ? "

Joe joined us and Suzette relapsed into silence. He was copper-bronze and made Dagobert and me look a pale tea colour.

" Race you to the raft ! " he challenged, tearing across the pebbles towards the water as though his feet were made of leather.

Dagobert and I hobbled after him more cautiously

while Suzette sensibly curled over to cook her other side. The raft was anchored a few hundred feet off-shore and Joe sped towards it like a speedboat, leaving a white wake behind him. Dagobert was a poor second, while I reached the raft, puffing badly, some minutes later.

Joe was basking like a seal on the raft while Dagobert was holding on to the edge to regain his breath. There was no one else there.

" Ever been blackmailed, Joe ? " Dagobert asked.

Joe stirred, like a seal who scents vague danger. " Wozzat ? " he said. " Hey ! " he called to me. " Why don't you bring that little Duffield kid swimming one day ? How about to-morrow afternoon ? "

I started to say yes, but swallowed a mouthful of water instead.

" You heard me," Dagobert said.

" No, why should I be ? " Joe drawled. " Oh, you mean ' protection.' Sure, you gotta give away a certain number of free drinks. Running a joint like mine, you gotta keep friendly with people ; you don't want no trouble with the police."

" I meant *blackmail*," Dagobert insisted.

Joe considered the word as though it were new to him. He shook his head innocently. " Nope," he said. " No, I never have."

" Then you're going to be," Dagobert said, hoisting himself up on to the raft.

" Who by ? "

" By me," Dagobert said pleasantly.

" Oh, yeah ? "

" Yeah," Dagobert nodded.

" Before you start that routine," I gasped, "give me a hand, somebody."

Joe gave me a hand. I was half-way on to the raft when Dagobert said : " I'vc been going through the late Hugh de Courcy Arkwright's private papers."

I may have missed some of the subsequent conversation. Joe let go and I was submerged for the next few seconds. When I came to the surface Joe was saying:

" The guy that got killed ? "

" That's the one."

" He didn't leave any papers."

Joe had forgotten my existence, and it was Dagobert who ultimately helped me up on to the raft. " You mean you *heard* they were all burned," he suggested.

Joe was non-committal. " You hear a lotta things in a job like mine," he mumbled. " I wish somebody had a cigarette. You mean they *weren't* ? "

Dagobert avoided a direct answer. " A couple of years ago you used to go to the Universal School, didn't you ? " he said.

" Sure," Joe nodded. " I got free tuition on the G-I Bill of Rights. *J'entre dans la classe—J'y entre.* All that kinda stuff. What good is it ? Everybody speaks English."

" Arkwright used to give you lessons."

" Lots of people used to give me lessons. I wouldn't remember."

" They keep weekly schedules at the school," Dagobert said. " Some of the old ones haven't been thrown away. For your information, Arkwright gave you private instruction for two hours a day for nearly three months."

" Okay, so what ? "

" When you're closetted with a person for two hours a day for three months running it's amazing how you run out of small talk," Dagobert said. " You begin to say anything that comes into your head, just to say something. I know. Even in a week, struggling along in Provençal, I've practically recounted the story of my life."

Joe had risen and was standing poised on the edge of

the raft. "That must be something," he said dryly flexing his muscles.

" Nothing to the details you told Arkwright," Dagobert smiled. Joe's arms were raised and his chunky, perfectly co-ordinated body made an arc towards the water. " Such as . . ." Dagobert continued.

But Joe had already dived. He remained under water for a good minute.

" Such as what ? " I asked.

Dagobert shrugged. " Search me."

Joe's head appeared beside the raft. He repeated my words verbatim. " Such as what ? "

Dagobert gave him a hand up. " I understand you have one of those rifles, like the one Arkwright was shot with."

" Is there any law against that ? "

" Probably," Dagobert nodded. " From the first floor balcony just over the Brooklyn Bar one can see the place on the Promenade des Anglais where Arkwright was killed." Dagobert, too, posed for a dive. " I mean," he corrected, just as he hit the water, " murdered."

Joe looked at me uneasily. " Say, what is this ? " he asked.

I shrugged. " He never takes me into his confidence."

" Is he some kinda cop ? "

" Not officially," I reassured him. " In fact even at Scotland Yard no one's *quite* sure of his status."

Dagobert bobbed up. " What was that ? " he asked, climbing on to the raft. " This kind of thing ruins consecutive conversation."

" I said," Joe spoke aggressively, " what's the big idea ? "

" No, you didn't," I corrected. " You asked if he were a cop."

" Members of the *Vingt-Troisième Bureau* do not normally describe themselves as ' cops', " Dagobert said with dignity.

" Then what the hell is this all about ? " Joe exploded.

" I'm so sorry," Dagobert apologised, sitting down beside us. " I thought I explained. I'm blackmailing you."

Joe remained for a moment deep in thought. He seemed to be doing a little mental calculation. The result was apparently unsatisfactory, for he churned the water viciously with the leg he trailed over the raft.

" Yes," Dagobert interpreted, " you were in your room at half-past five on Wednesday."

" But I didn't go near the balcony. I was shaving."

" But you were alone and you have no witnesses to prove you didn't go near the balcony."

" Does everybody have to have a witness," he said in exasperation, " every time a guy gets bumped off ! "

" It's handy if you happen to have a reason for wishing the guy to be bumped off."

" What have I got against Don Diego ? Sure, he's passed out a couple of times in my place—who hasn't ? But I've nothing again the guy."

" The one who got killed was Arkwright."

" Sure, but . . ." Joe broke off, staring at Dagobert, aghast. " Say, do you think it was Arkwright they . . . *meant* to get ? Who'd . . . ? "

" Someone he was blackmailing," Dagobert suggested, " like you."

" Look, let's get this straight, fella. You know darn well Arkwright had nothing on me. Well, practically nothing."

Dagobert obviously knew nothing about it at all. He looked innocent and waited.

" In fact you couldn't really call it blackmail. Maybe I shot my mouth off a bit during those lessons, boasted how I was doing the Government over my subsistence allowance—everybody did—they practically expected it. Even Arkwright said he figured it was just a joke, and asked what would happen if for fun he wrote in and laid information against me to the Veterans' Administration."

" What did happen ? "

" He was kidding, of course. But, well, just in case, I used to give him specially good rates of exchange when he brought dollars or pounds to me. Sure, you could call him a ' blackmailer ' if you want to, but it was such small-time stuff it wasn't worth getting excited about."

" In that case," Dagobert said, " let's don't get excited. I'll just carry on where Arkwright left off—with small-time stuff."

" If you got dollar bills," Joe said cautiously, " I can't let you have more than three eighty. . . ."

" Barioli, at the Grand, will do better than that," said Dagobert, revealing a knowledge of the local Black Market *Bourse* I had no idea he possessed.

" Barioli," Joe said sullenly. " I wouldn't know."

" You sell to him yourself, don't you ? " Dagobert said. " In fact he's the big shot."

" Look. My business is my business. I give you the best rate I can and if you can do better, well, go somewhere else."

" Yes," Dagobert nodded. " Barioli is your clearing house. The interesting thing is he's never had those Santa Rican pesos from you."

I heard Joe inhale swiftly and hold his breath for a moment. Then he said very casually : " Do they have pesos in Santa Rica ? I thought that was the Argentine."

" Those Santa Rican pesos you changed about ten days ago," Dagobert explained patiently. " The day Jane and I first discovered the Brooklyn Bar. The day that Santa Rican tramp steamer, the Carrabia, called at Villefranche. Do you remember, you told us about them that night when we were getting into the taxi with the three Marines ? "

Joe was fidgeting by this time and I could see he was inwardly debating whether or not to deny all knowledge of the transaction. He eyed Dagobert, then appealed to me, not very hopefully :

" Did I say anything about pesos ? "

I nodded, and he swallowed a couple of times. " I always did shoot off my silly mouth," he murmured. " I was thinking maybe you'd forgotten. Say ! " he exclaimed suddenly, " what's to prevent me from swearing I never said anything of the kind ? "

" Why haven't you handed on those pesos to Barioli ? " Dagobert said. " Have another swim and think of an answer to that one. We'll both have a swim and both try to think of an answer."

Dagobert dived off the raft again, but Joe had lost interest. He watched Dagobert thoughtfully, ignoring me. When Dagobert climbed on to the raft again Joe said :

" I'm holding on to them until the rate of exchange goes up."

" I've got a better answer," Dagobert said. " You hid them somewhere or even destroyed them so the police wouldn't come round and start asking you where you got them."

Dagobert's guess was obviously lucky. Joe glowered at him almost with admiration. " In a business like mine," he said, " it doesn't pay to get mixed up in things. All right, say I decide to forget the cash in order to avoid questions, I take a loss."

" How much of a loss ? "

Joe winced slightly at the question. " Plenty," he muttered. " Eight hundred of the goddam things ; in other words, four hundred bucks or nearly a hundred and fifty quid. . . . Then," he added, suddenly struck by the unfairness of it all. " I get asked questions all the same ! "

" Who gave you the pesos ? "

" A guy."

" Named ? "

" Look. My business is supposed to be confidential. Maybe I wouldn't know his name. Probably he was that guy off the *Carrabia*—what's his name, Pedro Garcia."

" I suggest he was an Englishman, fair-haired . . ."

" Okay, okay," Joe broke in with resignation, " if you know so much, why do you keep asking me ? "

" And indubitably off the *Carrabia*," Dagobert continued.

Dagobert's words affected Joe and me differently, though I was at first too preoccupied with my own reactions to notice Joe's. The *Carrabia* had called at Santa Rica before crossing the Atlantic and Henry Makepeace. who was not supposed to arrive in Marseilles until yesterday, had not written to Iris for weeks. I edged forward on the raft, nearly falling off it in my excitement. It was then that I observed the bewildered look on Joe's broad face.

" With," Dagobert concluded rather smugly, " freckles."

" Freckles ? " Joe repeated, plainly baffled. " That's funny—I never noticed Major Arkwright had freckles."

Chapter

12

DAGOBERT ORDERED A *CARPANO* FOR ME AND A *CAMPARI*
for himself. I was thirsty after our swim back from the
raft and the Chesterfield cigarette (for sale to the U.S.
Armed Forces only) provided by Suzette, and I eyed the
tall glasses of beer at the next table longingly. Dagobert
was moody and thoughtful; something had discouraged
him.

" *Que'l sens deia saber guidar,*" he said reflectively,
" *segon que l'ome e l'avers es; Mas ses mezura non
es res.*"

" Sir ? " said the waiter, hovering.

" Bertran de Born," I explained quickly.

" Oh."

" Has it any intimate bearing ? " I asked Dagobert
when the waiter, scratching his head, had drifted on.

" It means I'm losing my grip," he sighed. " ' Man
should be guided by his judgment, but without measure
nothing exists.' It sounds better in Provençal."

" Yes," I agreed.

" It's from a *sirvente,*" he began, cheering up as he
always does when he wanders from the matter in hand,
" or, if you prefer, a Provençal lay, called ' Against the
General Decadence.' "

" Was there much of it at the time ? " I asked
absently, forgetting for a moment what I was letting
myself in for.

" Magna Carta had just been signed. An heir to the
throne of France was born who turned out to be a saint.

They'd begun building Rheims Cathedral three years previously, and the father of modern experimental science, Roger Bacon, was one year old. In fact the outlook seemed reasonably bright."

"There's a moral somewhere," I said.

"All ages are on their last legs—according to those who live in them who ought to know."

"Is that a cheering thought?"

"I'm trying to work myself up into thinking that prosperity is just around the corner," he admitted. "The darkest hour precedes the dawn."

"Can spring be far behind?" I contributed.

"Yes," he said, and returned to his *Campari*. For a while he remained gloomily silent. "Henry," he muttered to himself as though the name depressed him. "Henry."

"Yes, isn't it time you explained those freckles . . . and the trip standing up in the bus in Villefranche?"

"The whole thing was crystal clear," he complained. "I was working up to my big moment. All Joe had to do was give the right answer : Henry. *Not* Arkwright. This thing is going to require a bigger brain than mine, Jane."

I patted his hand and gave it an affectionate squeeze. "I'll bet Joe doesn't know Roger Bacon was one year old in 1215."

"Thanks, Jane. By the way, you'd better verify that before you repeat it. Meanwhile, here's the waiter? Had you anything special in mind?"

"Yes," I said. "luncheon. But let's be late while you tell me what was crystal clear."

"Let me see if I can remember how it went," he said. "Oh, yes. Henry Makepeace for reasons which are immaterial, changed his mind about coming to Marseilles on the *Scythia* and jumped on the tramp steamer *Carrabia* about a fortnight earlier. He wrote Iris

about this change of plan, but Arkwright intercepted
the letter and kept it. When the *Carrabia* docked
ten days ago in Villefranche, Arkwright met it. He
suggested to Henry that for, say, the usual modest
fiver, he could give him some interesting details about
his wife's behaviour during the past two months in
Nice. Henry—a man of action—gave him a black
eye. You remember the black eye Arkwright had in
the Monte Carlo Casino that same night. Henry then
took a taxi to Nice, but having no money except Santa
Rican pesos, asked the driver where he could get
change. The driver took him to the Brooklyn Bar—and
there he changed the pesos. He had a drink and began
wondering if there could be anything in what Arkwright
had insinuated. Could the little woman have been up
to any tricks in his absence and if so with whom ? It
might be worth investigating before making known his
arrival. He lurked for the rest of the morning around
the Pension Victoria. Now Arkwright took Iris out to
luncheon that day as he did again, you may remember,
on the day he was shot. He did this sort of thing when
he was in funds. Luncheon out with Major Hugh de
Courcy Arkwright was one of the minor rewards which
sometimes fell to unattached females staying at the
Victoria."

He paused to finish his drink. I did not interrupt.

" So Henry saw his wife emerging from the Victoria
on the gallant Arkwright's arm. Knowing Iris, she was
probably clinging to that arm affectionately. Henry's
head began to swim slightly. For one reason he had
just realised—or rather thought he'd realised—that if
Iris had had a skid in his absence it was with Arkwright
himself. For another reason, more practical, Henry *is*,
as Iris told us, subject to attacks of malaria. One came
on at this moment. At any rate, he returned to Villefranche, where he'd left his luggage and went to the

Hotel Petit Marguery. He went to bed with quinine
and stayed there until Wednesday. During his fever
he thought a great deal about Iris and decided to give
more than a black eye to Arkwright. On Wednesday
afternoon at about five he went, as he told the proprietor
of the Petit Marguery, ' for a short walk.' He returned
about six-thirty and had dinner for the first time downstairs. He seemed weak and rather shaky. Of course
if, during that hour and a half, he'd come into Nice and
shot the man he thought to be his wife's lover, he *would*
seem rather shaky.

" He went to bed early and after seeing the papers
next day conveniently had a brief relapse. He wasn't
completely restored again until last night, when it seemed
a good idea to arrive suddenly as though he had just
disembarked that afternoon in Marseilles from the *Scythia*
as originally planned. And that is the story. How do
you like it ? "

" There are loose ends," I said cautiously.

" One very loose one," he said. " It isn't true."

" Yes. I can see that's a disadvantage. If Henry *had*
arrived ten days ago on the *Carrabia* . . ."

" He did," Dagobert interrupted.

I swallowed a mouthful of *Carpano* the wrong way.
" Then . . . ? "

" All the unimportant parts are quite true," he said
in a tone of discouragement. " Even the Petit
Marguery and the malaria. And also someone who
exactly answers to the description of Arkwright did
meet the *Carrabia*, though Henry says he didn't notice
him."

" Henry *says* ! " I echoed.

" How do you think I knew he had freckles ? I spent
half an hour with him yesterday afternoon in Villefranche."

" Why don't you tell me these things ? "

" I like to impress you," he explained simply.

" You do. Go on."

" I was having a glass of red wine with one of the dockers who helped unload the *Carrabia.* Running out of small talk, I happened to describe Arkwright. He said that a man who sounded like Arkwright had chatted with the Englishman who got off. What Englishman ? I asked. The one who's ill and staying at the Petit Marguery, he said. When I saw on the hotel register that the Englishman's name was Henry Makepeace, I decided to chat with him, too. I introduced myself as a friend of Arkwright's."

" Any reaction ? "

" I think his temperature went up a degree or two. But all he said was : ' Who's Arkwright ? ' I explained that Arkwright was the man who'd been shot Wednesday afternoon—the man he'd been reading about in all those newspapers spread over his bed. He said he couldn't read French ; he'd only been looking at the pictures. So I told him all about it. I told him that it took place on the corner of the Rue Ravel and the Promenade des Anglais, near that bar, you know, the Brooklyn Bar."

" A further rise in temperature ? "

Dagobert shook his head. " No, this time he looked blank. He said he didn't know the Brooklyn Bar because he hadn't yet visited Nice. He'd come straight from the *Carrabia* to the Petit Marguery. As a matter of fact he had not—except for that short walk on Wednesday afternoon—even left the hotel. I said, ' Indeed ' in a mysterious manner and, after expressing appropriate sentiments about his health, withdrew. I walked all the way home, reconstructing the story of how he'd murdered Arkwright. There was one bad flaw in it : his statement that he'd never been in Nice. I had to prove that he was lying, and that's where Joe was going to help. For I was certain Henry was the man who'd changed those Santa Rican pesos. I was wrong. He wasn't . . ."

" Do we start again ? " I said bravely.

Dagobert misinterpreted the suggestion and brightened. " Why not ? " he said, calling the waiter.

Chapter

13

It was Sunday morning and I don't remember what excuse Dagobert made for rising at some unholy hour— to check up on why the Makepeaces hadn't come home last night, I think. At any rate, I was dozing gently when the telephone beside the bed roused me. Mrs. Andrioli's voice said that Villefranche wanted me. I said 'Hello' sleepily, wondering whom we knew in Villefranche. It was Dagobert.

"I hope I didn't drag you from the typewriter," he said in a hearty voice. "Do you remember those mysterious telephone calls that upset Don Diego?"

"No."

"The day we arrived. The day the *Carrabia* docked. The man who twice phoned the Santa Rican Consulate and left no name."

"Pedro Garcia?"

"No. His name was Henry Makepeace. Make a note of it."

"Why?"

"In case I forget. This is getting complicated."

"I mean why did Henry telephone the Consulate?"

"Wheels within wheels. Work it out."

He rang off and I tried to go back to sleep. Then I tried, as he suggested, to work it out. Henry, just arrived from Santa Rica, could have had a personal message to deliver on behalf of someone in Santa Rica to Don Diego. But why not leave his name? And why telephone Don Diego before he'd telephoned his own wife ? Why, for that matter, had he not let Iris know he was laid up with malaria in Villefranche ?

I dozed off, and about half an hour later the telephone rang again.

" Got the answer yet ? " Dagobert's voice inquired.

" No."

" Pity," he sighed. " Neither have I. . . . I have another one for you. Arkwright's black eye."

" For a man with malaria Henry seems to have spent a busy day," I said.

" No. Joe Orsini was the author of the black eye. Am I holding your interest ? "

" Yes. Go ahead. I'll have my nervous breakdown later."

" Joe socked him the day after Sophie suddenly stopped taking her Universal lessons. Work that one out."

He rang off. I lay back and watched three flies revolving eccentrically around the frosted electric light bulb over the bed. One would pause in mid-air, dart suddenly towards one of the others, change its mind in mid-flight and shoot off in the opposite direction. I tried for a while to distinguish a pattern in their movements, a suggestion of system. Presumably they were up to *something*. But, apart from some blind biological urge to erratic movement, the entire performance was utterly lacking in design or motive.

The resemblance between the behaviour of the flies and that of the inhabitants of the Victoria Pension was so depressing that I got up and decided to have a bath. Sophie had abruptly broken off her lessons in French because, according to Elinor, she'd lost interest. A wise move, according to Mrs. Andrioli, because Major Arkwright was a very attractive man. The following day Joe Orsini had given Arkwright a black eye.

Yes, there was a possible connection between these three statements of fact, perhaps even an obvious

one. The missing link—supplied by Joe, but which Dagobert didn't explain to me until later—was already apparent
As Joe said, " Arkwright made a pass at the kid."

Meanwhile I went into the bathroom. The water was
cold, but I decided it would wake me up. Afterwards I
should ring down for coffee, sit on the balcony and completely alter the patterned silk frock I'd bought last
week at the Galeries Lafayette. I was considering the
hem when I remembered that Elinor Duffield had been
having a bath—also cold—at the moment Hugh Arkwright
was killed. Or so she said.

Did people in their right minds take cold baths?
Leaping out of the tub with a gasp, I decided they didn't.
On the other hand, I just had—which didn't really dis-
prove the point.

The hem was only the beginning of it. I should have
to do something " clever " about those tucks at the waist,
and then there were the shoulders. . . . Why I had
bought the thing I couldn't imagine. I rubbed myself
down viciously with a hand-towel. All right—Elinor
Duffield had stolen Dompierre's rifle and shot Arkwright
with it ? Why ? Just for practice—wasn't she keen
on clay pigeon shooting ?

The behaviour of those flies was relatively compre-
hensible. I clutched my dressing-gown around my half-
dried body and went back to the bedroom. Staring me
in the face was my typewriter (opened yesterday by
Dagobert), and in it the same since untouched sheet of
paper with (typed at the top by Dagobert) CORPSE
DILPOMATIQUE, Chapter One.

I regarded it without pleasure. In the first place, the
title wasn't fair. The only character who could be loosely
described as a member of the diplomatic corps, namely,
Don Diego, was, according to the latest available information, far from being a corpse. Possibly he was meant to
be, but if so I had no story.

I was not, at this stage, really convinced that Major Arkwright *had* been murdered. True, I was living with a man who was convinced he was, and to live with Dagobert is tantamount to inhabiting the same fantasy world and sharing the same mental aberrations. But I still reserved a doubt. I think there *are* such things as accidents, though Arkwright's death may not have been one.

This was not a very constructive reflection, and I removed the flowered silk dress from its box on top of the wardrobe, where I had hidden it from Dagobert in order to avoid discussion. I tried it on. Though it was plainly made for someone of a different shape, I still liked the pattern of tiny scarlet and yellow pimpernels. Perhaps without the shoulder pads. . . .

The telephone rang again and I nearly leapt out of my skin. So much for cold baths steadying the nerves, I said :

" And another thing, Dagobert. Why do you keep telephoning ? "

" I thought you might be wondering what's happened to me ? "

" Has anything happened to you ? "

" Nothing at all. Remind me to ask the concierge if he collects postage stamps."

" Why ? "

" I'm trying to work up an atmosphere of mystery," he explained. " And, oh. Tell the waiter we'll be three for dinner to-night. Ask him if he could put on something special, something rather expensive."

He hung up before I could ask for details. About five minutes later there was a tap on the door and Mrs. Andrioli came in with morning coffee. I hadn't ordered it, but it was exactly what I needed.

She put the tray down on the table beside the typewriter and said : " I have told the chef to make *moules à la marinière* for your guest to-night. It is five hundred francs supplement."

I remembered that mussels were her own favourite dish, but having no ideas of my own, I did not argue.

" Oh," I said, slightly taken aback. " I was just going to . . . But since you already know . . ."

" I listened when your husband telephoned," she explained simply.

" Yes, of course."

" No, not *of course*," she corrected me with a faint smile. " I listened because he meant me to."

" Do you think so ? " I murmured stupidly.

" He is not a fool."

" I won't argue that point. But obviously *you* are not."

" No," she agreed.

As she showed no signs of leaving, I asked her to have a cup of coffee with me. She said thank you, and only then I noticed that there were already two cups on the tray.

I gave her a cup ; her hand, as she took it, was considerably steadier than my own. She put it down and twisted the diamond rings I had noticed on her roughened fingers that first night in Monte Carlo. It was a gesture not of nervousness, but of uncertainty as to where she should begin. Finally she said :

" Yesterday I buried Major Arkwright. It is best that he remain buried."

I handed her the sugar-basin and waited.

" Perhaps he died by accident," she said, taking three lumps. " Perhaps not. . . . It really makes no difference. People make a great deal of fuss over these things."

" They are often considered important," I nodded.

She watched me as I poured out my own coffee. Her eyes were friendly but shrewd. " You," she said, stirring her coffee, " believe Major Arkwright was murdered."

I tried to look non-committal. " And you ? "

" You are pouring coffee on to the tray-cloth," she pointed out. " Yes, probably he was."

" And you think one ought to do nothing about it ? "

" Yes," she said, and dismissing the subject, " I think that would be best. I have brought some *gâteaux*. I thought you would like them."

I shook my head. " Thanks. Do you mind if I have a cigarette instead ? "

" Of course not. Perhaps you will let me have one." She chose a meringue filled with whipped cream and bit into it greedily. " He is dead," she said with her mouth full, " and it will do no good to find out who killed him."

" It's an original point of view." I admitted, feeling slightly outraged by her coolness.

" It might even do harm. . . ."

" To the murderer," I suggested dryly.

She nodded. " Yes, chiefly to the miserable wretch who killed him."

" In these cases one usually thinks of the murdered man as the ' miserable wretch '. "

She ignored my sarcasm. " You," she shook her head, " *and I* . . . we have never killed a man. It is hard possibly for us to understand the suffering and the anguish which would drive a person to commit this crime. The man or woman who would do murder to escape such torture of mind must indeed be a miserable wretch. . . ."

" Yes, but . . ."

I broke off in exasperation. Obviously there were a hundred things wrong with her argument. Analysed, it was simply a justification of murder.

" Yes, but . . ." I repeated lamely, " but don't you want to know who murdered Major Arkwright ? "

She shook her head again with maddening calmness and finished the meringue. I puffed at my cigarette and found I'd forgotten to light it. I said :

" Or do you *already* know ? "

Again she shook her head ; this time a faint smile played about her big good-natured mouth. " It is always

wise to know as little as possible about people," she said,
" especially about murderers, I imagine. . . . They make
quite the best meringues in Nice at the Marquise de
Sevigny," she added, helping herself to another. " Had
Major Arkwright listened to this advice he would still
be alive."

The third match I had applied to my cigarette went
out. I gave it up and gulped my coffee, which was
luke warm.

" You gave Major Arkwright this advice, too ? " I
murmured.

" Frequently," she said. " But he never listened to
it. . . . And now he is dead."

" And—er—now," I said, my throat feeling very dry
in spite of the coffee, " you offer the same advice to us."

She nodded indifferently. " For what it is worth.
You won't listen to it."

At the moment I was by no means sure of this, but I
said nothing.

" For many years," she said, " I have been afraid
something like this would happen. "

" That somebody would kill him ? "

" Yes."

" But everybody liked him."

" Yes, he was a very charming and likeable person."
she agreed. " He was popular because he himself liked
everybody and was interested in everybody. He was
warm-hearted and people confided in him. He had the
natural gift of sympathy. I think on the whole he caused
more happiness to people than unhappiness. To everyone except perhaps, perhaps . . ."

She paused and I supplied : " Except the person who
killed him ? "

She nodded. She sipped her coffee for a moment in
silence, then she said : " You know I suppose that Hugh
sometimes blackmailed people ? "

I nodded vaguely, noting the use of his first name. I refilled her empty coffee-cup.

"No man is perfect," she said tolerantly, "but Hugh was better than most. He was weak, but at least he was kind. He loved himself, but he also loved others. Yes, he blackmailed people, but he hated doing it. It was, he used to say, the only way he knew of making a living."

"Did he make a good living out of it?" I asked, a little bewildered by this defence of her late lodger.

She shook her head. "There were a hundred and eighty francs in his wallet when he died," she said. "His needs were few—he liked to dress well, a relic of twenty years ago. Hugh Arkwright was a professional dancing partner originally. He liked occasionally to take a pretty woman out to luncheon. Women were attracted to him and he was flattered by this, though it rarely went beyond innocent flirtation. He had no other expenses. He gambled little. He paid no rent."

"You mean . . . ?"

"No, he wasn't blackmailing me," she said briefly.

"Do you know whom he was blackmailing?"

"No, I do not. He never told me and I never asked him. I didn't want to know."

"Did he keep any, what you might call, documentary evidence against people? Letters? Pages out of hotel registers and so forth? The sort of thing you might find in his room, I mean?"

She glanced at me shrewdly. "You heard me in his room Wednesday afternoon?" she suggested.

"I heard someone."

"It was me. Yes, he may have kept certain papers of the kind you mean. I burnt them."

"Then . . ."

"I didn't examine them," she interrupted. "There were a few letters not addressed to him, some old newspaper cuttings, a faded snapshot or too. You will probably not believe me, but I burned the entire collection without going through it."

" Why did you search his room last Wednesday ? " I asked, leaving for later consideration the question of whether she had or had not examined Arkwright's papers, " I mean, if he'd been blackmailing people for years why didn't you do it years ago ? "

" Because he'd never before blackmailed anyone for more than a few thousand francs," she said. " He'd played safe. He'd found out only *little* things about people, modest misdemeanours, venial sins. Things which permitted him to borrow insignificant sums and keep almost on good terms with the people he took money from. He said it was like gambling : you needed great self-control. You had to set yourself strict limits. The big stakes, the big gains and losses, were not for him. *He* would always play safe."

A kind of anger had come into her voice, and at the same time I saw, to my astonishment, that she had begun to sniff. She put a handkerchief to her eyes, jabbing at them savagely. It was hard to tell whether she was angry with Hugh Arkwright in retrospect or with herself for betraying emotion.

" But he *didn't* play safe ! " she muttered. " I knew some day he wouldn't ; it would be too much for him. He'd find out *too* much. He'd ask for *more* than a few thousand francs. And then . . ." She gestured vaguely, helplessly, as though the situation had gone beyond her control. " I shall miss him," she concluded abruptly.

She blew her nose. I offered her a third meringue.

" And you think that's what happened," I said quietly. " He found out too much about someone."

" The day before you came here," she said, holding out her left hand, " he gave me this diamond ring. He said it was paste, like all my other rings. I had a jeweller

look at it yesterday. It's real and it's worth a hundred
and fifty thousand francs."

One hundred and fifty thousand francs, I remembered, were roughly a hundred and fifty pounds, or just
the amount Joe had given Arkwright that morning for
eight hundred Santa Rican pesos.

" I would like to return that hundred and fifty thousand
francs," she said.

" That would mean finding out whom he got them
from."

She nodded mechanically.

" And therefore," I suggested, " who shot him. . . ."

" I don't know . . . I suppose so. I didn't sleep very
much last night trying to think about it. Yesterday
morning, during the burial service, I tried to pray. I
still don't know what to do. Hugh left me more than—
well, rather lonely. . . . He left me with this heavy
debt, towards someone I don't know. I shall, I think,
give the ring to charity as I did his clothes and personal
belongings. I have only one way of discharging my debt
towards the unhappy creature who was tortured into
taking human life . . . and that is by *leaving him hence-
forth in peace*. That's why I've told you all this."

" But this ' unhappy creature,' as you call him, is a
murderer," I tried to reason. " And he's still at large."

" Hugh Arkwright *made* him a murderer," she said
dully.

A sense of unreality crept over me : we were on a
plane of morality far beyond my pedestrian grasp. I
said practically :

" That's not really our responsibility Mrs. Andrioli."

" It is mine," she said. " I knew it many years ago
when, instead of turning him over to the police, I married
him."

Chapter

14

I LIKED MRS. ANDRIOLI—I HAD EVER SINCE MY FIRST glimpse of her in Monte Carlo, breaking the traditions of the *Salons Privés* by treating roulette as though it were a game and immediately transforming her winnings into food and drink. I liked what I'd seen of her during our stay at the Pension Victoria, her good sense and good cooking, her firm but courteous manner towards her guests. She was, she told me, five years older than Hugh Arkwright ; but the difference between them was deeper. She was an adult and he was a child.

I had accepted every word she said without question ; she felt a deep and terrible sense of responsibility for the perennial play-boy she had taken on when she bought the Pension Victoria just before the war. They had been married the day war broke out, and at Hugh's request they had kept the event secret. It would, he said, be bad for his career to be known as a married man. Giving in on that point was her first mistake ; for already she had guessed what his career was. She had loved him the way a mother might love a child whom she knew to be weak and vicious, with the same swiftness to rush to his defence and the same underlying anxiety. She had borne the burden of his guilt for so long that it had become her own.

His death had lifted that burden, and it was possible to understand why she wished his murderer to go in peace. Perhaps, even, the murderer had, as she suggested, paid in advance for his crime, and should be left not to human justice, but to heaven's.

In brief, by the time Mrs. Andrioli left me that morning I was in a bad state of moral confusion. It was confounded still further by the sudden thought that Mrs. Andrioli herself could have killed him in order to discharge her debt to society. As Dagobert said, the thing was getting complicated. I felt a strong urge to take Mrs. Andrioli's advice and have no further part in it.

Just before noon I heard the Makepeaces in the room next door. They had come back from celebrating their reunion. We heard later that they'd spent yesterday at Juan-les-Pins and the night at Cannes—an ecstatic time getting " re-acquainted." Iris was bubbling with girlish joy and excitement. She was the heroine of a novelette in which Henry's dramatic return was the last-page happy ending.

We found ourselves neighbours on the balcony, separated only by the iron spikes, a few minutes later. I began tactfully to withdraw, but Iris stopped me. None of us had met Henry two nights ago in the sitting-room and Iris was dying to introduce him to *all* her friends.

In fact why not a cocktail party in Room Twelve immediately for this purpose ? Henry and Dagobert would have dozens of interests in common. Henry would be *most* amused by Elinor Duffield and Sophie, and there was a rather pleasant little Frenchman who played the piano divinely called Dieudonné Dompierre, but whom *everybody* called Pierre.

There were two bottles of gin, and Iris would go and warn everybody at once while I entertained Henry. Henry and I would *adore* each other.

After she had gone we eyed each other doubtfully across the iron spikes. The beach at Juan-les-Pins had left Henry looking pink and fit in spite of his recent bout of malaria.

He was in his late twenties, though his fair hair with a wave in it was thinning. He had slightly protuberant blue eyes and, of course, the famous freckles. It was one of those jolly, open faces that motor salesmen have when they're about to sell a car that needs new pistons.

" If you don't want to be entertained you needn't be," I tried to reassure him.

Henry never smiled, but he had a loud and hearty laugh which more than made up for it. In a most disconcerting way and without warning he would explode with laughter at practically anything anybody—including himself—said.

" There was a book of yours," he said, sobering down, " in the ship's library. I read it."

The prospect of a *tête-à-tête* with Henry became more attractive. " Which would that be ? " I asked eagerly.

He glanced around to make sure that Iris had gone. " The—er—*Carrabia*, as a matter of fact."

" No, I mean which *book* ? "

" Which book ? " he echoed vaguely. " Oh, I see what you mean. It was jolly good, damn clever, I thought. I can't remember exactly what it was called. There was a murder in it, I think. Or maybe it was a suicide. Bloke jumped off a cliff for some reason, I seem to remember."

" Anyway, it made a deep impression," I suggested.

" Absolutely," he agreed. " Don't know how you think of it all. How about a quick one before Iris comes back ? "

The gin bottles were already set out on the balcony on the iron table beneath the striped umbrella. He measured out two quadruples in tooth-mugs and added a flavouring of vermouth. He handed one of them through the bars.

" Where's Dagobert ? " he asked.

" I never know," I confessed.

" There was a type called Dagobert in that book, now that I think of it."

" It was probably the same one," I said. " He's practically the only man I know by that name."

He shrugged. " It's a damn silly name when you come to think of it—un-English. He was a sort of detective, wasn't he ? "

" Sort of," I nodded, " is the operative phrase."

He looked blank for an instant, then exploded with laughter. He stopped laughing as abruptly as he'd begun and frowned into his tooth-mug.

" I wanted to talk to you about Dagobert some time," he said. " Privately. He—er—did he mention having —er . . . ? "

" Called on you at Villefranche ? "

" That's it. It's about Iris. I suppose I shouldn't shout." He examined the iron spikes which divided us. " Perhaps," he began, putting a cautious foot on the outer edge of the balcony and steadying himself, " I mean if you don't mind. . . ."

" There *is* a door which leads into our room," I pointed out.

But he was already half-way over. I averted my eyes from the fifty-foot drop to the pavement.

" This is the sort of thing that gives the place a bad name ! " he said, exploding again, but luckily retaining his grip on the ironwork. " What's that about iron bars not keeping the sexes apart ? No, that's ' do not a prison make.' "

He paused in mid-air to work it out. To shorten the ordeal I suggested Love Laughs at Locksmiths.

" That's it," he said, landing safely on my balcony. " I'll bet I'm not the first to have climbed over those spikes. The old Pension Victoria's probably seen plenty of fun and games of that sort in its day. Eh ? "

To bring the conversation down to a more practical level I pointed out that he had left his drink on his own balcony. He was about to repeat the acrobatic performance when I hastily offered him my own plastic tooth-mug. This gave immediate rise to allusions to sharing tooth-mugs, and I rather hoped Iris would come back.

"D'you know, I pictured you as older in that book I read," he confided, glancing at me over the rim of the mug. "And more snooty."

"I am," I murmured vaguely. "What was it you wanted to talk about privately?"

"There's no hurry," he said, walking from the balcony into our room. He glanced at the blank page in my typewriter and helped himself to a Gauloise. "As a matter of fact I like mature women," he said, flicking his lighter and holding it to the cigarette. "Always did. They're more, you know, sophisticated, you know, more . . ."

The Gauloise caught him unexpectedly and he gasped. I was only moderately distressed. In theory I had been a little sorry for Henry in view of the Iris-Dompierre situation. I began to wonder if sympathy were uncalled for.

"Wasn't it about Iris?" I prompted.

"Iris is a good type," he said loyally. "She's mad about me, but she's broadminded too. I shouldn't wonder if she left us alone together on purpose!" He laughed heartily and added: "Oh well, we're only young once."

"Thank heavens for that," I said. "Dagobert, by the way, is singularly narrow-minded. . . . What was he checking up on when he visited you in the Hotel Petit Marguery?"

Henry looked worried. "That's what I can't quite understand," he said, sitting down in the one comfortable chair. He sipped his gin critically, or rather he sipped my gin critically. "I hoped you might help me out. This is all confidential, of course."

"Of course."

" He said he was a pal of this Major What's-his-name, you know : the one that stopped the bullet meant for the Santa Rican Consul . . ."

" The one whose room you now occupy," I nodded.

Henry choked over the remainder of our gin. " Gosh ! Was *he* in Room Twelve ? Iris didn't tell me. Not that one's superstitious or any rot of that sort, but . . . I mean to say ! Did, er, Dagobert know this major fellow very well ? "

" They went to school together," I said, forgetting to add that the school was the Universal.

" Oh . . . But weren't they different generations ? "

" There is that," I admitted.

Henry remained lost in thought for a moment. " I suppose Dagobert looked after his things, more or less. After he died, that is."

" He had nothing to speak of."

" I mean—you know—old papers and things."

" I know," I nodded. " As a matter of fact, Mrs. Andrioli *burned* all his old papers—and things. Without looking at them."

" Did she ? Did she really ? " he murmured, sucking at the empty toothmug. " Er, what was this Major What's-his-name like ? "

" But surely you remember Major Arkwright ! " I exclaimed with my most ingenuous smile. " He met the *Carrabia*."

" Oh . . . did he ? I had a stinking fever at the time. You get muddled . . . malaria, you know. Santa Rica's full of it. One reason I jumped on an earlier boat. You wouldn't have any gin in here, I suppose ? Excuse me a sec and I'll fetch some from next door."

When he came back via the door he was carrying a gin bottle, vermouth and a packet of " Players." He was looking quite cheerful again. There was, he reported, still no sign of Iris and the guests.

" We could throw a little private party in here ! " he suggested. " How about it ? Yes, d'you know, I thought you were a blonde. From that book I mean. Everybody's a blonde these days—even in Santa Rica, except up country, of course."

He refilled the toothmug and handed it gallantly to me. " What I really wanted to say was this," he frowned. " Business first, pleasure afterwards, eh ? The other night when I arrived—here in Nice, I mean— like an idiot I told Iris I'd just come from Marseilles. I mean, that I'd just landed on the *Scythia*. Whereas, as you and Dagobert know . . . I say ! Does anybody else know I was laid up ten days in Villefranche ? "

I shook my head. " I don't think so."

" Good. Having told everybody I came on the *Scythia* I'd look a damn fool if I suddenly said I'd been in Ville-franche all along. Would you two mind keeping it under your hat ? "

" Why didn't you let Iris know ? " I asked curiously.

" Have you ever seen a man with malaria ? " he asked. " Not a pretty sight. No sex appeal. Besides I was really too dam' sick at the time to want to get in touch with anybody. Too much fag."

" You could have telephoned."

" Telephoned ? " he repeated, rather sharply I thought.

He looked at me for an instant and I thought his pro-tuberant eyes were uneasy. It was, however, tempting to read into his expression more than was there. After all I *knew* he had telephoned Don Diego that morning.

" Telephoned ? " he repeated a second time in his nor-mal manner. " Forgot they had such things in France ! No, the point is, I'd be grateful if you'd not say anything to Iris about my being only three miles up the coast during these past ten days. She'd probably get the idea I'd been spying on her."

The thought delighted him, and he broke into hearty

peals of laughter. " It wouldn't have been such a bad idea at that ! What d'you think ? "

" I try not to think."

" When the cat's away, eh ? " he continued, charmed with his own wit. " They say this Arkwright chap was a smooth customer, rather Iris's type, I gather. Confidentially—between ourselves, Jane—were there any fun and games ? Any bits of nonsense ? I won't let it go any farther."

" Let's not let it go even this far," I said, rising.

He rose, too, and with his drink followed me towards the balcony. " Sauce for the goose, sauce for the gander, eh ? " he suggested.

" You have a proverb for every situation," I said. " And a one-track mind."

" Why not ? " he said.

" It's on the wrong track."

" Maybe you *are* a bit snooty at that," he murmured, leaning against the balcony railing beside me. " I like them snooty."

" You like them. Period." I said, making a tactical error.

He laughed happily. He'd been to the cinema and the witticism was apparently familiar. He put a negligent hand over mine and whispered :

" You read me like a book, Jane."

" This is getting absurd."

" Why ? " he breathed earnestly. " I love your hair Jane."

" If you don't know why, there's nothing I can do about it," I said, beginning to be irritated.

" Then why do anything about it ? "

I glanced at him witheringly and risked no comment. But Henry did not wither readily. He said :

" Of course it's absurd. That's what makes life interesting. Things like this are sometimes inevitable . . ."

I hoped for a moment that our Henry was developing a sense of humour. But his pop eyes were solemn—possibly the gin.

" I suspect you have snappy come-backs like that for all occasions," I said.

" Yes, rather," he nodded, vaguely feeling that it was a compliment.

" In that case," I said, completely losing my head. " think of a snappy come-back to this one : why did you give Major Arkwright eight hundred pesos the morning you got off the *Carrabia* ? "

He dropped the tooth-mug hc'd been holding with his free hand. It fell from the balcony and hit the pavement four floors below. I saw it bounce out and across to the Promenade des Anglais, rolling in a symbolic sort of way towards the spot where Major Arkwright had been killed. I heard Henry muttering something about " being dam' clumsy " and Iris' voice on the adjoining balcony laughing merrily.

" Hello," she said, " I was afraid iron bars wouldn't keep you two apart."

I should, of course, have been studying Henry's reactions, but the peregrinations of the tooth-mug still held me spellbound. It had come to a final pause at the feet of a man who stood exactly where Major Arkwright had stood at five-thirty last Wednesday afternoon. The man was gazing idly up at the Pension Victoria, and the man was Dagobert.

Chapter

15

IRIS DID HER BEST, BUT HENRY'S INTEREST IN ME SEEMED to have slackened. I may have been, as she insisted, exactly his type, but during the cocktail party he left me strictly alone. I remained wedged on the bed between Elinor Duffield and a forbidding woman called the Countess Gluttonsen who talked to me in French about (I think) Swedish court circles.

I'm not mad about social gatherings in Pension bed-rooms—especially at midday. You are already only too familiar with each other's faces. In fact you have been keeping your distance twice a day in the dining-room, and in the drawing-room taking refuge behind newspapers. Then suddenly Miss So-and-So has a few people into room twenty-seven for cocktails. You all change your clothes. You all shake hands and chatter animatedly as though you haven't met for years. There are usually about twelve women and two men. There is nowhere to sit. You chain-smoke and spoil your meal with cheese tit-bits. The ice runs out and you drink warm sweetish mixtures which taste non-alcoholic and make you sleepy all the afternoon. Everyone agrees it is a great success, and before you realise what you're doing you've invited the entire crowd to your room the following day.

Dagobert, who seems to be guided by instinct on these occasions, did not turn up. But Dompierre had some-how been persuaded to come. He wore his most shabby corduroy jacket over blue jeans and had not brushed his mane of dark chestnut hair. I think he was trying to look like the poor, struggling musician who has strayed by accident among his social betters. He stood uncomfortably in one corner, looking out of place. Elinor tried to make him talk to us, but he was in one of his not-understanding-so-well-English moods.

Henry was *bonhomie* itself, filling glasses, handing things round, laughing uproariously and exerting his charm on everyone in the room under the age of sixty— except me. We all agreed he was delightful, and " so typically English."

The third male whom Iris had dug up was the Countess Gluttonsen's son, a very stiff and correct young man of about twenty. Elinor had promptly introduced him to Sophie and settled them together on the balcony where they sat side by side without exchanging a word. Mrs. Andrioli had been invited but excused herself. On the other hand the three new Belgian women, eager to practise their English, were there in force.

At one o'clock Mrs. Andrioli on the floor below rang the luncheon bell in a marked manner, but only the Countess and her son, who were always dead on time for meals, responded. I moved over to make more room for Elinor. She followed the departure of the Swedish mother and son with a glance of regret.

" I wish Sophie would show a little more interest," she sighed. " I suppose it's something to do with her father. I sometimes think a psycho-analyst . . ."

" She was very fond of her father, wasn't she ? " I said.

Elinor nodded. " She used to follow him around like a dog. It was sweet, in a way. Everyone in Buffalo used to say so. Even as a baby he dragged her with him everywhere and when she grew up they were inseparable. I felt almost like an outsider. When he died this spring she had a kind of, I suppose you'd call it, a nervous breakdown. That's why I thought of bringing her abroad."

I agreed that that sounded reasonable.

"I wanted her to meet people, preferably young men of her own age, and—if I may say so—her own station in life. Of course I've gone the wrong way about it, grabbing every eligible young man I could lay hands on and thrusting him at her. I'm afraid it's been rather obvious."

I said not at all, and suddenly asked if by any chance they'd known Joe Orsini in Buffalo. The name meant nothing to her, and I explained that the proprietor of the Brooklyn Bar was a fellow townsman and graduate of the Buffalo High School. She shrugged and explained that Buffalo was full of Italian immigrants of the kind.

"America is a very democratic country," she told me with a slight smile. "Up to a point. We all go to the same schools, but we also have a phrase: 'the wrong side of the railroad track'. After school we generally return to our own side of the railroad track."

"It sounds tricky," I said. "Why did you come straight to Nice? But of course you'd been here in nineteen twenty-seven yourself."

"Yes, I thought . . ." she hesitated, sipped her cocktail and glanced at me with an apologetic smile. "But it doesn't make any difference what a woman of forty-five thinks, does it?"

As the question was not only cryptic but also rhetorical I smiled back vaguely and said nothing.

"We dream . . . we wake up," she continued. "I know you're thinking I came to Nice as much for my own sake as for Sophie's. You may be right . . ."

"Where did you stay in nineteen twenty-seven?" I asked, refusing the pink concoction Iris tried to put in my glass. (The gin and vermouth, getting low, was being reserved for Henry, Dompierre and Dagobert, if he ever arrived.)

"At the Negresco," Elinor said. "The slump didn't hit us until two years later! This time the Pension

Victoria seemed more our style. But it's very, very comfortable," she added hastily.

" How did you find it ? Cooks ? "

" No," she said. " I knew someone who stayed here and for some reason the name stuck in my mind all these years."

Henry arrived from the balcony with the prettiest of the Belgians in tow and a large glass of almost neat gin. She was having trouble understanding him, partly because of her imperfect knowledge of English, partly because of Henry's increasing difficulty with enunciation.

"What is this *mat choor* that he is saying ? " she appealed to us. "*Qu'est-ce que veut dire* mat choor, *au juste ?*"

" Mr. Makepeace likes mature women," I translated.

Henry glared but she laughed happily and immediately explained it all to her two older companions. Mrs. Andrioli rang the luncheon bell again and everyone realised with cries of amazement that it was after half past one. I'd thought it was later. Elinor invited us all for cocktails in her room the following evening and the party broke up. Dompierre was the last to leave ; as he was not lunching in the Pension that day he was sensibly finishing up the snacks.

Dagobert still hadn't come home and I lunched alone, though Iris pressed me to join Henry and her. They were going to buy a motor car that afternoon and why didn't I come along ? If Dagobert hadn't turned up, perhaps I could persuade Pierre to make a fourth. I said I had to have my hair washed, and after luncheon escaped into the sitting-room for coffee. Only the Countess was there, snoring over *Svenska Dagbladet*, and the Duffields. Elinor was knitting and Sophie was deep in the *Saturday Evening Post*. We again agreed what fun the cocktail party had been and how charming Henry was, and settled down to half an hour's peace and quiet.

By half past three there was still no sign of Dagobert, Elinor was dozing off and Sophie was still going through the motions of reading, turning a page about once every fifteen minutes. Through the half-closed shutters there was a glimpse of the Mediterranean, bright blue and sparkling. I put down Hugo's French Grammar Simplified, and said to Sophie : " Let's go swimming."

She came out of an article on the Far Eastern Situation, if indeed that's where she'd been, and said :

" What for ? "

" It might wake us up. Besides I more or less promised Joe to bring you swimming this afternoon."

Her eyes flickered towards her mother, then back to her magazine again. " I don't think I will." She had lowered her voice, so as not to awaken Elinor. " But thank you all the same," she added.

She began to read again, or rather she pretended to read. I rose. " Have it your own way," I said, and began to go.

But I lingered in the door, giving her another chance. Just as I was going she said, still speaking softly :

" Are you going anyway ? "

" Yes."

" It isn't very polite to let you go alone, is it ? " she stammered. It was the first time I'd ever heard Sophie worried by such a small item as politeness. I said :

" I don't mind in the least." Then relenting : " I wish you'd come with me."

She eyed her mother again. Elinor's glasses had fallen forward on her nose and her mouth was half-open. The lines, normally kept at bay by her animation, had regained possession of her face, and she looked weary, worn and old. Sophie regarded her with an expression I had never seen on the girl's face. I was so unused to any expression on Sophie's face that it took me a moment to identify it. It was affection.

" I might come and watch you," she said. " I'm not sure I'll swim."

I went upstairs and changed. I tapped on Sophie's door a few minutes later. I thought she said " Come in," and I pushed the door open.

Sophie hadn't heard my knock and she spun round in embarrassment as I entered. She was wearing a one-piece bathing dress not unlike my own, and she had been examining herself critically before the mirror. She had the thin body of an under-fed child, all arms and legs and angles. She had combed out her straight mousy hair, and it straggled unevenly towards her bony shoulders. Her colourless face flushed as she seized a dressing-gown and wrapped it hastily around her. I guessed suddenly why she didn't want to go swimming in front of Joe.

But it also struck me that her reasoning was wrong. The truth was she looked rather appealing in her bathing suit. I said, " Come along," and when she wanted to change back into her frock I told her not to be silly.

" Joe is used to voluptuous curves," I said bluntly, remembering Suzette, "and if I know anything about him he is not impressed by them."

She came with a mixture of unwillingness and eagerness. As we passed the sitting-room door she instinctively walked on tiptoe. But training triumphed. She put her head inside and said to her mother, who had wakened up :

" Janes' asked me to go swimming with her, Elinor. Do you mind ? "

"Of course not," Elinor smiled. " Have a good time." She added, just as we turned away : " Which beach are you going to ? I may come along later and watch you."

" The Beau Rivage," I lied promptly, thinking of the furthest beach in the opposite direction.

Elinor added a perfunctory warning about not swimming out too far and beamed at me gratefully. I wondered if her smile would have been so warm had she known I was leading her daughter to a rendezvous on " the wrong side of the railroad track."

Chapter

16

BUT OF COURSE JOE WASN'T THERE. SOPHIE SAID SHE
hadn't for a moment expected he would be—in fact on
the whole she was glad he wasn't. She'd only come to
keep me company, anyway.

Such companionability from Sophie Duffield was new
to me, but I said it was very nice of her and we plunged
into the sea ; that is, Sophie plunged. Like all Americans, she swam like a fish. By the time I reached the
raft she had dived from it and was streaking again towards the shore. I suspected someone had just arrived
who from a distance resembled Joe. But it wasn't Joe
after all, and we stretched out on our towels to enjoy
the sun. Sophie relapsed into her normal state of silence.
After about ten minutes I offered her a cigarette. She
hesitated, then accepted it. She smoked as though she
weren't used to it.

" Dad used to give me cigarettes when we went out
dancing together," she said. " He used to laugh when
they choked me. I got into the habit of pretending to
choke just because it amused him. I can't get out of it."

It was the longest speech I'd ever heard her make,
and I gave her another ten minutes to recover from it.
Then I re-introduced the subject.

" What was your father like ? "

" Like ? " She came to, gave the question consideration and said : " I guess he was just a swell guy."

The portrait seemed sketchy, but I recognised in it

the sentimental under-statement, the illiterate cliché in which educated Americans so often cloak their deeper emotions.

" He wanted a son, of course," she added. " But he got me. He used to call me Slump because I was born in nineteen twenty-nine. On the twenty-sixth of December—too late even for Christmas, he used to say. It's funny with parents. One of them teases you, pushes you around, treats you rough and you worship him. The other spoils you, is unfailingly sweet, and . . . oh, I don't know ! " She flung a stone across the beach. " If only," she murmured between her teeth, " she wouldn't try to treat me like her sister ! *He* could. But she can't ! No one can take his place. *No one !* "

She relapsed on to the pebbles, her head in her arms. Her fists were clenched and her thin body twitched. I put out a hand towards her shoulder, but thought better of it. I spoke harshly, keeping the sympathy in my voice under control.

" Don't be so egotistic, Sophie. No one's trying to take your father's place. But your mother—being your mother—may feel she deserves a place in your affections, too."

She made a brief affirmative gesture with her head without removing it from her arms. " I know," she murmured. " You're right, I guess. And she has—sometimes. I do love her really. It's only when she talks about men. Uhh ! " she shuddered. " I loathe men." She propped herself up suddenly on her elbows and looked at me with the wide eyes of a schoolgirl. " Don't you, Jane ? That Henry Makepeace, for instance—disgusting ! "

I laughed at her intensity. " I see what you mean," I admitted. " But they vary, you know."

" Dagobert's all right," she said. She frowned judicially, looking in her seriousness about fifteen years old.

" Or, anyway, he will be in a few years. To tell the truth, I like older men."

" Marry one roughly your own age and they get older."

" Umm," she reflected thoughtfully. " I suppose so.
. . . It means waiting. Not that *I* mind."

She glanced round suddenly. I wondered if the word
" waiting " had reminded her of Joe. I said :

" You've never been in love."

" Yes, I have," she said quickly. " Once. With Dad."

" Don't they have courses in psycho-analysis in the Buffalo High School ? " I said dryly. " You know what I mean."

She crinkled up her nose, half in disgust, half in amusement. " You're as bad as Elinor," she said. " Let's have another swim. We might as well."

When we emerged again we lighted cigarettes—this time Sophie did not cough—and discussed clothes. Sophie was surprisingly constructive on the subject of what to do with my new silk frock. Dagobert has a charitable theory that women do not spend the major part of their time discussing men and clothes. I was rather glad he wasn't there that afternoon, for after we had theoretically reconstructed most of our respective wardrobes, Sophie herself said :

" You think I'm keen on Joe, don't you ? "

" Aren't you ? "

She shook her head. " You can talk to him. As a matter of fact you and Joe are the first people I've talked to since I left home."

" Us," I nodded, " and Major Arkwright."

She went on rather quickly, I thought. " Joe's all right. Not that he's even noticed me—not any more than his other clients, but . . . to tell the truth, I first became sort of friendly with Joe because I knew it would annoy Mother. She'd be horrified if she thought I'd gotten friendly with the owner of the Brooklyn Bar. Not that I have, of course."

" And yet you told him that Major Arkwright had made—what did Major Arkwright actually make— advances ? "

She blushed suddenly. " I—I," she began, " I don't know what came over me. I *did* say something vague . . . maybe it was the atmopshere of the place with Suzette and all those girls. I guess I suddenly wanted to show off. There's no other explanation."

She looked so ashamed of herself that I laughed out loud.

" You made quite an impression on Joe," I said. " He gave Hugh Arkwright a black eye just to keep him in his place."

" Did—did Joe do that ? " she stammered. " Gosh ! How did you know ? " she added suspiciously.

" He told Dagobert. Nice is a small town."

" Apparently," she gasped.

" The interesting point is whether the black eye was deserved," I said.

She ignored the remark, her mind elsewhere. " The crazy guy ! " she murmured, tossing pebbles accurately towards a rusty tin. " The poor sap. . . . Dad once gave the clerk at the drug store on the corner a black eye because he got fresh. I was sixteen and he asked me if I'd ever been kissed." She stirred uncomfortably at the memory.

" For a young woman who loathes men," I said, " you seem to have caused lots of damage."

She blushed again. " I suppose it's a girl's own fault really, these things. Maybe I loathe women as much as I loathe men—me, anyway."

" Tell me about Hugh Arkwright," I said.

She missed the rusty tin by several feet, searched carefully for another pebble and said :

" How do you mean? "

" Had he asked for the black eye Joe gave him, or were you merely boasting ? In other words, did he get fresh, or did you just imagine it ? "

She tossed another stone, missing her target by yards this time. " I—I—don't know."

" You're twenty-one, Sophie. Old enough to vote," I said in exasperation. " Of course you know."

" I mean, I don't know whether it was his fault or mine."

" *It !* " I exclaimed, my brain reeling. " What on earth are you talking about ? "

This time she laughed at me. " Nothing very fatal," she hastened to reassure me. " At the School one day . . . oh, it's all very silly and boring, really. It can't possibly interest you."

" Go on."

She had turned her face away, but I could see that even her ears had gone red. She was digging a hole in the stony beach and badly damaging her fingernails in the process.

She said : " I know French pretty well—at least the grammar part—and we'd closed the books. We'd started chatting, the way you do. About life generally. Major Arkwright was nice to talk to. You felt very at ease with him, kind of intimate, and yet—it's hard to express —safe. He told me he knew I was a lonely, rather special sort of person—he knew because he was too. It sounds corny the way I say it, but it wasn't the way he did. Anyway . . . suddenly I realised the conversation wasn't safe at all. In fact he was subtly making love to me . . ." She broke off and looked up at me with those shocked, wide-open schoolgirl eyes which made it sometimes difficult to realise she was an adult.

" And," she repeated with a catch in her throat, " and *I was liking it.*"

" Oh," I said inadequately.

" Of course, the first thing I did," she continued hastily, " was to tell the school I was too busy to finish my course . . . and, well, that's really all."

" What did you tell your mother ? "

" That I wasn't getting anything out of the lessons, and that I'd lost interest."

" Had you, in fact, lost interest ? " I asked curiously.

Sophie considered the question seriously. " I think really I had," she said finally. " Anyway, I certainly have since. It was just one of those things. But, well, I did see him again, I mean in private. In his room, that was the awful part of it. By the way, don't for heaven's sake tell Mother anything about this ! She'd be terribly shocked, in spite of her nineteen-twenty ' modernism.' It was in the middle of the night a couple of days later. I think you and Dagobert had arrived."

" As a matter of fact," I nodded, " I thought I heard girlish laughter in Room Twelve late one night."

Sophie began to laugh, something between a giggle and hysteria. Not that my memory could be trustworthy at this remove, but I imagined it was the same laugh which had puzzled me that night.

" I know ! " she gasped. " I—I don't quite know why I went. He'd more or less invited me, of course, but I shouldn't have gone. I had some idea I ought to explain to him why I'd broken off my lessons so suddenly. Then —well, to tell the honest truth, I *had* wondered about the black eye and if it was anything to do with what I'd said to Joe. Major Arkwright wasn't expecting me. I tapped on the door, and when he opened it—Jane ! You'll never guess. It was awful ! He was nearly bald ! He wore a toupet and he'd taken it off for the night ! I guess I shouldn't have laughed. But I couldn't help it."

" On the contrary, it was exactly the right thing to do,"
I said.

She stopped laughing abruptly. " Poor Major Arkwright," she said, apparently remembering for the first
time that he was dead. " I wonder if he really was as
lonely as he said. Still, it doesn't matter much now,
does it ? " She threw a stone with restored accuracy
at the rusty tin, this time sending it spinning. She
sprang to her feet. " Shall we go in again ? "

I was about to say no when I saw her stiffen. She
went slightly pale and dropped on to her hands and
knees. But before she could clutch her dressing-gown
around her Joe Orsini had joined us. He said " Hi ! "
and stretched out on the pebbles beside me. With his
rippling muscles a deep bronze, he looked like a professional life-guard.

He stared at Sophie with a broad grin. " Don't they
feed you at that Pension ? " he said. " You're as skinny
as a rabbit. Come around some time and I'll give you
a decent steak with French fried."

Sophie squirmed miserably and I said : " Speaking of
food, has Dagobert invited you to dinner with us to-
night ? "

He shook his head.

" He's asked somebody," I said.

Joe frowned and tapped a cigarette out of his packet
of Lucky Strikes. He dismissed the thought which had
evidently crossed his mind. " No," he drawled, " even
Dagobert wouldn't do that."

" Do what ? "

" Invite Suzette—not when there are people like the
Duffields."

" Oh, wouldn't he ? " I murmured, accepting a cigarette.

He lighted it, lighted another and tossed it to Sophie,
saying, " Catch."

She caught it, took an awkward puff and immediately

choked. Joe burst out laughing and Sophie flushed. She looked wretched, but distinctly appealing.

" You don't know how to smoke ! " Joe said. " Don't pretend. Gosh, what a sophisticated type old B.H.S. is turning out these days ! "

He was on his feet again and had grabbed her by the hands. He jerked her up as though she weighed nothing.

" Come along, kid. I'll race you to the raft."

I watched them hit the water simultaneously, making two silver streaks through the blue water. They reached the raft at exactly the same moment. Joe must have been impressed. I was.

I chose that moment to fold up my towel and silently steal away.

Chapter

17

I WENT HOME AND CHANGED INTO MY NEW SILK FROCK, deciding it wasn't so bad after all—and besides, who cared? Dagobert was obviously never coming back; Joe and Sophie would not even notice my disappearance, and even Henry had lost his taste for maturity since my tactless question about Santa Rican pesos.

Doubtless I could have joined Elinor in the sitting-room and discussed the idle dreams of the middle-aged and the cruel awakening, or perhaps Dompierre wouldn't have minded if I sat quietly with folded hands and listened while he made depressed sounds on the piano.

Midday cocktail parties usually take me like this at about five-thirty in the afternoon, especially when I have missed tea. I glanced through a footnote in Hugo's " Simplified Grammar " and learned that the imperfect of the subjunctive is almost never used in contemporary French conversation ; but even this did not cheer me greatly.

I wandered downstairs, where the smell of cooking reminded me that one consolation still remained. I have never understood how the French manage to make the preliminary odours of dinner so ravishing. At home I always have to open the windows.

There was a slip of paper in my letter-box ; a telephone call at four o'clock. No message and no name left. Mrs. Andrioli had pencilled in: " I think it was Mr. Brown." It was nice to know he still remembered me.

There were three similar slips in the adjoining letter-box, Room Twelve. I was dying to look at them, but, luckily, didn't, for at that moment Henry himself joined me in the hall. It was our first moment alone together since the balcony scene this morning.

" Oh," he said, glancing round as though he hoped someone might come to his rescue, " I—er—there's a Sunday afternoon post, is there ? "

" I think they're telephone calls," I said, lingering.

" But I don't know anyone in Nice," he rumbled. " Perhaps the chap at the garage."

He took the slips from his letter-box, glanced at them and crushed them hastily into his trousers pockets. He had just washed and shaved, and he looked fresh and spruce, except for a kind of worn, worried look in his pale, protuberant eyes.

" No name left ? " I suggested.

He glanced at me sharply, then turned away to search for a cigarette. " No," he said. " No, there wasn't."

He obviously assumed I'd already examined the contents of his letter-box. I detained him as he prepared to leave.

" Any luck with the car you were going to buy ? "

" Yes, we got it. One of those little Renaults with the engine at the back. It's parked outside now, as a matter of fact. Iris hopes you and your husband will take an excursion with us some day. She'll arrange it with you."

" Where is Iris ? "

" Upstairs." Again he gave me one of those piercing glances and lowered his voice almost to a whisper. " Straightening up the mess."

" The mess ? Oh yes, the cocktail party."

" No," he said darkly, " *not* the cocktail party."

" I see," I supplied when he did not elaborate. " Just the usual mess."

The piercing gaze was more uncertain this time. Plainly he was beginning to be as puzzled as I was. He straightened his old school tie and said diffidently :

" If you're not doing anything, Mrs. Brown . . . I mean, it's six . . . and Iris is bound to be hours."

" Are you inviting me to have a drink, Henry ? "

" That was the idea, more or less. Of course, if you're waiting for Dagobert, or anything . . ."

" It's too late to talk yourself out of it. I accept."

Going down in the lift I said to him : " Do you want to clear up the mystery of the mess at once, or shall we work around to it gradually over our second dry Martini ? "

He laughed much too heartily for the confined space in which we found ourselves. " It's damned annoying all the same," he said, sobering down abruptly. " When we were out this afternoon someone got into our room. I had the key with me. Nothing was stolen, but my things were chucked all over the place. I thought probably you knew."

" You mean," I forced a smile, " you thought I'd done it."

" Oh, I say ! " he sounded shocked. " No, but Iris and I were making rather a lot of noise about it next door. You could scarcely have helped hearing."

" I didn't," I said, and added thoughtfully : " If your door was locked, one could, of course, get in from our balcony . . . "

" That's right," he nodded.

" But what could they have been looking for ? "

" It beats me," he shrugged. " Still, no harm done. Nothing's missing."

" Until the day before yesterday Major Arkwright's things were in that room," I said slowly, watching him fumble with the lift gates. " They could have been looking for something of his."

He got the lift open with a certain effort. " But Arkwright's belongings were all cleared out," he said. " Even his old papers and things. Didn't you say Mrs. Andrioli burned them ? That's the Renault. What do you think of it ? "

I admired the new car enviously and he opened the door. " We could drive along the Promenade somewhere," he suggested. " There are some cafés out by the airport end."

" Why not ? " I agreed.

Henry behind the wheel of the motor-car completely regained his self-confidence. He explained at length the technicalities of the engine at the rear and the engineering principles involved. He told me about petrol consumption and demonstrated the terrifying way you could weave around in traffic.

When we started I should have said that it was Henry who was slightly jittery and I who was all assurance. By the time we approached the airport the rôles were reversed. Perhaps Henry was not so stupid as I assumed. I always underrate vulgar little men.

I found I wasn't following his lecture on mechanics very carefully. Instead I was remembering that Henry Makepeace had given the late Major Arkwright not the usual fiver which seemed to have been the standard charge for minor peccadilloes, but the very considerable sum of one hundred and fifty pounds. I was remembering how Mrs. Andrioli believed that Hugh Arkwright had finally succumbed to the temptation of playing for higher stakes, found out too much, and driven someone to murder.

That this someone could be Henry Makepeace had never seriously occurred to me. He didn't look like my idea of a murderer. The wavy hair, the freckles, the regular Anglo-Saxon features were not at all my picture of a murderer. I expect something more esoteric. Of course in the newspapers actual murderers usually look about as common and uninteresting as Henry . . .

Nor did he act like a murderer. I expect cunning and subtlety in my murderers, enigma or else a bland air of total innocence. How, of course, actual murderers act when they aren't murdering is another question.

Then he had an alibi. He'd never been in Nice before Friday night and Arkwright had been murdered on Wednesday afternoon. On the other hand, people with alibis are, for some reason, the very ones to suspect.

In this frivolous fashion I sought to restore my self-confidence and mentally to reduce Henry to the minor rôle which nature had surely intended him to play. I was slightly shaken, however, when he forked right where the Promenade des Anglais ends and took the road marked CANNES.

" I know one shouldn't speak to the driver," I said. " but wasn't there a café near the airport ? Of course there are doubtless cafés in Cannes, too . . ."

" It would be rather a joke if we didn't turn up to dinner ! " he said.

" It would make us laugh, but probably not the others," I pointed out.

" Iris wouldn't mind. She'd think it was rather romantic."

" But I think Dagobert would notice."

" He's a bit of a lad himself, if you ask me."

I raised an eyebrow. " All right," I said after a moment's pause. " I'll ask you."

" My theory of marriage is live and let live," he divagated maddeningly. " Of course if there are kiddies it's different."

" I want to hear more about your theory of marriage sometime," I said, " but wasn't there some talk about stopping to have a drink ? "

" Any time you like," he said expansively, accelerating

to pass a tram on, I think, the wrong side. " Just say the word."

" I've been trying to say it," I complained mildly.

" Take a married woman, for instance," he said. " Why should she spend the best years of her life bent over the kitchen sink ? " He glanced at me rather pityingly, I thought. " Getting prematurely old, grey, wrinkled. . . . She wants to enjoy herself just as much as a man does. She wants to have fun. To live."

" I couldn't agree with you more," I said hastily, drawing attention to a lorry which was charging down on us. " There is also a car behind with obviously lethal intentions. It's been hooting furiously for the last five minutes."

Henry accelerated impatiently, muttering something about " these frogs " taking a few driving lessons, and we left the limousine behind in a cloud of dust.

" Personally," said Henry, " I like married women."

" Before we get on to the depressing subject of maturity again," I interrupted, " tell me why you brought me for this delightful drive. Business first, you know."

He laughed heartily, recognising the quotation. " You know, you're a scream, Jane. Iris said you were. Give me a woman you can have a laugh with, every time." He suddenly assumed that bland air of total innocence which had been one of my requisites for true murderers. " Now where was that place ? It's called La Réserve. . . . As a matter of fact there *was* a little matter I wanted to mention," he said, as though he couldn't quite recall what it was. " Let's see . . ."

He had let his foot slip from the accelerator and we slowed down to a crawl. Behind us, outraged motorists hooted indignantly. Henry waved them past.

" That dam' limousine's been following us ever since we started ! " he growled.

" The little matter you wished to mention," I prompted.

" Oh yes. What was it ? Oh yes, this chap Ark-wright. That's the pub over there, isn't it ? I believe it's a reasonably decent place. Shall we ? "

He swung the little Renault perilously across the road and we came to a halt before La Réserve, a roadside inn with little tables set out beneath dusty plane trees. A sign assured us that they had " *Salons particuliers* ", but I disappointed Henry by insisting on sitting outside beneath the plane trees facing the road and watching the game of *boules* which is the normal Sunday afternoon occupation of the Midi.

I paid for this a few minutes later. The sandy mouth of the river Var behind La Réserve made an excellent breeding ground for mosquitoes and even before the arrival of the beer — which, taking advantage of Dagobert's absence, I had ordered — we were eaten alive.

Henry returned to the subject of the " *Salons par-ticuliers* "—the phrase sounded cosy to him and rather " French ". We could, he pointed out, have dinner here.

I reminded him : " You were talking about this chap Arkwright. Remember ? "

" Okay, I'll make a clean breast of it," he said, with his frank, open expression which made me instinctively clutch my handbag. " I gave this Arkwright fellow some money. Why be mysterious about it ? "

" Why, indeed ? "

" He was short. I was flush. I didn't know him from Adam, of course, but he was a fellow Englishman in foreign parts and when he explained—what was it ?— something about being cleaned out at Monty—naturally I dug into my pocket."

" That was nice of you."

" You get like that, knocking around foreign parts," he explained modestly. " Some people would say I'm generous, maybe gullible. But I've always been like that. Easy come, easy go."

"That was quite a bit to go—all at once," I said admiringly.

He took a deep swig of beer. "Oh, I don't know," he deprecated, "a fiver doesn't mean much nowadays."

"A fiver!" I repeated, slightly startled.

"Forty pesos, if you prefer," he said, killing a mosquito. "That's what I gave the fellow."

This time I took refuge in the beer. Henry had spoken so casually that I'd almost believed him. A fiver had an air of verisimilitude. Henry might just have handed over a fiver, exactly as he said. In view of Arkwright's known methods, the recurring sum carried momentary conviction; it was his normal fee.

But Joe had cashed one hundred and fifty pounds worth of Santa Rican pesos that day, and even men of Henry's confessed gullibility do not part with a hundred and fifty pounds without a reason. Henry, in fact, was lying; and he did it so well that I glanced at him with new respect.

He was also eyeing me with a touch of that suspicion which so frequently marred our relationship. He said, cupping a lighter to his cigarette :

"Why you should be interested in all this I can't imagine."

I smiled brightly. "Some people just can't help taking an interest in other people's affairs."

Henry did not smile. "No," he said in a rather sinister way.

"Curiosity," I babbled stupidly.

"Curiosity . . ." he began heavily.

"I know—killed the cat," I interrupted. "I'd forgotten how good you are at proverbs. Are you trying to frighten me, Henry ? "

"A good fright," he said, flicking the lighter suddenly and making me start, "sometimes does a woman good."

He put the cigarette-lighter in front of my glass, facing me. It was an ordinary Ronson, with only one peculiarity. It bore the initials: J.H.B. They were my initials.

" And, er . . ." I murmured, finishing my beer, " you found my cigarette lighter among the things flung all over your room ? I see why you reasoned that I must know something about it. I, to make a clean breast of it as you say, I probably left it there during the cocktail party."

He shook his head grimly. I was aware of feeling both absurd and a little frightened.

" No good ? " I queried.

He shook his head again. I suddenly wished I hadn't come along on this excursion.

" I found it," he said, " in my suit-case under the bed."

" When I rifle a room," I said, " I always leave some little token of my visit, generally a skull and cross-bones scrawled in lipstick, sometimes only my cigarette-lighter. May I, er, have it back ? "

He nodded. He continued to stare at me with his pale pop eyes. It was a slight consolation to realise that he was as frightened as I was.

" What are you trying to find out ? " he said slowly.

" Who killed a man," I said, rising. " Shall we get the bill and go home ? "

The proprietor of La Réserve arrived with the bill on a saucer. It was eighty francs. Underneath this was written in crude block lettering: " CAREFUL, HENRY."

The plan for a cosy little supper party together was not again broached. Henry drove straight back to the centre of Nice. Neither of us was very talkative. I spoke once to call his attention to the fact that the black limousine—or one remarkably like it—was still behind us. It had, I noticed, the C.D. plate of the *Corps Dip-lomatique.*

We passed the familiar awnings of the Bar d'Angleterre a few hundred yards before we reached the Pension Victoria. It was still only seven and I suggested we have a drink. I don't know whether this was consideration for poor Henry or for myself. Our nerves were in much the same condition.

This time Henry had whisky, an immense one, and I had a dry Martini. But even when we'd finished them and Henry had gloomily insisted on " the other half " our conversation did not sparkle. We spoke monosyllabically at about five minute intervals, like a happily married couple on their annual holiday. I made an occasional comment on a passer-by and got friendly with a poodle at the next table. Henry confined himself to brief incoherencies such as : " It isn't fair ! " and " Damn it all, they can't . . ." incompleted and probably meaning-less.

An Arab carpet-seller—the same one I think who sold us the prayer-rug at the Negresco—tried to liven us up, but Henry dealt with him in his best Empire-destroying manner, telling " the dam' nigger to buzz off ".

I tried to read the back of the newspaper of the man opposite while Henry again fell into a brood. He came out of it to mutter : " Whatever he got, he deserved ! "

" Yes," I agreed, " but . . . but what are we talking about ? "

I don't think Henry heard me. He was looking over my shoulder and he had gone a kind of sickly green. I don't know anything about malaria but it struck me that he might be having a sudden attack of it. He had begun to shake violently.

" Is anything the matter ? " I asked in alarm.

" No," he said, clutching the edge of the table. " No, I thought . . . Let's go."

I agreed gratefully and glanced round for the waiter. Behind me our Arab carpet-seller was vanishing into the crowd. He looked round at the same time I did and winked at me broadly. He was stooped over, but he looked much taller than usual. He also looked uncommonly like Dagobert.

Chapter

18

W HEN WE REACHED THE PENSION VICTORIA WE FOUND a gendarme chatting amiably with the concierge. He broke off to regard us narrowly as we entered the lift. When we emerged from the lift a second gendarme was waiting in the Pension hall. He stared at us searchingly, but said nothing.

" There must be some perfectly simple explanation," I murmured kindly to Henry.

" I don't feel very well," Henry said. " Excuse me."

But before he could escape, Iris had come out of the sitting-room. She looked surprised to see us.

" Hello," she said, " I saw you two driving off. I'd have taken a small bet you wouldn't turn up again until the wee hours. He told me this afternoon, Jane, that you were just his cup of tea. I was prepared to spend the evening holding Dagobert's hand."

She laughed, but she sounded a little disappointed in us. Not being good at this kind of badinage, I changed the subject.

" Why the police force ? "

" I don't know," she shrugged. Then, observing the gendarme more closely : " He's rather a sweetie-pie, isn't he. . . . Oh, by the way, darling, I've asked that poor Monsieur Dompierre to have dinner with us. Otherwise he'd only have something out of a tin in his room. I hope you don't mind."

" Not at all," Henry said indifferently. " If *you* can stick the little frog. Anyway I may not have dinner. I may dose myself with quinine and go to bed."

" Don't be a bore, darling," Iris smiled sweetly.

Henry bolted without giving me the chance to say " thank you " for the drive. Iris's sweet smile became a little fixed.

" They're so funny about each other," she complained. " Pierre is just as bad."

" Did you expect them to fall into each other's arms ? "

She frowned. " No, of course not. But, well, neither of them takes the other *seriously*. Henry's more or less accused me of carrying on with every man in Nice— *except* Pierre. And now Pierre, who's been worrying for days about Henry, laughs every time I mention his name. He calls him a *foutriquet*, whatever that means. It's really rather confusing."

" But a relief, I should have thought."

" I suppose so," she sighed. " Men are so stupid— and sometimes a wee bit dull, don't you find ? . . . The trouble is they do quite mad things for one, and then one gets involved, half out of gratitude."

" What particular mad things had you in mind ? " I asked.

Her eyes flickered towards the gendarme, who was smoking a cigarette at the entrance door.

" Nothing especially," she murmured. " Just neglecting his work, that trip to Beuil. . . . I'd better see what's happening to Henry."

When I went into our room Dagobert was drenching a corner of his handkerchief with Lenthéric's *Repartie* and opening my new bottle of Renoir's *Future*. He was wearing his grey flannel suit and looking rather distinguished and pleased with himself.

" Oh, good," he said, " you've already changed." He inspected my new frock with the nod of approval husbands always give when it's too late to do anything about it. " I'm glad you finally decided to take it out of that box on top of the wardrobe."

"Don't change the subject," I said, reaching for a cigarette.

"Was there a subject?" He poured *Future* on another corner of his handkerchief and opened my *Carnet de Bal*. "How's your boy friend? Still finding you just his cup of tea?"

"Henry is in a very bad state," I said, sinking down on the edge of the bed. "On the other hand, what you've done to Henry's nerves is child's play to what you've done to mine."

The *Carnet de Bal* went on the third corner of his handkerchief and for the fourth time he hesitated between Piguet's *Bandit* and Caron's *Fleurs de Rocaille*. He said in a tone of disappointment:

"You didn't find my unseen presence reassuring?"

"I don't mind going prematurely grey," I said, "if it serves some useful purpose. But . . . are *you* responsible for the gendarmerie?"

"Indirectly," he nodded. "By the way, *foutriquet* is distinctly N.D.U. I mention this in case we meet people."

"N.D.U.? You'll have to make these things simpler. I've been out of touch for so long."

"Not in Decent Use," he explained. "It's a very rude way of saying 'nasty little squirt,' surely an exaggeration for a man who shows such sound taste in women to hold hands with on balconies!"

"Poor Henry," I sighed.

To my astonishment—and, I must confess, my delight —Dagobert looked suddenly angry.

"Poor Henry!" he snapped. "Poor Henry rubbish! Are you aware, Jane, that you've been having flirtatious little tête-à-têtes on balconies, cosy glasses of beer in roadhouses of dubious reputation, expensive cocktails in the intimacy of fashionable Côte d'Azur cafés, with this man whose reputation stinks all the way from Santa Rica to

British Honduras, with this, this *foutriquet* who is also very probably a murderer ! "

I raised an eyebrow. " Henry said *you* were a bit of a lad, now I think of it."

Dagobert calmed down slightly. " Did he ? In—er —any particular connection ? It's these *choux à la crème* and éclairs," he murmured. " I swear off every day, but . . ."

" I only hope they haven't spoiled her appetite for mussels," I said sweetly, " which is what she's going to get . . . among other things."

" We were discussing Henry. You must watch a tendency you're developing, Jane, to introduce extraneous elements into the conversation."

" Did Henry murder Arkwright, then ? " I asked bluntly.

" Probably not," he admitted with reluctance. " But I'm keeping an open mind—at least where Henry is concerned."

" Let's talk about nicer things," I said. " We see so little of each other these days. What are we going to do this evening ? "

He " borrowed " my cigarette. " I've had a fairly full day," he said. " I thought a quiet evening . . ."

" Not *another* quiet evening ! " I protested. " I haven't recovered from our quiet evening with the U.S. Marines. Couldn't we go to the cinema or something ? By ourselves ? "

He thought for a moment and then said : " Yes ! That's exactly what we'll do. . . ."

He sat down beside me on the bed, handing me back my cigarette and taking a fresh one for himself. He took my hand. The dinner bell rang. Neither of us moved.

" You know we don't have to solve this murder," I murmured, " if we don't want to."

He sighed. " Just this one. Then we'll go to Algeria. Yûssef was telling me about an oasis on the edge of the Sahara where . . ."

" Who's Yûssef ? I don't know any of your friends any more."

" The carpet seller. . . . Which movie shall we go to ? "

" The new Marcel Pagnol that *Nice-Matin* was so excited about."

" Umm," he said doubtfully. " The only thing is . . ."

" You've seen it," I suggested.

" As a matter of fact, yes. The other day, more or less."

" I hate the way we're drifting apart. We used to have such lovely lives together." I nestled my head sentimentally against his shoulder. " The dinner bell has rung. Is it polite for us to ignore it, what with guests ? "

" The oasis," he said, " is fifty miles from the nearest town. You take a camel . . ."

" Iris," I said, " is making heavily-veiled insinuations that Dompierre shot Arkwright for her sake."

" Yes, I overheard the bit about the ' mad things men do for one.' I was lurking at the hall door. I hope," he added anxiously, " that Dompierre hadn't anything to do with it."

" He couldn't have," I said. " I heard the Bach *chaconne* and I'd have noticed if he stopped playing it in the middle."

Dagobert nodded in an unconvinced way, as though he didn't entirely trust my evidence. I was sure of few things, but one of them was that Dieudonné Dompierre was playing the piano uninterruptedly at the time Arkwright was shot, and I resented the doubt in his manner.

" In fact," I said, " Dompierre and Henry himself are the only two people we know who have cast-iron alibis."

" And Don Diego," he added.

" And you," I said patiently, " and Commissaire Morel *and* Buckshot. Wouldn't it be less confusing to confine our limited energy to those who just conceivably might have killed Major Arkwright; such as Elinor, who remembers the name of the Pension Victoria from way back in nineteen twenty-seven; Sophie, who broke off her Universal lessons because she thought she was falling in love with him; Iris, who fled from the Pension the night he was killed; Mrs. Andrioli, who was—I hope these little details aren't wearying you—Mrs. Andrioli, who was his *wife*. And, for all I know, your Suzette ! "

Dagobert had listened to my speech with admiration. " Why don't I stick to Bertran de Born and leave these things entirely to you ? " he exclaimed ruefully. He rose and looked for a match for his still unlighted cigarette. " The only thing is I seem to detect a slight anti-feminine bias in your list; your five suspects are all women."

I explained in greater detail my reasons for the list. He listened with flattering absorption, and his cigarette remained unlighted for so long that eventually I gave him my lighter. He flicked it open before he recognised it.

" Oh ! " he said, looking foolish.

" Next time," I said mildly, " leave something with your *own* initials on under Henry's bed."

The telephone rang. It was Mrs. Andrioli to say our guest had arrived. I asked her to send her into the sitting-room. I don't quite know why I had been assuming that Dagobert had invited Suzette to dinner ; it had become an *idée fixe*.

I was, therefore, unprepared when we entered the sitting-room, to find Don Diego Sebastiano de la Torreda waiting for us.

Chapter

19

I WAS NOT CONVINCED THAT DAGOBERT HAD INVITED Don Diego to dinner merely to discuss a scheme for putting the treasures of Santa Rican archæology on the tourist map. That may have been his intention—he said it was—but I doubted it.

So, I think, did Don Diego. He sipped his pre-dinner orangeade in a distracted way while Dagobert warmed to the subject. It was the first time that Don Diego had been outside the Consulate since what he persisted in calling the attempt on his life, and he eyed the gendarme in the hall with evident satisfaction. Dagobert had spent over an hour this morning persuading Don Diego that there had been no attempted assassination, but simply a straightforward murder. Dagobert was, as Don Diego ruefully told me, a very persuasive man ; but, he added, he had sent his bodyguard along before him just in case.

Though this explained the presence of police in the Pension, it did not add to the tranquillity of dinner. We were not our usual happy family gathering that night in the dining-room. There were few bursts of spontaneous gaiety, and even the three Belgian women— who had had iced port in the sitting-room before dinner —talked in depressed whispers. The waiter seemed to tiptoe more softly than usual and you could hear—in fact you frequently did hear—a fork drop.

Only Dagobert seemed unaware of the atmosphere and of the fact that several people in that room were straining to overhear every word he said and pretending not to. During the first course all they could possibly have learned was a great deal about the Mayan creator god Kukulcan —" the feathered snake that goes in the water," according to the chronicles of Tutul-Xiu—and Chac, the rain god with the pendulous nose. This was clearly all fresh to Don Diego, too, and failed to grip him.

My own attention strayed and I tried for a while to untangle the various strands of tension surrounding us. Some were relatively simple. For instance, the entire dining-room was wondering how we managed to be having a special dinner and planning to have a few swift words with Mrs. Andrioli about it afterwards. They were impressed when Dagobert ordered champagne, but I think it would be an exaggeration to say that people jumped guiltily when the cork popped. Everybody wondered who Don Diego was ; the most widely accepted theory was that he was a police commissaire, which would account for the gendarmes. It is significant that the presence of police can affect even people with nothing on their consciences. And someone in the dining-room to-night, I remembered uneasily, could have murder on his conscience.

I caught a glimpse of Mrs. Andrioli's anxious face in the doorway, and I knew that the same thought had crossed her mind.

There were other emotional cross-currents which may or may not have been connected with this basic tension. At the next table Iris was in difficulties. Henry had apparently been persuaded to give up his threatened attack of malaria and dine with his wife and Dompierre. Iris was proposing the new Montmartre Night Club which had just opened in the Rue de France. Both men were being very self-sacrificing about it, Dompierre insisting that Iris and Henry couldn't possibly want him along, Henry pointing out that Iris could dance with him at

any time and that he might join them later if he felt
up to it. Iris was beginning to be a little short-tempered
with both of them.

But the most astonishing situation in the room was
that at the Duffield's table. They, too, had a guest
to-night and the guest was Joe Orsini ! I learned afterwards that Elinor had found Sophie and Joe on the beach
together and immediately insisted that Joe dine with
them. They sat at the far end of the room, and all I
could make out was that Elinor was being very gracious
and *noblesse oblige* while Sophie had relapsed into her
familiar mood of taciturn unsociability. Joe, I thought,
seemed reasonably at home, though slightly subdued and
distinctly on his good behaviour.

I gave up trying to understand the emotional strains
and stresses which doubtless surrounded us and concentrated on the *moules à la marinière*, thus gaining
Mrs. Andrioli's approval. Mussels were not only her
own favourite dish, but her speciality as a cook, and she
had prepared them with her own hands. She hovered
round our table, waiting for praise.

She and Dagobert had a fascinating technical discussion
about their cultivation, varieties and preparation. They
omitted no detail and at the end of five minutes I felt I
knew each mussel personally. It made a change from
Kukulcan and Chac, of course, but I hate hearing about
the private life of the things I'm eating.

So evidently did Don Diego, for he didn't touch his
plate. Nor had he touched his champagne. He was,
he explained, on the wagon ; but did I mind if he smoked
a cigarette ?

I have often thought that I was unfortunate in my
two modest conquests in Nice. Both had started so
promisingly : Don Diego with that delightful little mis-
apprehension about *Mademoiselle* being *charmante*, Henry
with his gallant avowal of preference for " mature women."

Both had known me for about ten minutes when they were attacked by violent jitters—fleeing precipitously from Negresco terraces, dropping tooth-mugs from balconies, and regarding me ever afterwards with alternate nervousness and gloom.

To-night Henry was in the nervy phase, eyeing me as though I might at any moment go off with a bang. Don Diego was going through a period of deep depression, not eyeing me at all.

Don Diego had, of course, things on his mind. The thought that last Wednesday's assassin, if not apprehended, might strike again was only one of them. His chief source of worry was the alterations which his Uncle Don Geronimo had made in the Consular set-up before returning to the Paris Embassy this afternoon. In the first place the Santa Rican Consulate was now to be open between ten and twelve every morning and between two and five every afternoon except on Mondays. Don Diego was to eschew the company of Suzette and her like and to give up drink entirely. The car with the C.D. plates, which actually belonged to the Embassy—and which apparently Dagobert had borrowed for the afternoon—was to be returned to Paris, together with Juan. Don Diego would be looked after by a char whom Don Geronimo had engaged to come for two hours a day. All of this was being put into a confidential report which Don Geronimo was sending to the new President, to show him that the French section of the Santa Rican diplomatic service was on its toes. Finally Don Diego's salary had been cut by twenty-five per cent.

" But you'll make that up on the exchange," Dagobert suggested sympathetically. " The peso has risen that much since the elections."

Don Diego shook his head glumly. " I get paid by my uncle from Paris," he said, " in francs."

" Pity," Dagobert sighed ; and he did something I've

never seen him do before : he lighted a cigarette between courses.

At that moment Mrs. Andrioli arrived to say that someone wanted Don Diego on the telephone. Don Diego and Dagobert exchanged a glance and looked quickly towards Henry. Don Diego excused himself and left the room. Henry's eyes, popping more than usual, followed his departure.

" Would you care to let me in on all this ? " I asked Dagobert, dropping my voice to the conspiratorial whisper which was the tone of to-night's dining-room conversation.

" We sent a cable this morning to Santa Rica," he murmured. " Juan's waiting at the Consulate for an answer."

I noticed Henry also murmuring to Iris, and a second later Iris looked round and said :

" Who's your guest ? "

Dagobert said casually, but so that the whole room could hear : " Don Diego Sebastiano de la Torreda, the Santa Rican Vice-Consul."

" He's rather sweet," Iris said, filling in a sudden gap of silence which had fallen over the dining-room. " You must introduce him to Henry. They'll have things in common—dark-eyed señoritas probably ! "

Henry did not echo her merry tinkle of laughter. He finished the whisky he always had with his meals—" Can't stick this dam' wine, doncha know "—and glared round for the waiter. The waiter was at our table, removing plates. He had just rescued Don Diego's untouched dish of mussels from Dagobert, who regretfully watched them disappear from his grasp to be deposited on the sideboard.

" We're going to that new night club after dinner," Iris continued. " The one with the ' Dix Atomic Beauties.' Why don't you come and bring him along ? "

" We're going to the films," I said, glancing at Dagobert, who was still smoking his cigarette.

" I," Dompierre contributed firmly, " have music to compose. I am sorry."

Dagobert came to slightly. " Did you make that piano arrangement you play of the unaccompanied violin *chaconne* ? " he asked, changing the subject.

Dompierre was nearly as bewildered by the question as I was. Not knowing Dagobert as well as I do he may have felt it had some bearing on something. He frowned.

" No," he said slowly, " it's the Brahms version. . . . Is there any reason for the question ? "

" None at all," Dagobert admitted. " I like it."

Which—I reflected—showed remarkable musical appreciation ; for Dagobert had never heard Dompierre play the Bach-Brahms *chaconne* !

Iris said she *adored* music and that the " Montmartre " was supposed to have a divine band. Don Diego returned looking baggy-eyed but inscrutable and the waiter brought us a *Blanquette de Veau* in a silver dish. The Countess Gluttonsen, who had raced through the cutlets and fried potatoes which everybody else had, stared at us, recorked her bottle of Graves Supérieur and, followed by her son, left the dining-room in a marked manner.

" It was Juan," Don Diego said. " No answer yet." He glanced towards me inquiringly.

" I have no secrets from Jane," Dagobert said, exaggerating. He stubbed out his cigarette. " I've been thinking . . . Juan himself wouldn't have taken a shot at you, by any chance ? "

" What ? " said Don Diego, swallowing suddenly. His podgy fingers fumbled for the tumbler of water beside his plate but found the champagne instead. " You said *nobody* shot at me ! "

" Yes, but I keep changing my mind," Dagobert

explained ingenuously. " Juan was in the car outside the Brooklyn Bar at the time. It was facing the Promenade and from the car window he could have done it."

Don Diego had gulped down the champagne under the impression that it was water. His thin butterfly moustache twitched but he forgot to mop the champagne bubbles off it.

" I wish you hadn't said that," he muttered. " *Blanquette de Veau* is my favourite dish. Now my appetite is gone."

Dagobert refilled his champagne glass. Don Diego supped it moodily. " But no," he continued. " It could not be. It could not be."

" Then," Dagobert shrugged, " I withdraw the suggestion, and return to my original theory that Arkwright was simply murdered, and no attempt at all was made on your life."

Don Diego wasn't listening. " You do not understand," he murmured. " Juan Moro is like a son to me. Anything he does for me. All he owes to me. I raise him from the gutter. We do not have gutters in Santa Rica but you know what I mean. His family, too, owes all to me. His little sister Consuelo," he concluded, clinching the argument, " was the first woman I ever loved."

" The one that looked like me ? " I asked.

He shook his head absentmindedly. " No, that was another." He toyed with his *Blanquette de Veau*, found it good and ate it thoughtfully, reflecting on the sorry pass that civilisation had come to when doubt could be thrown on faithful servants like Juan Moro. " She was just fifteen," he added dreamily.

Possibly I had misjudged the subject matter of his reflections ! We all ate for a while in silence. I caught the sound of Elinor's voice occasionally, asking Joe kindly about his life in Buffalo, his family and plans for the future. I wondered whether she were simply checking up on him or trying to make him feel uncomfortable. If the latter, she would have, I felt, singularly little success.

Henry nearby had ordered his third whisky—excessive indulgence in whisky seemed to be another characteristic of my admirers—and Iris was talking intelligently to Dompierre about " modernistic music," a term with which Dompierre seemed to be unfamiliar. Other pensionnaires were already leaving the dining-room, taking their oranges with them.

Dagobert leaned back and said conversationally to Henry : " How did you discover ' La Réserve ' ? Been there before ? "

Henry started at the question, as well he might, and looked at me with reproach.

He stammered : " No. I . . . I . . . Isn't it well known ? I just seemed to have heard of it somewhere, old boy, somebody or other mentioned it. I . . ."

" It doesn't matter," Dagobert said with that elaborate casualness which makes everybody sit up in their seats and wonder what it's all about.

I saw Henry's forehead sweating slightly as he returned to his cutlet, and for the next ten minutes I'm sure he was trying to figure out the catch in Dagobert's probably meaningless question. I did think, however, that Iris, although she continued to talk about what she called " these awful people like Stravinski," had not been unconscious of the question. My own interpretation of this phenomenon—if it was a phenomenon—was that La Réserve had probably been a sentimental haunt of hers and Dompierre's before Henry's arrival, and that Iris in her extravert way had recommended it to Henry this morning when they drove back from Cannes.

Don Diego looked up suddenly from the plate of

Blanquette de Veau which he had polished with a piece
of bread.

" Besides," he said in a more optimistic tone, " Juan
Moro would not have missed ! "

He emptied the remainder of the champagne bottle
into his own glass and Dagobert hastily ordered another.
I said unnecessarily :

" You mean, if Juan had shot at you he'd have hit
you. That eliminates Juan."

Don Diego nodded. He was feeling much more
cheerful suddenly, either because he'd at last had something to eat and drink or because his faithful servant
was no longer under the cloud of suspicion. He stroked
his moustache and regarded the dining-room with
deliberation.

" Of course it may well be," he said, " as Señor Brown
believes that the Colonel Arkwright was murdered. It
may well be also that the murderer finds himself at this
moment in this room. This would be a weight off my
mind." He shrugged. " Naturally."

Unless, I thought, he lowered his voice it would be a
weight off no one else's mind ! Even Joe at the far end
of the room had half glanced round. Don Diego continued imperturbably, addressing me :

" But I like better Commissaire Morel's husband."

" Yes, of course," I nodded hastily.

Don Diego looked grave but he also looked pleased
with himself. " Husbands," he said, " are sometimes
very uncertain. They misunderstand, they come home
suddenly, they get excited." He sighed, not without
satisfaction. " This could be. Commissaire Morel has
asked me for the names of such husbands. Naturally I
do not tell him. I am a gentleman. The *petits pois*
are delicious. My appetite returns. Afterwards we go
perhaps to a night club and drink to the departure of
my uncle, Don Geronimo Estaven de la Torreda, hein ? "

Mrs. Andrioli reappeared discreetly at our table. I wondered for a moment if she were going to tell us to ask our guest to lower his voice. Instead she told him he was wanted again on the telephone and followed him out of the room, looking distressed. Again it was Iris who filled in the conversational lacuna Don Diego had left behind him.

" I know who he reminds me of ! " she exclaimed. " Charles Boyer." She lowered her voice. " Does Dagobert really think Major Arkwright was murdered ? Wouldn't that be rather awful ? I mean for all of us. I mean questions and things."

There were scarcely half a dozen people left in the dining-room by this time, all at the Duffields' end of the room, and Iris was overheard only by ourselves and Henry, Dompierre having left the table to fetch an ash-tray from the sideboard, also at the far end of the room. Henry himself was deep in his fourth whisky. He had the red, boiled, healthy look of the confirmed whisky-drinker, and he held himself with the rigidity and alert dignity of a person about to fall flat on his face. He looked as though he were listening to Iris, but I don't think he heard—or rather understood—more than every fifth word.

" I've never been questioned," Iris added in an eager whisper.

I wondered if she could possibly be as silly as she obviously was. Dagobert grinned at her with that tolerance men always extended to Iris Makepeace.

" Do you want to be ? "

She blushed prettily. " Well, no. Naturally not."

" All right," Dagobert said, " where did you dine last Wednesday ? "

She screwed up her soft face in a thoughtful pout, then opened her gold-flecked eyes very wide. " At Raynaud's," she gasped. " With Major Arkwright."

" That was luncheon," Dagobert reminded her.

" Of course it was ! You mean *dinner*."

" After the row with Dompierre—when you left the Pension in a—a, what was it ?—a huff ? "

" Oh ! " she said, making a round O with her mouth. " That ! "

Dompierre came back with the ash-tray and Iris looked at him with a return of her old affection. She tried to catch his hand surreptitiously as he passed behind her chair, but he forestalled the move.

" *Chéri* . . ." she whispered reproachfully.

Henry stirred, shuddered slightly, stared at our table and blinked at no longer seeing Don Diego there. Don Diego returned and Henry blinked again.

" To hell with this," he muttered cryptically and tried to rise.

Realising his own limitations he sank back into his seat and remained apparently unaware of the whispered conversation which subsequently took place at our own table about himself. Don Diego glanced at him, then moved his chair nearer to Dagobert.

" You were right ! " he exclaimed softly. " Juan's got the details, though the actual cable won't be delivered until to-morrow morning. M-A-K-E-P-E-A-C-E, isn't it ? "

Dagobert nodded. " The Roquefort's good. Let's see, you eat it before the meringue glacé, don't you ? Do you mind if Jane and I stick to our rude Island customs and do it the other way round ? "

Don Diego nodded conspiratorily. But he was too excited to leave it alone. " The police being here might be convenient," he whispered. " Though I'd better telephone my uncle in Paris before doing anything definite."

" Yes, do that by all means," Dagobert said. He caught Dompierre's eye fixed upon him. " We're trying to put the wind up Henry," he explained. " But I'm afraid we're wasting our time."

" What *is* a *foutriquet, chéri* ? " Iris asked Dompierre earnestly.

The waiter cleared his throat and deposited a fruit plate in front of Henry. The Belgian women left the room, the youngest one giggling. Dagobert compared the differing merits of Roquefort and Gex. When I wasn't wondering what Juan had just telephoned about I was wondering how late we'd be for the films. Don Diego finished his own meringue glacé and accepted Dagobert's. We ordered coffee and brandy, but before it arrived Don Diego was called to the telephone for the third time. Dagobert followed him out of the room while I smoked a quick cigarette. It had been a most restless dinner party.

Dagobert came back a moment later, but remained uncommunicative. I know him too well in these moods to bother asking questions. Iris, finally facing the fact that her husband was in no fit state to dance anywhere to-night, was telling Dompierre that now he *had* to come with her. She added something in a whisper which I didn't catch ; but I would have taken a small bet that it was . . . " our last night alone together *chéri*."

The Duffields had risen, smiled vaguely in our direction and gone into the drawing-room. Joe lingered behind to say " Hi." He paused at the sideboard to pinch a carnation for a buttonhole and strolled over to us.

" This place is getting as bad as the Brooklyn Bar," he grinned, " what with Don Diego and me lowering the tone."

" How are you doing ? " I inquired.

" Search me." Joe shrugged. " Okay, I guess. Jeeze ! Can she talk ! " He paused awkwardly, swaying on his heels, glancing after his departed hostess. " Maybe I'd better high-tail it after them. For my *demi-tasse* and liquors in the lounge." He winked broadly and began to go.

Dagobert detained him. " You know those papers," he said briefly, " the ones in his room that you knew were burned."

I remembered that yesterday on the raft Joe had said he knew that Major Arkwright's papers had been destroyed.

Joe hesitated, then said : " Yeah ? "

" How did you know that ? "

There was something about Dagobert's voice which made Joe suddenly decide not to stall.

" The maids, the waiters, everyone in this place knows it," he said. " *She* told them all, quite openly. I'll be seein' you."

" Just as she told you," Dagobert murmured thoughtfully after Joe had disappeared.

I nodded. Mrs. Andrioli, we knew, had her own special reasons for wanting all the world to realise that Major Arkwright's private papers had been burned unread. She wanted those whom her husband had blackmailed to believe that their secrets had died with him. But *would* they believe this ? When she told me the unlikely story that she had not even glanced at the papers I happened to believe her. Would everyone else be equally trusting ?

Iris had got her two escorts out of the room. Henry went under his own steam but it was uncertain how far he would get. Dompierre trailed along after them, in a resigned, hang-dog sort of way. He had evidently fallen again for the " our last evening " line and looked as though he despised himself almost as much as he despised the Makepeaces.

Don Diego was still in the office at the telephone and we were alone in the dining-room when Mrs. Andrioli herself brought in our coffee and brandy. We thanked her for an excellent dinner. That is, I thanked her. She and Dagobert were both curiously constrained, as though each were preoccupied with a subject which neither wished to broach. Finally she cut short my very uninteresting remarks about the *Blanquette de Veau* and said to Dagobert :

" There was once some trouble between a chamber-maid at the Pension and this Juan Moro. Afterwards I think Hugh may have had a few hundred francs out of Moro."

" Why do you mention this ? " Dagobert asked.

She sighed anxiously. " Just to show you how hopeless it is ever to untangle all the ramifications of my husband's affairs. Please stop trying to."

" In other words," Dagobert said quietly, " you do know *some* details of Hugh Arkwright's activities. You must be frank with me, Mrs. Andrioli. *Other people* must think you know such details, perhaps more details than you really know." He looked at her unsmilingly and I could see that he was as in earnest as she was herself. " If you will go at once to the *Préfecture de Police*, Mrs. Andrioli, and tell them everything you know, I promise on my word of honour to have nothing more to do with the business."

She shook her head quickly. I had seen that same look of stubborn unreason in her eyes this morning in our room.

" In that case," Dagobert said reluctantly, " I shall go on interfering. To start with, everyone in the Pension and several people outside the Pension want to know how much you actually saw of those papers you burned on Wednesday afternoon. You told Jane you didn't examine them. Jane believes you. I do, too. But the faded snapshots. You must have caught a glimpse of them."

She didn't reply. Unaccountably there was moisture

in her eyes. Dagobert tried not to notice. I felt sorry for him, knowing how he hated this kind of thing.

"The concierge told me that a letter with a Santa Rican air mail stamp arrived about three weeks ago," he said, not pursuing the snapshots. "It was addressed to Mrs. Makepeace, but she never received it. Arkwright, I believe, intercepted the letter and kept it. I'm not suggesting that you read it. But you must have noticed the large triangular red and green foreign stamp."

"I may have," she admitted. "I don't remember. . . . Yes, I think there was such a stamp. I didn't look at the address. Please believe me."

"Hugh Arkwright was living at the Pension Victoria in nineteen twenty-seven," Dagobert said. "Mrs. Duffield was in Nice—at the Negresco—during that spring. Did he know her?"

Mrs. Andrioli shook her head.

"When the Duffields arrived about three weeks ago are you certain that Major Arkwright didn't recognise Elinor Duffield?"

Mrs. Andrioli nodded. "Quite certain," she said. "He would not have told me. But I would have known."

"Pity," Dagobert murmured for the second time to-night. He looked composed, but I realised that a pet theory of his had received a nasty shock. "I may have to take your advice, Mrs. Andrioli," he smiled, "and stop trying to untangle your husband's affairs after all."

"Please do," she repeated more briskly. She poured out our coffee for us and replaced the silver pot on the tray. "I haven't had my dinner yet," she said, livening up noticeably at the prospect. There was a touch of her old cheerfulness as she explained: "I'm not having the ordinary dinner. I'm having the same one you had."

Dagobert said to her just before she turned away :-

" Those old snapshots, Mrs. Andrioli." She stiffened, but this time he persisted. " Couldn't one of them have been of Elinor Duffield twenty-three years ago ? "

Her back was turned to us and I saw her shoulders slump slightly. She was fighting back the tears which had threatened a moment ago when the same subject had been approached. Her voice was controlled but throaty.

" If you feel you must know," she said, " they were both snapshots he took years ago . . . which he'd kept . . . I don't know why. They were snapshots of me . . ."

Chapter

20

WE WERE STILL FEELING RATHER CHASTENED A MOMENT later when Don Diego returned. It was a curious glimpse into the blackmailer's character—snapshots of his wife, sentimentally guarded among the documents of his profession. It was a private glimpse we felt we had no right to have had.

Don Diego's appearance left us no time for self-reproach. Other matters were plainly brewing.

"A bad thing has happened which I do not understand," he said in a puzzled, worried way. "I think it is illegal. I have tried to telephone Paris, but my uncle is not yet arrived."

He sat down and reached for his brandy glass, but started to his feet again without touching it. "I go at once to the *Commissariat Central,*" he announced abruptly. "This is my duty. You will please to understand."

"That would be easier if you'd tell us what's happened," Dagobert said.

"They have arrested Juan Moro."

Don Diego brought a most unsatisfactory dinner party to an end by leaving almost at once. He was excited and outraged, and it was hard to get a coherent account of Juan's arrest out of him.

I, too, had been excited until I learned that Don Diego's chauffeur, driving to the Pension Victoria to take us—as Don Diego put it—"to some night clubs" had ignored traffic signals and been taken along to the *Commissariat Central* from which, presumably, Don Diego could immediately obtain his release.

The alarm, then, was false ; and I wondered why Don Diego took it so dramatically and why Dagobert took it so calmly. Don Diego's attitude was that diplomatic immunity had been violated and the Santa Rican flag insulted. Dagobert merely murmured to me : " Good ! Now we can go to the movies." I felt both of them were over-playing their parts.

Later, Dagobert made a single further reference to Juan Moro. It was during a tense part of the Pagnol film when I hoped he was concentrating on the dialogue, so I could form some idea afterwards of what the film had been about.

" I hope," he murmured. " Commissaire Morel will find Juan more informative than I did this afternoon."

Meanwhile the concierge had found Don Diego a taxi, the gendarmerie had withdrawn and the Pension Victoria had settled down to its normal post-prandial state of silent battles over the wireless, half-hearted efforts to find a fourth for bridge, uninstructive conversations in three languages about knitting.

Iris and Dompierre had crept out. Henry had fallen somewhere by the wayside ; probably he'd gone to bed. Joe, on the horsehair couch in the sitting-room, was balancing a cup of coffee on his knee and, with mingled fascination and respect, was watching Elinor talk. Sophie, beside them, sat without expression. Her eyes wandered occasionally towards the *Reader's Digest*, unopened in her lap.

We sneaked in to look for my handbag which I'd left there before dinner. Elinor was saying to Joe :

" The Orsinis, you know, were one of the most illustrious families in Rome. I believe no less than five popes have been Orsinis."

"That doesn't sound much like our branch of the family, ma'am," Joe grinned. "We've always gone in more for selling ice creams."

Elinor smiled. "And the best ice cream in Buffalo it used to be, too," she said. "On the corner of Elm and 17th, you know, Sophie. I used to buy cones from Papa Orsini when I was a little girl."

Dagobert had rescued my handbag from the couch. There was the ghost of malice in his smile as he said to Elinor:

"And what was *your* name in those days, Mrs. Duffield?"

Elinor did not hesitate, but I thought the smile was a little fixed. "I was a Miss Hickenfinkle," she said.

Joe's face remained grave but Sophie unexpectedly giggled. Both Elinor and Joe rightly ignored her and I followed Dagobert towards the lift, reflecting that *he* was scarcely in a position to be facetious about people's names! On the other hand he had doubtless brought the rather patronising "Orsini" conversation to a merited conclusion.

It wasn't until we were half way down in the lift that I thought to ask: "How did you know her name was Hickenfinkle?"

"I didn't," he grinned. "Wasn't it lucky?"

We walked down the Promenade and through the public gardens towards the Place Masséna. We admired the cinerarias under the park lights and paused to listen to the band. Dagobert vacillates between a love of brass bands and Palestrina *a capella*, and we had to wait until they'd finished Selections from *Faust*. We arrived at the cinema at ten, just in time for the last showing of the principal film.

In London I follow the latest French films at the Academy and Studio One with the enthusiasm of a regular *New Statesman* reader. In France, however, they have the unfortunate habit of omitting English sub-titles and I spent the next hour in silent despair.

At the end I had given up the French language once and for all and felt better. My future lay in Hampstead, not Nice. On the way home we stopped and had ice cream and talked sentimentally about the Freemasons' Arms, the cat and our two harlequin Great Danes. Though neither of us mentioned it, I think one of the most attractive aspects of Hampstead was that there we were not involved in murder.

It was after midnight when we walked along the Rue de France towards the Pension. We passed the new Montmartre night club, from which issued the savage noise of accordions, and though both of us thought of Iris and Dompierre, neither of us mentioned them. It is all very well to talk about "living with your characters," but when you suspect each one of them in turn of having committed murder, it is a relief to forget them for a while. I won't say that I had entirely forgotten mine during the evening, but it was pleasant being alone with Dagobert discussing new curtains for the flat.

We met no one when we got out of the lift. We found our key and crept quietly towards our room. The day hadn't been perfect, but at least this was the end of it. Dagobert opened the door with a sigh of relief. It had, of course, been too good to last. Our light was already on.

Henry Makepeace rose from the arm-chair and blinked at us. His hair was wild and his mouth twitched. He was in a dreadful state and it remains until this day a mystery how he had climbed over the balcony partition without breaking his neck.

" All right," he said in a voice which started with defiance but ended in a squeak. " I'm ready. Can't you see I'm ready. Bring them in."

" Bring what in ? " Dagobert asked.

" Your cops ! I can take it. I know when I'm licked."

He fell back into the arm-chair. His teeth had begun to chatter and tears started from his eyes.. He let them roll down his cheeks without attempting to wipe them away. I tried not to look. The drunken degradation of the man filled me with something worse than disgust. I was thoroughly, horribly frightened.

" What are you waiting for ? " he whimpered. " For Christ's sake say something ! Do something ! " A sob racked his body. " I can't stand any more. *You* know all about it ! Please, please, dear Lord, let me have it now—quick."

His head sank into his arms. At least one did not have to look into those bloodshot eyes. I understood suddenly something of the agony Mrs. Andrioli had once described of the person driven to the edge of sanity by fear and remorse.

" You know all about it ! " he repeated in a hoarse whisper. " *You* know I killed him . . ."

Chapter

21

THE SUNLIGHT, REFLECTED FROM THE WRINKLED BLUE sea, was shimmering across the white ceiling over the bed. When I opened my eyes the flies were describing their aimless orbits around the opaque glass bowl beneath the electric light. There were only two of them this morning, but their gyrations remained as inexplicable as ever.

I gave it up and studied the wall-paper. It had a design of cabbage roses, interspersed with alabaster urns. By half closing your eyes you could make a face, with slanting red cabbage-rose eyes and a startled triangular mouth made from an urn. By making the urns into eyes and using a rose for the mouth you got a jolly fat-faced cherub, yawning.

It was Monday morning when half the shops are closed and already groups of cyclists were off for a day in the country. Dilapidated vans, piled high with sheaths of carnations and marguerites were coming down from Grasse and surrounding villages for the flower market in the *Vieille Ville*. In the distance an early morning train gave a hysterical little squeak.

I smelled coffee from somewhere and my imagination quickly supplied the honey and *croissants* which ought to accompany it. I eyed Dagobert. He was sleeping angelically beside me, arms and legs straddled out, occupying about three-quarters of the bed.

He opened one eye, said : " It's Monday," and closed it again. I said nothing. " Day of rest," he explained, as though I had queried the statement. He sighed deeply and pretended to breathe regularly. I thought his last remark over. Perhaps it is a mistake to think before breakfast.

" In what particular way," I asked, " does that set it off from the rest of the week ? "

He stirred, rubbed his eyes and looked at me. He decided not to pursue the discussion and rang the bell for breakfast.

" Iris," I said, " didn't get in until three. I heard her."

He looked puzzled. " You heard her not coming home? Oh yes, of course. Shall we talk about all these fascinating things over coffee ? "

I agreed. Dagobert is not one of those people who consider it indecent to utter a word before breakfast. We seldom spend that meal behind the fortification of our newspapers. But I could understand his reluctance to plunge immediately into matters where they had left off last night. Dagobert had enjoyed the scene with Henry even less than I had, and he'd had the unenviable job of getting Henry undressed and into bed.

Breakfast came and we balanced the tray on our knees and poured out coffee. We spilled it into our saucers ; we got crumbs between the sheets and honey all over the knife-handles ; but there is something about breakfast in bed which makes these minor hardships worth putting up with.

Espoir and it's left-wing enemy the *Patriote* were folded on our breakfast tray. I read through the entertainment section of *Espoir* while Dagobert studied the political news in the *Patriote*. This seemed to depress him.

" One of these days," he concluded in a sinister tone of voice, " history is going to repeat itself once too often."

I glanced at what he'd been reading ; it was something about the Foreign Ministers meeting somewhere to discuss a *modus vivendi*.

" Why," I wondered, " when three or four politicians are gathered together are they always called the *Big* Three or the *Big* Four ? "

Dagobert didn't know either and we returned to our respective papers. I got tremendously excited by the children's crossword puzzle because the first clue was : " Le Roi d'Angleterre " and " Georges " fitted. I decided that there was hope for my French after all, but ten minutes later I had got no further. I lighted my first cigarette and thought about Henry, and of how I should employ his unexpected admission of guilt in the unlikely event of *Corpse Diplomatique* ever being written. It seemed unfair to use his unadorned statement : " I killed him," as a chapter ending, since the explanation of this outrageous confession was immediately forthcoming. Nor of course would any reader, seeing that the book was only two-thirds finished, for a moment believe it. It would, however, be extremely ingenious if, after confessing freely to the murder and having been therefore dismissed as a suspect, Henry should indeed, turn out to be the assassin of Hugh Arkwright.

This thought shook me so badly that I almost tore Dagobert from his newspaper (he was deep in the sports page, reading an article called " *Chez Nos Boulistes* ") to discuss it. If Henry had the ingenuity and the aplomb to stage that ghastly scene last night in order to mask a greater crime then I had certainly from the beginning misread and misrepresented his character.

Before I got too complicated I mentally reviewed the facts as they had emerged last night.

About a month ago Henry Makepeace, down from the hills after a two months' geological survey, had made for the nearest dockside café in the coastal town of Santiago da Santa Rica. There he had gone on a protracted binge, during the course of which he must have made that discovery, confided to me, that even in Santa

Rica " they were all blondes " these days. The blonde whom Henry had been most struck by also had a Lascar admirer. There was a rough-house and " the swine pulled a knife on me." Henry got the knife away from him and " before I knew what was happening, old boy, the little rat was sprawled over the bar with the knife in his side."

Though these things happen " daily " in Santiago " and no one pays much attention to them " Henry, afraid that the man might " pop off," decided to leave town hurriedly. The *Carrabia* was in port and leaving at once for the Mediterranean. Henry bribed the Captain to take him along.

But just before he sailed he wrote an air mail letter to Iris, telling her that he had found a ship which would get him to Villefranche ten days sooner than the *Scythia* on which he had previously booked a passage to Marseilles. He'd been half tight when he wrote the letter and " like a dam' fool I said there'd been a spot of bother." He had, in fact, given Iris sufficient details for Arkwright (who intercepted the letter) to work on.

Arkwright met the *Carrabia* at Villefranche. He was very sympathetic. He didn't tell Henry how he, Arkwright, happened to know so much about the business, but he had regretfully to inform Henry that the Lascar had died, and that—technically—Henry was a murderer. A mere bagatelle, Arkwright had shrugged charmingly, which he, Arkwright, would be delighted to put straight. Luckily he happened to be a great friend of the Santa Rican Vice-Consul in Nice. He was certain that with Don Diego's aid the whole matter would blow over at once. In fact the only reason Arkwright had met the *Carrabia* was to assure Henry that there was nothing in the world to worry about. All he need do was leave it to Arkwright, rejoin his delightful wife and not give the incident a further thought.

There was only one small thing. In order to gain Don

Diego's invaluable help a little money might be required. Arkwright hated to raise such a sordid subject, but Henry had lived in Central America and he knew how these things were.

Henry said he did, and it was at this point that he felt his attack of malaria coming on. Arkwright took him to the Petit Marguery Hotel, borrowed a fiver to carry on with and promised to come back and keep him informed. After Arkwright had gone, Henry staggered downstairs from his bedroom and tried to telephone the Santa Rican Consulate. Henry had suddenly decided to check up on this fellow Arkwright, just to see if he really were a friend of the Santa Rican Vice-Consul. Don Diego was out. He tried again an hour later but Don Diego was still out.

Then the fever had really got him and he did no more telephoning. Arkwright returned with a grave face to say it was going to cost more than he'd at first realised. Henry had parted in all with a hundred and fifty pounds which seemed to depress Dagobert even more than it depressed Henry himself. By the time he was fit enough to do anything further about it he had heard of Arkwright's death. Some instinct warned Henry to drop the whole business. If he were actually to be accused of murder in Santa Rica, Don Diego could get in touch with him himself.

At this point Dagobert had turned up in Henry's hotel bedroom with vague hints which had made Henry's hair stand on end.

For Henry had no alibi between five and six-thirty on Wednesday afternoon.

Actually, he told us, he'd taken a bus into Nice, had a glass of beer at one of the dozens of cafés near the bus terminus (*he couldn't remember which one*), felt too weak to walk anywhere, and had simply ridden back on the six-thirty bus to Villefranche. The famous walk—for

which he had witnesses, namely the wife, proprietor and
daughter of the Petit Marguery—was the first thing
which had come into Henry's mind when Dagobert visited
him.   Subsequently Henry had bribed the wife, proprietor and daughter of the Petit Marguery to back up
the fiction of this walk.   When Dagobert discussed it
with them on his second visit to Villefranche on Saturday
morning it had not occurred to him that they were lying.

I had also played my part in Henry's nervous dis-
integration.   The balcony-scene, followed by the discovery of my cigarette lighter in his rifled room, our
conversation at La Réserve and the feeling that we were
being followed were advanced stages on the way to his
final breakdown.

The last straw was Don Diego himself turning up for
dinner.   The net had closed and Henry waited for the
kill.   The gendarmes in the hall and the telephone calls
were just added torture.   Obviously we were playing
with him, diabolically baiting him before finally accusing
him of murder.

He had waited, waited.   Don Diego had vanished.   We
had gone off calmly to the films.   Henry knew that he
could not get through that night without a showdown.
He had gone on drinking in his room after Iris and
Dompierre went dancing.   Even whisky (he said, exaggerating slightly) had not affected him.   He climbed over
on to our balcony and waited for our return. . . .

Needless to say the story had been less coherent
than this last night.   Henry had been in a drivelling
state of mental and moral chaos, of tears, defiance,
threats, remorse, self-justification, self-accusation.   At
one moment he was blubbering that it was none of our
dam' business, the next he was abjectly begging us to
turn him over to the police at once.

When this kind of thing had gone on for about half an
hour Dagobert made—at least from the amateur detective

angle—a mistake. Instead of keeping Henry in this
miserable but pliable frame of mind until every point in
the story was cleared up, Dagobert suddenly threw in
his hand.

" If I tell you you're not a murderer," he said to
Henry, " will you go quietly—I mean to bed ? "

Henry had looked dazed, suspicious, hopeful and
extremely pathetic. Dagobert explained briefly what
the cable Don Diego had received from Santa Rica
during dinner had said. It was a cable in reply to one
Don Diego and Dagobert themselves had concocted,
asking for confidential information about Henry.

The Lascar had recovered from his knife wound and
had never been fitter. In a word, Henry had not killed
a man after all.

" Unless," Dagobert amended, just before we finally
turned out our light, " he killed Arkwright."

It was a pleasant little after-thought to take to sleep
with you. Dagobert had succeeded in calming Henry ;
I tossed around listening to Henry snore until I heard
Iris come in.

Even this morning, I reflected grimly, Henry was
doubtless still sunk in swinish slumber, thanks to Dagobert, no longer troubled by a guilty conscience, while I
stared at the children's crossword in *Espoir*, wondering
what stinging insect started in French with a G. I was
hurt by the injustice of it.

Dagobert looked up from the *Patriote* suddenly.

" Hello," he said, " do you remember Jean Potin ? "

" The one who's irresistible to women and blows them
up by putting bombs under their beds ? "

" That's the one."

" That's where we started, Dagobert—months ago," I
complained.

" I see they've just pinched him in Marseilles."

Chapter

22

We poured out more coffee and changed newspapers. Dagobert infuriatingly filled in the word *guêpe*
which I'd known ever since the Lower Fourth and refolded
the paper. He found something which apparently interested him and for the next few minutes I heard nothing
further from him. I saw that his coffee remained untouched, a thing which rarely happens.

"Jane," he said finally, letting the paper fall from his
hands and reaching for a cigarette, "have you got on
very far with your *Corpse Diplomatique*? "

He knew I hadn't so I didn't reply.

"Because," he said, "it—er—seems to be finished."

This time I stared at him. He recovered the paper.
I made out a headline I hadn't previously noticed. It
was on the front page and I never seem to notice head-
lines on the front page. It said :

"*Le Commissaire Morel met fin au mystère de l'assas-
sinat raté du Vice-Consul de Santa Rica.*"

I never exactly devour French, but I struggled on with
bated breath. Commissaire Morel may have put an end
to the mystery, but at the end of five minutes I was
more mystified than ever. Dagobert rang for hot coffee.

"There's also an afternoon bus for Tourette-en-
Provence," he said. "Somehow I don't think Mrs.
Andrioli will mind if we leave on such short notice, and
just between you and me I've almost had life in a small
pension."

"But," I gasped, "Arkwright! The people he was
blackmailing—all the suspicious details we've dug up ! "

" For some time now," he said cheerfully, " I've been wondering if the blackmail angle might not turn out to be a vast red herring. The fact that Arkwright also turns out to be a red herring is, frankly, a slight shock. That's why I'm glad you haven't wasted your time writing a book about him."

I sank back against the bolster with very badly mingled emotions. I was too dazed even to point out that it had been he, Dagobert, who had first guessed that Arkwright was a blackmailer. So sold had I been by Dagobert himself on the fact that I was in the midst of complex and sinister events that it took a minute or two to throw off the nightmare.

That it should all fizzle out like this, over breakfast and newspapers in bed, was an anti-climax which left me both relieved and disappointed.

" It will be colder in Tourette," Dagobert said, ringing again for coffee. " We brought your tramping boots, didn't we ? "

I nodded absently. " Dagobert. Start very slowly, remembering I only understand every second word of how Commissaire Morel solved the mystery. It was Juan Moro, wasn't it ? "

" Yes. We under-estimated Juan Moro, right from the beginning. Luckily Commissaire Morel didn't. Of course, of your original ten characters Juan was the most unlikely and therefore the obvious one to keep an eye on. Juan and Suzette. I forgot to keep an eye on Juan."

" He drove you out to La Réserve yesterday," I reminded him.

" So he did. We talked about Mayan temples. He'd never heard of them. He mentioned Consuelo."

" The first woman Don Diego ever loved ? "

Dagobert nodded dryly. " She's now one of the coastal-town blondes Henry was telling us about. As Don Diego told us he gave Juan's sister a start in life."

"In some ways it's a pity Juan missed," I said.

"Don Diego, I think, was sincere last night when he refused to believe his faithful Juan Moro had attempted to murder him."

"He was sincere, but the suggestion upset him violently just the same."

"The de la Torreda tribe have been badly disillusioned lately," Dagobert said. "Thousands of faithful Juan Moros arose at the last elections and kicked them out of office. The down-trodden are frightfully ungrateful these days."

"Why," I asked, "didn't Juan quietly knife him one night in the Consulate instead of picking out the most public place in Nice? And shooting, incidentally, from such a distance that he missed?"

"It wasn't so stupid as it seems," he said. "Don Diego himself probably gave Juan the idea. If you'll remember the first time we saw Don Diego he was living in terror that an attempt might be made on his life. He was seeing phantom assassins everywhere. Juan knew this. If Juan himself assassinated him, suspicion must immediately fall on one of these creatures of the Vice-Consul's imagination. The police would look for mysterious Santa Ricans. Actually the only Santa Rican around was Juan himself. This doubtless occurred to Commissaire Morel. That's why he at once let Don Diego have police protection. But you've read the paper."

"Yes, but tell me," I said hastily.

"Commissaire Morel has, it seems, been biding his time to have a little talk alone with Juan, when the Vice-Consul was not around. As you know he had Juan picked up last night on some trumped-up charge, ignoring traffic signals. Unfortunately Morel couldn't prevent Juan's telephoning Don Diego who—again as you know —rushed off to the rescue, swearing that the Santa Rican flag had been insulted. Morel had to release Juan before the *interrogatoire* was completed. But Morel knew the history of Consuelo and he has witnesses who are willing to swear that the gun was fired from the spot where the car was parked. He hasn't found the rifle—though he knows Juan had one—and he realises, of course, that you can find witnesses who'll swear the gun was fired from anywhere. Even you, Jane, haven't the faintest notion where the sound came from. Personal opinions on the subject are legally valueless. I've even found a waiter in that café on the corner who swears it came from *this* room.

" Anyway," he continued after relighting his cigarette, " Morel's intention was to pick up Juan again this morning. He did not wish to frighten Juan or upset Don Diego, so he let them go back to the Consulate. Naturally a guard was put outside the door and a gendarme slept in the car in the adjoining garage. When Don Diego interrupted the *interrogatoire* Morel had only asked general questions, giving Juan the impression—or so he hoped— that Juan himself was not under suspicion. But Juan is brighter than he looks. He got the wind up. And late last night he decamped."

" What about the gendarmes ? "

" Juan did not take the car. Nor did he leave by the front door. There is a courtyard behind the Consulate and a wall which separates it from another courtyard which is at the back of a block of flats in another street. Morel's men only discovered this after Juan had escaped ; and I believe there is shortly to be a slight reorganisation of the Nice police force."

He rang for the third time for more coffee, but the service at the Pension Victoria was not at its best that morning. He refreshed his memory in the columns of *Espoir* and quoted :

" The Brigade Mobile expects shortly to make an

arrest. Juan Moro cannot have got far. Swiss and Italian border officials have been given his description. We await with confidence the outcome of the man-hunt which will conclude the tragic affair of last Wednesday."

" I hate man-hunts," I said. " I hope Juan gets away."

" The end," Dagobert said, stretching, " is not very satisfactory, but at least it's unexpected. . . . Will it take you long to pack ? "

I nodded and wished more coffee would come. Next door I thought I heard the Makepeaces stirring. A moment later Henry's voice was audible from the adjoining balcony. He was singing ! The words were something about " my baby wouldn't go home." I looked at Dagobert. He winced and went back to *Chez Nos Boulistes*. I tried to remember the essential fact : the mystery was finished. Nothing more to worry about. No murderer lurking in the corridors of the Pension Victoria. Only some poor devil of a Central American peon fleeing for his life with half the police of the Côte d'Azur on his heels—*à ses trousses*, as the paper charmingly put it.

The only thing that kept worrying me was the docile acceptance with which Dagobert had taken it all. I know Dagobert, and he does not normally react so calmly when pet theories of his are exploded. I tried to lead him on.

" And," I said deliberately, " do you think that's the way it all was ? "

He came out of the bowling news with an effort. " The assassination ? " he murmured. " Yes, of course. What is good enough for Commissaire Morel is good enough for me. . . . To tell the truth, Jane, I've been getting a bit behind lately with Bertran de Born."

I got out of bed with the general intention of brushing my teeth. I felt let-down and dissatisfied. The sound of Henry's voice next door irritated me. It would be good—at least it ought to be good—to leave the Pension Victoria, and yet the prospect of Tourette-en-Provence left me apathetic. I rang the bell, this time impatiently, for our second round of coffee, though I didn't especially want it. I was suffering from the deadly sin which medieval theologians—and Dagobert—called Accidie. " The fourth head of the Beast of Helle is Sloth," I remembered from somewhere, " whyche is cally'd of clerkys accidie."

It was a poor thing if one had to have an unsolved murder on one's mind in order to savour life ! I felt acutely ashamed of myself. This morning's edition of *Espoir* had dispersed dark clouds of suspicion and terror from the Pension Victoria and all *ought* to have been, like the weather outside, sunny and bright. It wasn't.

I have found by experience that my intuitions are best ignored. I brushed my teeth furiously and tried to ignore the one which grew momentarily more insistent. It was vague and must be put vaguely. It was that there was *still* an unsolved murder on my mind. . . .

This may have been why I jumped and spun violently round at the tap on the door. Since it was only the maid and we had been ringing for her for the last twenty minutes there was no real reason why my heart should have begun to thump even before I caught sight of her face.

There was a second reason for my seemingly unaccountable behaviour. I had heard outside a sound which was subconsciously familiar. It was consciously familiar too, of course, since it was the urgent two-note hoot of all French police, ambulance and fire vehicles. But it had become ineluctably linked in my mind with the time I'd heard it last Wednesday, when Hugh Arkwright was shot. To this day the sound makes my pulse quicken.

Dagobert had thrust his feet into bedroom slippers

and wrapped a dressing-gown around him. The maid, I noticed, did not have further coffee supplies with her, though that was her habit when she answered our bell. Her face was very white and she was apologising for not having answered our call sooner. On the floor below all was in confusion. Yes, something dreadful had happened. The doctor was there, but it was too late. Would we please now excuse her.

Dagobert did not say anything to me when the door had closed again, but I had made out enough of the conversation. If I hadn't, his face would have interpreted it for me. He looked as shaken as I felt. His face was dark with anger and I saw his fists clench and unclench.

Mrs. Andrioli had just been found dead in her bedroom.

Chapter

23

MRS. ANDRIOLI HAD BEEN FOUND DEAD BY THE MAID who always took her a cup of black coffee at eight o'clock every morning. Her room was on the floor below ours. It was at the back of the building and was reached by a narrow covered porch over the well of the interior courtyard. Hence it was isolated from the visitors' rooms, and if she had made any sound in the night no one had heard her. The Pension staff—a cook, a kitchen boy, the waiters and the chambermaid—all slept out. The chambermaid and the kitchen boy came at seven in the morning and left before dinner in the evening. The cook and the waiters arrived in time to prepare luncheon and left about ten o'clock in the evening after washing up. They presumably had been the last people to see her alive.

I heard the technical name of what caused death late that afternoon after the pathologist's post-mortem examination. It wasn't acute ptomaine poisoning but that's what it meant. Something she had eaten—indubitably the mussels—had been fatal. She had probably died around three o'clock in the morning about the time I'd gone to sleep.

The inquiry was straightforward and so far as we learned no suspicion of foul play was suggested. The cook stated that Mrs. Andrioli had retired at ten, complaining that she had eaten too much and felt sleepy. Dagobert and I, the only other people in the Pension who had eaten mussels that evening, were briefly questioned as to whether we had felt any ill effects of the dish.

By the end of the day the *médicin-légiste* had done the
autopsy and issued his authority for the body to be
buried.

One thing about Mrs. Andrioli's death struck me
immediately. Both the cook and the waiter mentioned
it, but it apparently led to no further police inquiries.
Mrs. Andrioli had eaten not only the mussels which she
had kept back for herself, but also those which Don
Diego had refused, the plate which had sat on the sideboard all during dinner. . . .

Marie Andrioli had an older sister called Mrs. Camellini,
who kept another small Pension in Cimiez in the hills
above Nice. Mrs. Camellini was, since the death of Hugh
Arkwright, Mrs. Andrioli's nearest relation, and she was
her sole heir.

She was a small, energetic, bright-eyed woman with
much of Mrs. Andrioli's own forthright charm. She had
been fond of her sister, though they had seen little of
each other since the war. Mrs. Camellini, we later
learned, had known and disapproved of her younger
sister's secret marriage to Hugh Arkwright, whom she
despised. She considered Marie Andrioli soft, sentimental and hopelessly un-Latin.

Marius Andrioli, a *beau garçon* and a promising *com-
merçant* who had avoided conscription up until the very
beginning of 1918, had been killed in the second battle
of the Marne, and Marie, who was only eighteen at the
time and one of the prettiest girls in Nice, had been
inconsolable. She could have married again a dozen
times over. What she needed was children (Mrs. Camellini had had seven !), but no—Marie must make a cult of
Marius (who would have been the last to understand it)
which lasted for nearly twenty years, until, in fact, she
fell in love with this gigolo, this permanent lodger who
rarely paid his rent, this self-styled " Major " Arkwright

who aped the manners of an English *milord* so well that she, Mrs. Camellini, had seen through him at the first encounter.

Mrs. Camellini explained her sister's infatuation for Arkwright as a kind of thwarted mother-love, but she admitted that it was none the less profound.

It was Mrs. Camellini who pointed out a rather perplexing detail of her sister's death. There was a house-telephone beside Marie's bed. Even assuming that Marie had called out in the night during the pain she must have felt and not have made herself heard, why had she not used this telephone ? It worked ; Mrs. Camellini and Dagobert had verified this.

Mrs. Camellini had a theory which sent both Dagobert and me into deep thought. Her theory was that Marie had not *wanted* to be saved ! She had not exactly committed suicide—that would be a mortal sin—but she had done nothing to stave off death when it struck. Mrs. Camellini had been to Arkwright's funeral. She had seen then that something had been extinguished in her sister's soul ; a vital part of her—perhaps the will to live—had been buried with Hugh Arkwright in a corner of the English cemetery. Mrs. Camellini had recognised the symptoms because (she told us) she had known them herself—three times, when three of her own children had been buried.

But the normal person recovers from these crises of despair, is it not so ? One has other children, and a husband who spends his time playing bowls and drinking red wine in the neighbouring bistros. One has a Pension which is doing badly due to high taxes and the fact that the pre-war type of retired English gentry no longer spend the winter in Cimiez. But Marie was impractical. A heart is an *excellent* thing to have, but it must not rule the head.

The only comforting thing about Marie's death was

that she owed it to her favourite indulgence. Her *gour-mandise* was the thing which had prevented her from turning into one of "those good women." If she had to die it was fitting that she should do so after dining too well. Marie herself would have liked it to be so.

I do not think the possibility that her sister had been murdered ever crossed Mrs. Camellini's mind. She knew nothing of her late brother-in-law's blackmailing activities. Like the rest of Nice, she believed he had been mistakenly shot by Juan Moro in an attempt to assassinate Don Diego. I once asked her if she did not think it remarkable that both her sister and her sister's husband should have had fatal " accidents " within a space of five days of each other, but she considered this no more remarkable than that a number in roulette at Monte Carlo should turn up twice running, a coincidence by no means rare. Dagobert agreed with her on this point, or rather he said he did.

I am recounting my impressions of that Monday and the next day or two rather disconnectedly ; they remain rather disconnected in my own memory. I spent a good part of the ensuing forty-eight hours at my typewriter, out of the main current of affairs. This, I need scarcely say, was Dagobert's idea. For he had dropped all thought of Tourette-en-Provence and Bertran de Born. Mrs. Camellini, who had been grateful to us for consenting to remain on at the Pension Victoria, did not realise that it would have taken the Brigade Mobile itself to have evicted Dagobert.

Mrs. Camellini had been notified at once of her sister's death and she arrived at the Pension Victoria shortly after the police. By the time we were dressed she had already taken charge of the place. Not only had she fulfilled those formalities which the police demanded of her, wept briefly but sincerely at her sister's death, but she had already made out the menus for luncheon and dinner and seen that the servants were busy.

Her sister's estate consisted primarily of the lease of the premises and the goodwill and reputation of the Pension Victoria. It was a considerably better paying concern than her own Pension in Cimiez, and Mrs. Camellini was too good an hotelier to allow its efficiency to lapse even for a day. She was aware that two deaths within less than one week were scarcely good publicity, and she told all of us that she would quite understand if we wished to move. She added that she would be very glad to look after those of us who cared to remain.

Parenthetically the Pension Victoria improved noticeably from the first day Mrs. Camellini took charge. The hot water suddenly became abundant and the food delicious. There were fresh flowers daily in everyone's room, the beds were turned down and shoes were polished to twice their former lustre.

The Countess Gluttonsen and her son never benefited from these changes; they left that same morning in their open Mercedes-Benz, complete with goggles, crash helmets and dust-coats.

Elinor Duffield voiced the opinion in the sitting-room before luncheon that it was " really kind of mean " to desert the place in the circumstances and most of the rest of us agreed. Actually Elinor herself had decided only last night to leave this morning for Florence, but she asked Mrs. Camellini if she might delay her departure for a week. Mrs. Camellini looked relieved, but not so relieved—I thought—as Sophie looked.

Dompierre rented his room by the month and with his piano and paraphernalia was only too glad to be able to stay. Henry wanted to push along to Monty, where there was a bit of life, but Iris silenced him. They, too, would stay, glancing meltingly at Dompierre—" for poor Mrs. Andrioli's sake."

" And besides," she added in one of her terrifying stage whispers, " it would seem so *suspicious* to leave suddenly."

" Why would it ? " Henry growled.

Iris looked prettily confused. " Because—I mean," she glanced swiftly at Dagobert and began to stammer—" I mean, because, well—to run away, you know, after two people have suddenly died—er—people might begin to wonder why. Don't you think ? "

" On the other hand," Dagobert smiled, " isn't it even more suspicious *not* to run away ? I mean people might begin to wonder if you were afraid to make yourself conspicuous by bolting."

" It's beyond me, old boy," said Henry.

But Dagobert had very successfully fixed it so that now no one dared change his mind again and leave.

Chapter

24

ELINOR CANCELLED THE COCKTAIL PARTY IN HER ROOM, but after dinner that evening she asked Dagobert and me to have coffee with her. The sitting-room would be crowded and she suggested we come on to the balcony of her bedroom.

We said we'd be delighted, and when we had finished our Brie and folded our napkins we made our way along the corridor towards Room Six.

"Every time someone is killed," Dagobert observed as we knocked on her door, "we are invited for coffee and confessions."

In much the same way, I remembered, Dieudonné Dompierre had invited us privately into his room after Arkwright's death. Over Dompierre's nescafé we had first learned that Arkwright was a blackmailer and we had heard of the gun which had inexplicably vanished.

I entered Elinor's room with even greater expectations. All afternoon at the typewriter I had wrestled with notes and queries, lists and tables. I had drawn up parallel columns of those who *could* have killed Arkwright and those who could have killed Marie Andrioli. I had struggled with ways and means, with alibis. I had sketched a plan of the Pension Victoria and a map showing the junction of the Rue Ravel and the Promenade des Anglais, complete with a large X to mark the spot. I had filled several sheets of paper, and then scribbled illegible footnotes, corrections, insertions, and large

question-marks all over them. In brief, I had probably
wasted my time.

I entered Room Six with expectation because the
column which Elinor Duffield occupied in my notes was
one of the least satisfactory. It contained a reference
to the fact that she was an enthusiastic shooter of clay
pigeons, that she *said* she'd been having a bath (cold)
at the time of Arkwright's death, and (most suggestive)
that she'd remembered the name of the Pension Victoria
since 1927. However (however was a word which
occurred frequently in my notes !), Elinor had certainly
not been near the dish of mussels on the sideboard during
dinner. I had been facing her table last night and should
have noticed had she left it. I had seen her and
Sophie go out and neither of them had passed the
sideboard.

Elinor welcomed us graciously, and I was glad she
could not read the thoughts which had been passing
through my mind. Unlike Dompierre, she did not at
once embark upon the subject of conversation for which
we had been invited. Instead she commented upon the
increasing quantity of tourists in Nice and their lessening
quality. I was afraid for a moment it was going to turn
into one of those I-can't-think-where-these-dreadful-
people-come-from discussions, and was relieved when she
said she thought it an excellent thing that the Riviera
has become a resort for plain people (like us ?) instead of
a playground for the rich.

She had arranged three chairs on the balcony and
coffee and a bottle of Benedictine arrived almost as soon
as we had seated ourselves. Room Six was at the opposite
end of the corridor from Dompierre's room and the
balcony faced up the Promenade, that is : away from the
Rue Ravel. From Elinor's balcony you could not, in
fact, see the spot where Arkwright had been shot ; and
it occurred to me that a much better alibi for the time

of Arkwright's death would have been to say that she was in her own room, instead of taking a bath. I had had a confusing afternoon with my notes and it did not occur to me that instead of seeking to establish an alibi Elinor had merely stated the simple truth !

" It was so nice of you to come," she was saying. " Perhaps Mr. Brown—or *may* I say Dagobert—will pour out the Benedictine. . . . There was something I rather specially wanted to talk to you about." She smiled anxiously. " I hope you won't mind."

" No, of course not."

She continued to smile, but her fingers, clasped in her lap, twisted uncomfortably. She wore no nail varnish to-night and she was dressed less youthfully than usual. She had lost something of that hard, smart, club woman look which I both disliked and admired, and the smile, less self-assured, was gentler. Plainly she found it hard to begin.

" If you don't mind I won't have any Benedictine," she said as Dagobert handed a glass to her. " I thought you and Jane might like it. It's about Sophie," she added.

She had already poured out coffee and I handed her the sugar-basin. She shook her head with a momentary return of her bright smile.

" No sugar, thank you. I still have to think of my figure, you know ! " The tight lines about her mouth relaxed. " Or do I ? " she added with a slight laugh. " The truth is, I like *three* lumps and I think I'm going to have them."

She took four. " It's about Sophie and Joe," she said.

She was looking at me and I moved a little guiltily. But there was no reproach in her clear grey eyes. " You know this Joe Orsini, I believe, better than I do. You two are nearer Sophie and Joe's age than you are mine, and you may be able to understand them." Her voice hardened. "I don't."

"In what way?"

"I try to," she went on, ignoring the question. Her voice had softened again and she seemed to concentrate on the coffee-cup in her hand. "You must believe that I've tried very hard to understand. . . . You see, there was an awful scene last night after you two went to the movies. I've no right to tell you this, but I've no one else to talk to, and sometimes you've got to have someone to talk to. Half-way through coffee Sophie suddenly announced that she and Joe were going to take a walk. Naturally, I said I'd come with them. Joe was very nice about it, I must admit. But Sophie!" She shivered slightly without glancing up. "Sophie said she didn't *want* me to come! She said I followed her around everywhere, I never left her alone. I tried to run her life. She said I'd ruin her life if she gave me the chance. She said that . . . that she *loathed* me."

She paused to sip the coffee which she had been mechanically stirring. Her hand was steady, but her lower lip was quivering. She made an effort to smile, then, to my relief, gave it up.

"Of course she was hysterical and didn't mean it," she continued dully. "I know she didn't mean it. It's silly of me to talk about it, isn't it? Do let me pour you another cup of coffee."

"Did they go alone for their walk?" I asked.

"Oh, yes. I excused myself. I said I had a headache, which was only too true. Joe—again I must admit —behaved very well. He tried to persuade me to come along and told Sophie to stop acting like a hysterical kid. He's a good-hearted young man, maybe a little uncouth, but . . ." She sighed and left the sentence unfinished. "Sophie marched into my room at about two o'clock in the morning. I was sitting here on the balcony. She was no longer hysterical, but I'd never seen her face so hard. She told me defiantly that she and Joe were in love and that they were going to be married whether I liked it or not. I told her that we were leaving for Italy by the first train this morning, and I ordered her to go to bed at once. She left without saying good night, slamming the door behind her."

We all sat for a moment without speaking. There was nothing that either of us could say and Elinor Duffield sat stiffly, her eyes fixed on the distance. I saw that her eyes were wet, and it was like the relief of the first rain from a sultry, leaden sky. A slight shudder ran through her.

"Pride is a horrid thing," she murmured. "I—I didn't follow her into her room. I wanted to, but I couldn't. I sat here all night. Even this morning I told her I had put off our trip to Florence only for Mrs. Camellini's sake. I couldn't bring myself to admit that it was for Sophie's sake. And yet," she added with a sigh, "I can admit it to you, who mean relatively nothing to me. . . ."

I broke the silence which followed by saying : "I had a long heart-to-heart talk with Sophie yesterday on the beach."

"I'm glad," Elinor said, "Sophie has *no one* to whom she feels she can talk."

"Like you," I suggested, "perhaps she finds it easier to admit things to people who mean nothing to her."

Elinor considered this and finally nodded. "Yes," she said reluctantly.

"It's extremely impertinent of me to say so, but Sophie told me how much she loved you."

It was an intolerably patronising remark to make to an older woman whom I'd known for less than a fortnight, and it was not strictly true ; but I was rewarded by the eagerness in her manner as she said :

" Did she ? Did she really ? I've sometimes wondered lately. I've thought maybe it's been my fault, but . . . What did Sophie say ? Did she . . . ? " She broke off and dabbed her eyes quickly with a small lace handkerchief. " Do forgive me. I'm being silly. It doesn't matter in the slightest. Dagobert's glass is empty. Do fill it." She was smiling again. " It's my only way of bribing you to listen to a foolish woman's domestic troubles—which I'm probably exaggerating, anyway ! "

" I think you are," Dagobert nodded gravely. " But as domestic troubles are the only troubles which matter in the slightest and the Benedictine is excellent, I consent to be bribed."

She watched him refill his glass with a kind of gratitude. " Of course I am," she said. " Exaggerating, I mean. It's very good for me to have someone hear my complaints who dismisses them as they deserve to be. . . . Er—I suppose she's with him now. . . ."

" Where else would she be ? " Dagobert grinned.

" She rushed away from the dinner-table without even saying excuse me."

" Doubtless to break the good news that ' the old woman ' had put off the threatened departure for a week."

I'd been a little uncertain of Dagobert's ' the old woman '. Elinor received it with a slight gasp, followed by a light laugh almost of pleasure.

" Yes, I guess that's exactly what I am to them," she said. " The old woman. The old woman." She repeated the phrase as though it were new to her and not altogether distasteful. " Tell me," she continued more animatedly, " you know Joe Orsini, I believe. Sophie, in one of her tantrums, said you both liked him. Do you really ? "

" Yes."

" But the idea of his *marrying*, I mean Sophie ! "

" What's wrong with it ? "

" I—don't—really—know ! " Elinor exclaimed slowly. The thought seemed revolutionary to her and, like the phrase "the old woman," not quite so preposterous on second consideration as it had been on first. " He's a good sort in some ways, isn't he. To tell the truth— though I wouldn't for the world say it to Sophie—he reminds me just a wee bit sometimes of her father ! Not really, of course. Arthur was, if you don't mind the word, a gentleman. But there's a certain air of solidity about them both, a kind of rugged, good-natured . . . I almost said *honesty !* Though Joe, I gather, has been making his living on the Black Market money exchange. Arthur," she added with a wry smile, " was a banker. I wonder if there's really so much difference."

Elinor, whose manners were always excellent if some-times a little professional, apologised suddenly for monopolising the entire conversation with her own affairs. She attempted to engage Dagobert in intelligent discussion of international politics. As she was an assidu-ous reader of *Time* and Dagobert's information was largely derived from the sports page of *Nice-Matin* she ran circles round him. She brought me into it by intro-ducing literature, but the fact was I hadn't read a good book lately. I hadn't even written one, though Dagobert told her I was going to.

She scrupulously avoided further direct reference to Sophie, though occasionally when her mind drifted I heard her murmuring such things as : " June would be a good month," and " announcements could be sent air mail." I also noticed her tendency to stop talking suddenly in the middle of sentences, as though to listen for footsteps approaching the door. But by ten-thirty, when we said good-night, Sophie had not turned up, and Elinor was trying not to notice.

By this time the conversation had sunk from the

heights of politics, literature, art and music to personalities, settling down inevitably to those of our fellow pensionnaires. And, of course, to Mrs. Andrioli.

We had already announced that we must go and were on our feet when Dagobert said :

" Did you know that Mrs. Andrioli was really Mrs. Arkwright ? "

Elinor sat down again abruptly. " No ! " she exclaimed, " I certainly did not. If I had . . ." She broke off exasperatingly. " But what makes you think so ? "

" She told Jane. Mrs. Camellini also knew about it."

Elinor seemed thoughtful, puzzled and I thought a little annoyed. My heart lurched slightly as I wondered why. " I knew she was fond of him," she said finally. " I went to his funeral with her and she cried. To tell the truth I did, too, just a little. It seemed so pathetic to be buried—with no one but your landlady and her sister, and an ex-Universal pupil and her mother. Are you *sure* ? "

Dagobert nodded.

" But why the secrecy ? "

" It was Arkwright's idea. It seemed that a wife, plump and older than himself, would have handicapped him in his profession—as a professional charmer."

" You mean as a blackmailer ! " Elinor snapped.

This time we both sat down again. It was the first hint we had had that Elinor even suspected the charming Hugh Arkwright of blackmail. She had flushed and I saw her bite her lip.

" I wish I'd *known* ! " she muttered.

" Why ? "

She laughed harshly. " I guess everybody hates to be made a fool of," she said. " I certainly do. And that's just what your fine aristocratic Major Arkwright did to me. I think I'm rather glad he got shot. No, that's a horrid thing to say. Nevertheless . . ."

"He wasn't *mine*," Dagobert pointed out with a smile. "You knew Hugh Arkwright back in 1927, didn't you ? "

She shook her head absentmindedly. "No, but . . ." She broke off with a sigh. Dagobert lighted the cigarette she had taken from the table. "Having gotten this far," she said resignedly, " I might as well go on. . . . More personal revelations, I'm afraid," she added with a faint smile. "That is, if you're interested."

"Actually," Dagobert said, " we're fascinated."

"Well, I knew the Pension Victoria back in 1927," she said, " when apparently Major Arkwright was already the occupant of Room Twelve. I knew . . . " she blushed suddenly and faltered, "I knew Room Six. This room."

She smoked her cigarette nervously, puffing at it in an awkward way, reminiscent of the way Sophie had smoked on the beach yesterday, like a girl just learning to smoke. Doubtless it was the evocation of a generation ago, but even while she spoke she seemed younger, girlish and a little silly.

"You were staying at the Negresco," Dagobert prompted gently.

"Yes, but I spent a night once in this very room ! " she gasped. "With . . . with that swimming instructor I sometimes still laugh about whose name was Hippolyte of all things and who was the colour of mahogany ! " she finished all in a breath.

"And Arkwright remembered and recognised you," I said.

"No, he didn't. That's what makes me so furious with myself. He didn't recognise me ! "

"No," Dagobert nodded. "Mrs. Andrioli said he didn't."

" Not," Elinor continued, " until I was fool enough to *tell* him. Then he did. Or said he did. I talk too much, just as I'm doing now, I guess . . ."

" You can't think what a weight you're lifting from my mind," Dagobert said almost gaily.

" Why ? "

" I'll tell you later. Go ahead."

Elinor lowered her voice confidentially. She now glanced towards the door for fear that Sophie might come in in the middle of her confession.

" Well," she said. " Well, Major Arkwright took me out to luncheon shortly after we arrived. To talk about Sophie's lessons in French, he *said*. We went to Raynaud's and I must confess he was very charming and delightful. I didn't realise until later that he was leading me on to talk about myself. I don't know what came over me but I couldn't resist talking about Hippolyte. I told him Hippolyte was the most beautiful creature ever made and that I'd been wildly in love with him. Then I told him why I'd come back after so many years to the Pension Victoria—a kind of sentimental journey. Finally I found myself confiding how I'd wanted to stay in exactly the same room where I'd been so divinely happy—twenty-three years ago. Why I was such a silly old fool I shall never understand."

" You mean to come back to Nice ? Or to tell Arkwright about it ? "

" Both ! " she said firmly.

" And then ? "

" Then, as Joe says, came the ' pay off '. Next day this Arkwright asked me if I could lend him twenty dollars. I said certainly not, and he explained that he only wanted it in order to take me out to luncheon again so we could talk about Hippolyte. Did Sophie, he asked, know about Hippolyte ? I said of course she did—I was

always boasting about my conquests as a girl in Nice.
Did she, he added, know about that romantic night in
Room Six ? "

Elinor put out her half-finished cigarette. " To cut
a long story short I gave him a twenty dollar traveller's
cheque. I gave him at least five more before he died.
That must be Sophie ! " She broke off to listen, but the
footstep in the corridor did not approach. She relaxed
and the animation she had displayed during this recital
of her scandalous past faded. She said anxiously : " You
won't say anything about this to Sophie ? No, *of course*
you won't. Forgive me for asking such a thing ; but
you can't realise how intolerant daughters can be . . .
Tell me, why did you say I'd lifted a weight off your
mind ? "

Dagobert looked embarrassed. He fumbled in my
handbag for a cigarette. " Since we're all making
confessions," he began, but he appealed to me to rescue
him : " What is the socially correct way of explaining
to one's hostess that you've been suspecting her of
murder ? "

Elinor looked blank and I hastened to say : " You
know that book Dagobert said I was going to write.
It's about the death of Major Arkwright and we are
amusing ourselves by assuming that one of us in the
Pension murdered him. Naturally you are a major
suspect."

" Oh, I see," Elinor said still somewhat bewildered.
" And the others ? "

" They are, if anything, even more suspect."

" You see," Dagobert enlarged cheerfully, " Arkwright
was blackmailing everyone in sight, including me. You
and Sophie are not only the wealthiest people in the
Pension, but until now you seemed to be the only people
he wasn't blackmailing. The apparent fact that you
were *not* being blackmailed may seem an odd reason for

your being especially suspect, but . . . You explain, Jane. It's your book."

" One always suspects the least likely person," I smiled, hoping that Elinor would enter into the spirit of the thing. She listened earnestly and without the flicker of a smile in response. I persisted, but it was uphill work. For I was quite aware that the subject was not one to be facetious about. " You had no visible motive for killing him. Now you have. One hundred and twenty dollar's worth. It puts you on a level with the rest of us."

" How awfully amusing," Elinor said indifferently.

" Now, if we could only discover," Dagobert said, " that he'd also been blackmailing Sophie . . . "

Elinor came to sharply. " That's absurd ! " she said.

" Of course it is," I agreed. " Dagobert specialises in making preposterous remarks which I later have to edit."

" Oh, I see," she said, regaining her equanimity. " It must be very confusing being an author and getting mixed up between the real world and the one of your own creation."

" It is," I agreed fervently.

" I've never read a—what do you call them ?—a Mystery ? " she said. " But I shall certainly read yours when it comes out. What's it called ? I shall put it on my library list at once."

We chatted desultorily for a few minutes more and again suggested leaving. I think she wanted us to stay, but she was too polite to be insistent. She thanked us touchingly for being so patient with her, and hoped she hadn't spoiled our evening. She said she was feeling infinitely better for our " nice visit together " and added rather vaguely :

" Papa Orsini was really one of the sweetest old men.

I believe there was some talk once of his running for the Buffalo Town Council. I must ask Joe if he ever did."

She saw us to the door. But though she said good-night cordially, her glance was towards the stairway and the lift along the empty corridor. I didn't look around as we walked away, nor did I hear the door of Room Six close behind us. I wondered how long she would stand there, waiting.

" I think," Dagobert said suddenly as we reached the stairs, " we'll go out and find Sophie and, if necessary, knock a little sense into her ! "

Chapter

25

AS AN ACCOUNT LIKE THE PRESENT ONE UNFOLDS I AM
aware that the persons involved in it should become
increasingly suspect. My trouble, as I again returned
to the struggle the following day, was that as I went
along everyone was getting *less* suspect.

I made out a list of those who had had the bare opportunity to kill Major Arkwright, but the more I studied it
the less convinced I was that it contained a murderer.

The list was :

1. *Elinor :* the bathroom, opposite Dompierre's room,
had a narrow window giving on to the Rue Ravel from
which the fatal spot was visible.

2. *Sophie :* she'd been lying on her bed reading, but
her window faced the spot marked X.

3. *Iris :* she couldn't remember quite where she was
at five-thirty—out shopping, she thought—but the
concierge said she'd come in before five.

4. *Henry :* he was in Nice at the time, having " a
beer " at a café (unidentified) near the bus terminus.
(Ten minutes' walk from the Pension Victoria).

5. *Mrs. Andrioli herself :* she'd been in Arkwright's
own room at the time.

6. *Joe Orsini :* he was shaving, but there was no witness
to prove that he hadn't gone to the window of his room
over the Brooklyn Bar.

7. *Juan Moro :* he was still at large and still (officially)
the culprit.

8. *Me :* I included myself to show Dagobert how
thorough I was.

I also had a list of those who had not had the opportunity of shooting Arkwright. It included:

9. *Dagobert*: who was eating pastry in the Rue de France.

10. *Suzette*: who had been in another part of Nice on business of her own.

11. *Don Diego*: who was only a few feet from Arkwright himself.

12. *Dompierre*: who had been playing the piano.

Arkwright had been blackmailing the following: Elinor, Iris, Henry, Joe, Juan. Also, from the list of those who physically could not have shot him, Dagobert and Dompierre.

He had not been blackmailing—*so far as we knew*: Sophie, Mrs. Andrioli, Suzette, Don Diego and me.

In other words, the list of those who had both opportunity *and* motive (i.e. blackmail) boiled down to Elinor, Iris, Henry, Joe and Juan.

Now, (I argued) the person who killed Arkwright must also have poisoned Mrs. Andrioli. The murderer had known she had seen Arkwright's papers. The murderer had feared that from these papers she had learned who had the strongest motive for killing Arkwright, and guessed who, in fact, had done so.

More of my scientific elimination (as above) and I must have the final answer! Who could have tampered with the mussels? I made out my list, first noting that no one had gone into the kitchen after the waiter had taken the plate from the sideboard. (This note was the result of a little private investigation of my own, which I hadn't told Dagobert about. I also arbitrarily eliminated the servants.)

My list of those who could have poisoned the mussels was: Dagobert, me, Don Diego—on whose table they had been; Dompierre—who had gone to the sideboard to fetch an ashtray halfway through dinner; Joe—who had paused at the sideboard to pick a buttonhole ; and (brilliant inclusion !) Mrs. Andrioli herself—who in this case might be said to have committed suicide after murdering her husband !

Those who could not have added poison surreptitiously to the fatal mussels were : Elinor, Sophie, Iris, Henry, Suzette and, of course, Juan Moro.

The rest was simply a matter of crossing out, like solving anagrams when you've half the letters filled in.

Of the five people who had opportunity and motive for murdering Arkwright, Elinor, Iris, Henry and Juan could not have poisoned the mussels. Of the five people who could have poisoned the mussels, Dagobert, Dompierre and Don Diego had had no opportunity to shoot Arkwright, and Mrs. Andrioli and I had no motive (at least I had no motive).

That left exactly one person who had had *both* motive and opportunity for killing *both* Arkwright and Mrs. Andrioli.

The one person was Joe.

As Joe was also the one person whom I was inwardly convinced had nothing to do with it, my despair may be understandable. Dagobert, arriving just before luncheon, found me in a state of dejection. He glanced through my notes with interest and congratulated me on my impeccable logic. I said nastily :

" If it comes to that what have *you* been doing ? "

" Floating around," he said airily. " I met a man who's going to teach me *boules*. By the way, the reason we couldn't find Sophie and Joe last night was because they were at the Fair. In one of those shooting-booths. Sophie won a celluloid doll."

Chapter

26

LUNCHEON WAS REMARKABLE CHIEFLY FOR AN EXCELLENT *soufflé* and Dagobert's good humour. We were late and half the guests had finished. The Duffields were just leaving as we came in. Elinor smiled pleasantly and Sophie gave us a look of recognition, without venturing to speak. Both of them were a little pink around the eyes ; but I noticed Sophie take her mother's arm as they reached the hall.

The Makepeaces were lunching alone. Henry was studying the car mart in the Paris *Herald-Tribune* while Iris had a book propped up beside her plate. It was Zola's *Thérèse Raquin* in translation. Their conversation was confined to occasional requests to pass the salt and pepper.

Dagobert ordered a bottle of Veuve Cliquot, though he does not normally like champagne, and attacked the Anglo-Saxon heresy that champagne ought to be very dry. Like all silly things it should be slightly sweet and, as it is not supposed to chill, it should not be too cold. It ought to go off with a resounding pop, the cork preferably bouncing from the ceiling on to someone else's head. It ought to have a reckless label designed by, say, Raoul Dufy, and the neck of the bottle should be festooned with plenty of gold and silver tinfoil. It should be wildly expensive.

"At least it's that," I nodded, as the waiter soberly removed the cork with a linen napkin. "Has your publisher offered you another five pounds on Bertran de Born ?"

" No," Dagobert admitted. " I'm glad you mentioned that. I'll write this afternoon and suggest it."

" Then what are we celebrating ? "

" It is pointless celebrating when there's something to celebrate. You need to celebrate when there's nothing in particular to get excited about."

" Quite," I nodded, " but what is it ? "

" Just a passing idea I had."

He was much too casual. My heart skipped about three . beats. " Dagobert," I murmured, lowering my voice, " you . . . you haven't found . . . you don't know who . . ."

" Who murdered Arkwright ? " He grinned. He shook his head. " Would I be so cheerful if I had ? No, the only satisfactory moments in these cases are when things are jogging along nicely and it doesn't even cross your mind that the people at the next table may be murderers."

The people at the next table were the Makepeaces and I pointed out that such remarks were making it extremely difficult for them to concentrate on *Thérèse Raquin* and motor car advertisements. Dagobert apologised to them.

" The idea that crossed my mind," he said, " was that there might be money in this thing. I mean, in carrying on where Arkwright left off. For instance, if we could dig up something more about Henry."

" Look here, old boy," Henry muttered darkly, " I don't know what you're talking about, but——" He didn't finish the implied threat and Iris gave him a brief glance of contempt.

" Henry's been a continual disappointment," Dagobert complained. " First because it wasn't Henry who changed those pesos at the Brooklyn Bar, and then because he handed over one hundred and fifty pounds' worth of them to Arkwright instead of only five pounds' worth as he so deceitfully told you, Jane."

" I can see how that would be a disappointment to Henry," I said, " but why to you ? "

" Because—do you mind my thinking aloud like this ? —because I'd decided that the person who'd paid up the other hundred and forty-five pounds must be Don Diego, the only other man in Nice who might be expected to have Santa Rican pesos. This would have opened up fascinating vistas to the imagination."

" We need a few more of those."

" Yes," Dagobert concluded with a sigh, glancing at Iris as he spoke and craning his neck to see what she was reading, " now that Arkwright's gone there's a good opening for an amateur blackmailer around the Pension Victoria. Of course you get bumped off occasionally——"

Iris continued to read *Thérèse Raquin*. It had been at least ten minutes since she had last turned a page.

Half-way through coffee Dagobert remembered a dozen engagements he apparently had for that afternoon. I chased out into the hall after him, fighting against an oppressive feeling in the pit of my stomach. He had already rung for the lift and was adjusting his beret in the hall mirror. A half-finished Gauloise was stuck to his lower lip.

" Where are you going ? " I asked a little breathlessly.

He came out of a deep brood and shrugged expansively. I recognised the gesture and the general manner from films of French detectives. Dagobert must have too, for he immediately relaxed.

" I met a French detective this morning," he said. " He was a remarkably ordinary, straightforward sort of chap. Most disappointing."

" Dagobert. Are you going to see Commissaire Morel ? "

" No, it's only that I've got this game of *boules* and I don't want to be late."

" Dagobert," I repeated, " I *want* you to go to Commissaire Morel. Please. And at once."

The lift had arrived and he was already opening the door. The unaccustomed champagne at luncheon may have affected me or it may have been Dagobert's persistent cheerfulness. But something made me feel uneasy and on edge. I have already explained that my intuitions are almost always wrong and the present one was not exceptional. Panic is an impossible thing to analyse, especially in yourself. I only know that it crouched somewhere behind me from the moment that I saw Dagobert's head descending in the lift that afternoon. It coloured and distorted my impressions until the time when the nightmare finally lifted. . . .

For it had suddenly become just that, a nightmare. Why it had become so at this arbitrary moment I cannot understand. We had received the very real shock of two deaths, but even after Mrs. Andrioli had been found poisoned, appalling though that was, I had been able to treat the situation as a kind of intellectual problem. Now it was no longer something to be dealt with by the intellect, by lists and motives and alibis. It had become something I longed only to escape from, blindly, without thought, almost without curiosity. I have heard that soldiers who have acquitted themselves with courage during the actual dangers of battle will sometimes awaken years later, in the security of a suburban bedroom, sweating with fear in retrospect, suffered for the first time.

On this sunny afternoon, after an excellent luncheon and a bottle of champagne with the man I happen to be in love with, I was inexplicably stricken with terror of a kind which two actual deaths had not until now caused.

Dagobert had flatly refused to let me come with him. He stuck to his story about *boules* and advised me to carry on the " good work " I had done that morning.

" Try eliminating people the other way around," he had suggested, more, I imagine, in an effort to find something for me to do than as a serious proposal. " Start where you finish. Obviously Joe did it. Then assume for a moment that the police doctor knows his business and that Mrs. Andrioli died quite simply by accident. That adds to your list of suspects those you had eliminated because they could not have poisoned the mussels. Your potential murderer is now : Joe, Elinor, Iris, Henry or Juan. Now make a further assumption : assume that the motive has nothing to do with blackmail. Your potential murderers are the same five plus those Arkwright wasn't blackmailing, namely : you, Sophie and Mrs. Andrioli."

" While we're about it," I'd said, " why not add the ones that have an alibi : in other words, you, Dompierre, Suzette and Don Diego ? "

" That, Jane, is a very sound suggestion," he had said, pressing the lift button.

I had watched him disappear, struggling against that unreasoned tremor of fear I have already lengthily described. I wandered upstairs to our room, less with the intention of filling in any more pages of futile conjecture than because I couldn't think of anything else to do. The french windows leading on to our balcony were open and a breeze was blowing in from the sea. It was probably the mistral or perhaps it was the sirocco ; I am vague about which is which. At any rate they are both notorious for adversely affecting one's morale.

I walked out onto the balcony. The air was balmy yet fresh, walking weather rather than swimming. The sea was choppy and of that intense emerald green merging into indigo blue that one sneers at in picture postcards. The line of Cap Ferrat rising in tiers of olive green, the shoulder of Mont Boron cutting off the bay of Villefranche, the hill of the Observatoire, dark green against a blue luminous sky, made one of those Provençal canvasses of Cézanne which, in the Tate Gallery, make you sick with longing for the Mediterranean. I pinched myself, just to remember where I was.

I glanced down at the Promenade beneath. Dagobert was crossing the road. A taxi was parked just opposite. I saw the driver, a pleasant-looking ruffian with an immense white moustache and a bald head, wearing battle dress trousers supported by braces and instead of a shirt a white under-vest, greet him like a long-lost brother and open the taxi door. A moment later the taxi drove off with Dagobert in it.

I was glad to see that he was no longer forced to stand in crowded buses !

On the balcony next door Iris was stretched in a deck chair, deep in *Thérèse Raquin*. She was so engrossed that she hadn't at first noticed me. She glanced up at the sound of my departing footstep.

" Have you ever read this thing ? " she said in a tone of mingled wonder and doubt.

I said I thought I had but I'd forgotten it.

" Pierre lent it to me," she explained. " He's trying to educate me, I suppose ! It all seems rather ' French ' to me : about an unwakened young woman with a dull husband. Suddenly she falls in love with a he-man. And, I must say, the things that then go on ! I'll lend it to you afterwards."

She returned to the book with shocked eagerness. I withdrew, changed my shoes and decided to take a long walk.

Chapter

27

THE PROMENADE DES ANGLAIS IS THREE MILES LONG;
I walked clear to the end of it. In theory a brisk walk
clears the mind and restores the spirit. As neither of
these things had happened by the time I reached the end
of the Promenade I determined grimly to walk back
again. By the time I had half retraced my steps
I had at least found a new subject to think about. My
feet hurt.

Brightly I had worn that new pair of *suède* sandals
which had looked so smart yet practical in Raoul's
window in the Avenue de la Victoire. Dagobert had congratulated me on their purchase, but wondered if it might
not have been wiser to have bought them in my own
size. With a further mile and a half to hobble before
I reached home I began to think how depressingly right
he had been.

Cars whizzed past unfeelingly, not one of them, of
course, a taxi, and I wistfully eyed the wicker chairs of
a pavement café, but remembered how fatal it is on these
occasions to falter. Walking in shoes too small for you
is like fighting against the temptation to sleep when
you're snowbound and in danger of freezing to death.
You must go on. If you pause you are lost.

It was at this point that I recognised the new Renault.
It was coming towards me, cruising along the kerb and
couldn't very well avoid my distress signal. Even a *tête-
à-tête* with Henry was preferable to becoming a permanent
cripple. I waved eagerly.

The car stopped, but it wasn't Henry. It was Iris and she was alone. I got in gratefully and she explained that she'd suddenly decided for no reason in particular to take a drive. Like me, Iris had her problems that afternoon and had decided that an excursion would calm her down. Unlike me she had a car to do it in.

In an unbelievably short time we were back again at the end of the Promenade which I had reached with such physical toil. We forked right towards Cannes, as Henry and I had done a few days ago. The dusty plane trees were familiar : I had been here before. In another five minutes we would reach La Réserve with its checked table-cloths and its *salons particuliers* where Henry had been so attentive. Almost by instinct I glanced around to see if a limousine with C.D. plates were following us. Nothing was following us.

For some reason Dagobert's words about history at breakfast yesterday came back to me : " One of these days history is going to repeat itself *once too often.*" My mind was working this way that afternoon. I asked :

" Where are we going ? "

" Nowhere particularly," Iris said, coming out of her brown study. " Anywhere you like. I only wanted to get away from the Pension for a while. We could have tea somewhere."

She had slowed down, though we were already going at less than thirty miles an hour. A faded sign painted on a whitewashed wall stated that La Réserve—*Sa Cave, Sa Cuisine, Ses Spécialités, Son Bar Américain*—was only a kilometre further on. I don't know whether Iris noticed the sign or not, but she suddenly turned right up a narrow side road which said : " St. Isidore, 6 kilometres."

" I believe there's a church there or something that one ought to see," she explained.

" Undoubtedly," I said, struck by her sudden pallor. I have never seen a woman who has just seen a ghost,

but I imagine she would look like Iris at this moment.
Since this sort of thing is catching I asked tremulously :

" Anything the matter ? "

" No. No, of course not. Nothing's the matter,"
she said, steering a little wildly up the narrow ascending
street. She swerved to avoid a dog which was sun-
bathing in the middle of the road. " Everything's the
matter ! "

When she didn't continue I said : " You wouldn't like
to be more explicit ? "

" Men," she said.

" Oh—that ! "

We continued our perilous ascent towards St. Isidore.
Dagobert once gave me two or three lessons in driving.
We broke them off because we felt that to remain on
speaking terms was more important than my learning to
drive. But I remembered about not going round blind
corners on the wrong side of the road. Iris apparently
didn't and this tended to make it hard for me to give my
full attention to what she said.

" I don't understand men," she said.

" No," I agreed. " I think that child's going to dash
across the street. . . . Nor women, either, when you
think of it."

She sighed. " You've got something there, Jane. Me,
for instance."

" Oddly enough you were the one I was thinking about."

The child didn't dash across the street and the road
became wider and less tortuous. We were following a
grey stone wall, covered with bougainvillea. Cypresses
rose behind it. It was the cemetery.

" Henry was half awake when I came in on Sunday
night. He'd been crying. I felt like an absolute bitch."

" Had you been acting like one ? "

" Yes," she nodded.

" Then that might account for it."

" You and Dagobert don't begin to understand people like Henry and I—me. You're too sure of yourselves, you know just what you want."

" On the contrary," I said, " I thought you two went after what you want in a fairly extravert, ruthless way."

She shook her head. " I knew you wouldn't understand. You don't even know what we're looking for. We're looking for . . . for love."

This kind of remark embarrasses me acutely and I said briefly : " I'm sure you find it."

She shook her head again, more violently. " That's where you're wrong ! We don't. We could have, but we let our opportunity slip. We could have found it in each other. Now it's too late."

" Why ? "

" I don't know," she said dully. " It just is. We let each other go and now we can't find each other again. . . . That night in Cannes together after Henry had just come back—that famous night which was supposed to be a kind of honeymoon all over again—it was a complete flop ! We couldn't bear to be alone together. We had nothing to say to each other. We were bored, bored stiff ! We had to get other people to make up foursomes. Even during the daytime when we had a picnic on the beach at Juan-les-Pins we had to pick up another couple to talk to. That night we attached ourselves to a bigger party so we wouldn't have to dance with each other all the time. Naturally we both got stinko and neither of us even remembers going to bed. We were actually *glad* to get back to the Pension Victoria where we knew people."

" You once went to Switzerland together, didn't you ? "

" Yes," she said. " Four years ago, just before we were married. That's when we decided to get married. We had a heavenly time."

"Why don't you go back?" I said. "I mean right away, to-morrow. No, better still, to-day."

"It wouldn't do any good."

I didn't argue. Probably she was right. She began again after we had negotiated the square at St. Isidore and, tacitly forgetting the church, followed the road which led down into the valley of the Var. She said:

"We first met at a tennis club in Streatham that we both belonged to. Henry had just been demobbed, he was twenty-two and he said he was looking for someone to spend his gratuity with. We had a marvellous time. There was a wizard gang in those days at the Club and we had parties every night. Until we went to Switzerland we didn't have time to realise that we were badly enough in love to want to get married. We had a slap-up wedding and the whole gang came. We decided right away that we weren't going to let marriage interfere with our both having a good time. We made a private pact about it. We were both young, attractive and hadn't seen much of the world. Just because we were married, we said, that was no reason for us to become middle-aged and stuffy. Henry had his friends and I had mine. Why should marriage mean giving them up?"

"I don't know," I said, as she waited for me to answer, "but it does."

"It didn't with us. Not even friends of the opposite sex. Especially friends of the opposite sex. That was part of our pact. We used to tell everybody about it. We were going to be really *modern*." Her voice broke slightly on the word.

I remembered from my first meeting with Iris her taste for histrionics; it vitiated what sympathy one might otherwise have felt for her, and I had again to remind myself that over-acting does not necessarily mean having no feelings.

"Modern!" she repeated with dramatic irony.

" The word was very popular," I said, " in Elinor Duffield's youth."

" It must have hit our set in Streatham a generation late," she said with surprising acumen. " I remember the first time—a week after we were married—when we put our code of modern morality into practice. Henry took my best friend, Mildred Hawkes, home after a dance and didn't turn up again until two hours later. I had to laugh about it and tease him and ask him if her technique was as good as mine. I confessed that I'd had a very enjoyable necking-party with one Bill Carfax. We laughed uproariously about it—and then had the row of our lives. Henry smashed up our wedding tea service and I spent the night in tears."

" And that didn't give you a slight indication that there was a catch in it somewhere ? "

She shook her head. " Oh no ! We were much too sophisticated. Besides as time went on it became easier. It *is* fun, you know, having flirtations. We even got to the stage when we'd boast to each other about our conquests, exchange details. To tell the truth they weren't so frightfully damaging," she hastened to add. " They were, well, rather petty and sordid, I suppose, when you think of it. . . . I didn't go *too* far, ever. Henry didn't either, that is I don't think he did, though he used to pretend in public that he was no end of a Lothario. Then about a year and a half ago he got this job in Santa Rica. I couldn't go along because he had to spend most of his time up-country in men's camps or something. Anyway . . . I didn't go. He wrote very regularly and the funny thing is his letters were more affectionate than he himself had been since Switzerland. At first there was a certain amount of silly teasing about the way I was probably carrying on with the boys in the office and about the dark-eyes Senoritas in Santa Rica. Then even that gradually stopped. He said he was missing me dreadfully and what a time we'd have when we met again this year. It was his idea that I come down to Nice and wait for him. He was making plenty of money and why didn't I give up my job and have a few weeks lazing around before he came. I was fed up with London, so I snapped at the idea. The first person I met was Dieudonné Dompierre."

She stopped and seemed to concentrate for a while on the road. I didn't prompt her, knowing that she would eventually continue without prompting. We had turned to the left on descending into the valley and after our pointless detour through St. Isidore we were again on the main Nice-Cannes road.

"You probably won't believe it," she said, "but I didn't particularly flirt with Pierre at first. At first I made rather a set at Major Arkwright, nothing very serious, just, you know . . . I think, yes, I *know* . . . I was a little afraid of Pierre. Even then. He wasn't a bit like the boys I'd known at home. He was so grave and solemn. He kept looking at me, almost as though he didn't like me. When he spoke to me he was half rude. When I smiled he would scowl. You can't *flirt* with a man like Pierre. He doesn't even understand the rules of the game. One day I told him I was interested in music. I'm not, but you have to talk about something. He asked me if I'd like to hear something he'd composed. I said I'd adore to and he played it to me on the piano. It sounded dreadful to me, but, of course, I said it was quite heavenly and he called me a liar. One thing led to another, and eventually to . . ."

Her voice trailed away in a slight shiver. I suggested : "To Beuil ?"

She nodded. "That ghastly night. Jane ! I've never been so frightened in my life ! "

"Why ? " I asked impatiently. "According to Dompierre nothing of a very irrevocable nature took place."

" That ! " she said indifferently. " No. As far as
that goes. . . . Here's something else you probably
won't believe : I'd never been literally unfaithful to
Henry. I wasn't that night. But that was the night
when I realised I was really in love with Pierre. And,
therefore, no longer in love with my own husband ! "

" I think, Iris, you're being a little too intense about
it all," I said.

" That's what *I* thought," she countered. " I said
I'd forget all about it as soon as Henry came. I'd
merely keep Pierre in his place until that time and then
. . . well, we'd see. Maybe they'd get on together and
it would be like those old threesomes back in Streatham.
Just fun. It wasn't. In the first place Henry and I,
well, we started the old game again of pretending we
both had little innocent *affaires de cœur* on the side.
Only this time it was different. I no longer cared
whether Henry's interest in other women was genuine
or not. I still don't. That's the awful part of if.   I
just don't give a damn. He can be picking up one of
those girls in the Brooklyn Bar at this very moment
for all I care. I almost hope he is."

" Have you," I inquired, " ever heard of divorce ? "

She ignored the question. " Only Henry still *does*
care ! " she whispered tensely. " He still loves me,
desperately."

I doubted this, but made no comment.

" I knew for sure on Sunday night when I came in so
late and found he'd been sobbing his heart out. I
knew," she repeated on a rising note of hysteria, " on
the very night when I'd just become Pierre's mistress."

Chapter

28

WE REACHED CAGNES-SUR-MER, WHERE DAGOBERT'S
Uncle Tancred used to have a hand-loom, and looked
vaguely for a place to have tea. As we didn't find one
immediately we drove on to Antibes and did the tour
of the Cap. It was well after six before we turned
round and drove back towards Nice.

Conversation had been desultory since Iris's melodramatic announcement. This was largely my fault.
She was dying to tell me all the delightfully sordid
details and for some reason I was reluctant to hear
them. She was an exasperating young woman. Just
as you began to feel almost sorry for her—sorry for the
silliness which had got her into such emotional straits—
you realised that she was half-enjoying herself. At one
moment she was snivelling over her lost innocence and
youth (she was just twenty-five) and the next moment
she was thinking how shocked and thrilled her friend
Mildred Hawkes would be when she heard about it.

She had persuaded herself that Henry meant all those
affectionate things he had written her from Santa Rica
and that he *needed* her. " He's my *husband*, Jane ! "
she exclaimed with a sob in her voice which made you
want to say roughly : " Why didn't you think of that
before ? " On the other hand, there was Dieudonné
Dompierre, the enigmatic, passionate Latin who was (for
all Iris knew) a genius, who moved depths of passion
and mystery in her soul that she had never dreamed of.
And who *also* needed her. " It's like tearing myself in

217

two, Jane! I can't let Pierre down—not *now*, after. . . ."

" Has he suggested you get a divorce and marry him ? " I asked practically.

" No-o-o," she admitted. " Not exactly. He's a Catholic, you know," she said, as though that explained everything.

" He may be, but you're not. Strictly speaking, you and Henry haven't been married at all, from Dompierre's point of view."

." Really ? " she said, her mind elsewhere. " I told him about that terrible knife-battle in Santa Rica when Henry nearly killed a man. Pierre said it was a pity Henry hadn't got knifed himself. . . ." She shivered and added with a gasp : " Sometimes Pierre's so *brutal*, Jane."

I didn't ask for details and we drove along for a while without speaking. The wind had dropped and the sea, absorbing the last rays of the sun setting in the mountains behind us, had gone like mother-of-pearl shot with grey and pink and pale green. The earth was still warm but from the Var Valley arose a faint curl of mist which sent a slight chill through you and made you wish you'd brought a cardigan. The treachery of the climate at this hour had been one of Mrs. Andrioli's favourite subjects. *Entre chien et loup* had been her pet phrase, and though my dictionary translated this without comment as " dusk," I began to understand more vividly what it meant : around us the friendly dog of daylight disputed dominion with the slinking wolf of night. Doubtless this incursion into etymology was fanciful, but I again felt a return of that uneasiness which had hovered just over my shoulder ever since the lift had disappeared with Dagobert. I wondered where he was. I wondered what he was doing. I wanted suddenly and quite desperately to see him and touch his hand. In brief, I was being almost as silly as Iris.

A signpost said that Nice was only ten kilometres farther on. In other words we'd be home in fifteen minutes. Iris switched on the headlights, but it was still too light for them to have any effect and she switched them off again. She said in an oddly worried tone of voice:

" Do you know that book *Thérèse Raquin.* It's really rather disgusting. I don't think I'll finish it. I can't think why Pierre wanted me to read it. Of course it's a classic, I suppose."

" I had the impression after luncheon you couldn't tear yourself away from it," I said.

" That was the early part. Where there was a lot of leaping into bed. The hero—I suppose you'd call him the hero—reminded me a little of Pierre. Of course he was only a peasant and Pierre belongs to a very old family, but he'd been an artist and, well, I've never read such violent scenes of physical passion ! "

She laughed shortly, colouring with embarrassment. In spite of the American tough novels which were her favourite reading matter, Zola still had the power to shock her.

" What's discouraged you ? " I asked, suddenly remembering the plot of *Thérèse Raquin,* and catching in advance some of the thrill of horror which ran through Iris.

" They—the lover and Thérèse—they murder her husband," she faltered. " So they can go on sleeping together. It's the ghastliest thing I ever read. I—I can't get it out of my mind. . . . And yet it's only a stupid old book. Why did Pierre insist on . . ." Her voice trailed away. She concentrated on the road again, and so did I. " I suppose one *could* go to Switzerland," she said.

I nodded. We were now on that section of the road we had by-passed in coming, and I recognised La Réserve on our right. Iris, deep in other things, had not I believe

been aware that we were passing it. Without thinking
I pointed it out. I felt her stiffen slightly and start.

Afterwards I realised we had gone through St. Isidore
on our outward journey because Iris did not want to
drive past La Réserve. The next moments were much
too crowded for me to analyse her whims.

We were driving fairly fast but the glimpse I caught
as we passed La Réserve made me want to bite my
tongue out for having called her attention to it. The
scene was outwardly a familiar one on the Nice-Cannes
road : a few parked cars, half a dozen people sipping
aperitifs at tables set under the plane trees, the inevitable
game of *boules* along the dusty side-road with the clank
of iron bowls and the eloquent group around the players,
suffering with the contestants, urging the bowls onwards
with cries, groans, gestures of hope and agony, the hot
argument which followed every throw, the appeal to the
measuring rod which restored peace.

The only remarkable detail about the scene was that
one of the parked cars was a taxi and its driver, a bald-
headed man with a colossal white moustache, was gesti-
culating in despair at the shortcomings of the player
who was at that moment bowling. The player, of course,
was Dagobert.

Iris recognised him at the same moment I did. I
caught a glimpse of her out of the corner of my eye, or
at least I think I did. At any rate I heard her gasp.
I also felt the car swerve and heard the screech of brakes.
I had an impression of headlights suddenly flashing on
and off just in front of my eyes, a panic signal. At the
same time there was the sound of splintering glass, the
wrench of metal all mixed up with the sense of hurtling
through space. Actually the space was only a foot or
two, for my head came with a smart rap against the
windscreen. I heard Iris scream—at least I hoped it
was Iris and not me. Then I blacked out completely.

Chapter

29

IT WOULD BE DRAMATICALLY TELLING IF ONE COULD start this chapter with something like : *At the above point Jane's MS. breaks off. What follows was supplied from notes in the possession of Commissaire Morel, edited by Dagobert.*

I suggested this to Dagobert, especially the part about his editing it, but he said the labour entailed would break the continuity of his work on Bertran de Born. And besides (he said) no reader would believe for a moment that anything fatal or even serious would ever happen to me. I don't quite know what he meant by this, but I don't like the implications. It seems to suggest a kind of callousness somewhere, or perhaps a failure on my part to depict my own character sympathetically.

For the exceptional reader who may, for the briefest moment, have worried about what happened to me when Iris crashed the new Renault into an oncoming truck, I hasten to say that it was one of the most disagreeable experiences I ever hope to have. Not only was I frightened to death, but my shoulder was bruised, my forehead was scratched—I was delighted when it even bled a little—and Henry said I was probably "concussed." I had a raging headache, and the doctor said " it was one of the most miraculous escapes he had ever known and that the average woman. . . ."

Dagobert, at this point, tells me that the doctor said exactly the same thing to Iris, who incidentally got off with a sprained wrist and—though I wasn't present that evening to witness it—a mild nervous breakdown.

Dagobert at the time, however, was much less offhand about the business. In fact my most vivid memory of coming to again—I thought it was a few days later, but apparently it was a few seconds later—was the sight of Dagobert's face over mine. He looked so white and frightened that I had to remind him it was me who'd had the accident. When I smiled (bravely) and told him I thought I'd live it was almost worth having been in the smash to see the blaze of relief in his eyes. I remember him during the drive in the taxi back to Nice. He held me in his arms so tightly that, had it not been for fear of hurting his feelings, I should have asked him to relax his grip. I dozed off once or twice during the return journey, awakening to feel his lips brushing my forehead and to glimpse a hard, angry jut around his jaw. When he saw that my eyes were open his expression became tenderness and solicitude itself.

None of this is at all surprising nor (as Dagobert points out) of the faintest interest to anyone. I put it in partly to annoy him and, to be frank, because I rather like to dwell upon it for sentimental reasons of my own.

We were alone in the taxi, Iris having been driven back by one of the *boulistes*, while a nearby garage took care of the unfortunate Renault. These details were vague to me at the time and when I attempted to talk Dagobert tried to quieten me. I did say :

" It was lucky you happened to be on the spot."

He nodded. " Yes, dearest. . . . Close your eyes."

I obeyed, and my mind wandered off—into Somerset, for some reason. We had just come in from a walk to Porlock Weir. It was drizzling and tea was waiting for us in front of a wood fire. It was very cosy and comforting. But there was something wrong, some detail out of place. No, the curtains were drawn and the scones under the cover of the silver dish were golden brown and oozing butter. Something else. . . .

Of course! You couldn't logically say it was lucky that Dagobert had been on the spot. If he hadn't been on the spot in the first place there wouldn't have been an accident! It was when Iris had suddenly seen Dagobert that she let the steering-wheel go—or whatever she had done which had caused the accident. And yet she had seen him lots of times before. It was most perplexing.

" Is Iris all right? " I asked.

" Yes." Under his breath I think he added: " Unfortunately."

" Why did she . . . you know? It's much too difficult to explain."

I dropped off again and immediately found the answer. Iris had never before seen Dagobert *at La Réserve*! It wasn't he, *it was his presence at La Réserve* which had upset her. But why was that? *I* might have felt upset at finding him there, but why should Iris be?

La Réserve had come into it before, somewhere.

" What do we know about La Réserve, Dagobert? " I asked.

Or perhaps I didn't ask the question out loud, for he made no answer. Somebody had been talking about La Réserve the other night at dinner. Dagobert had asked Henry where he heard of it and Henry had said. . . . No, *I* had decided that Henry had heard of it—from Iris. Then Dagobert had asked Iris where she had had dinner on Wednesday, after Arkwright had been murdered. And Iris had looked distressed at the question and not answered. It was on Wednesday evening she'd had the quarrel with Dompierre, packed her luggage, called a taxi and left the Pension Victoria—only to change her mind later in the evening and come back again. The taxi! There was a limited number of taxis in Nice as I had learned this afternoon when my feet hurt. You could trace taxis !

I got tremendously excited and struggled back to the surface.

" Dagobert ! " I cried, " the taxi ! "

It was not the sight of *Dagobert* which had terrified Iris, but the sight of the *taxi-driver* ! Iris, for some reason which was entirely beyond my grasp, did not want her movements of that evening to be known and the taxi-driver knew them ! We should have guessed this days ago. I seemed to be propped up on my elbows now. Dagobert was sitting beside me. I repeated :

" The *taxi*, of course ! How stupid of us. *This* is the very taxi Iris took to the railway station that night ! "

Dagobert grinned anxiously. " This ? " he murmured.

I blinked at him. The taxi seemed to have vanished most irritatingly. I was undressed and in bed in our room at the Pension. There was an ice-pack on my head and a tray beside the bed with chicken broth which I now remembered having eaten some while ago, and poached eggs, half consumed. I could also now remember the doctor and his saying there was not much wrong with me that a good night's sleep wouldn't put right. I had a tearing headache and my time-sense seemed to have got mixed up a bit. It was strangely reminiscent in this respect of that first night out with the U.S. Marines, though much less fun.

" I hope," I said, " you took that taxi-driver's number."

" Yes, and his name," Dagobert reassured me gently. " It's César Brandinelli, and let me congratulate you on your faultless deduction when half unconscious. It *was* César who drove Iris and her luggage from the Pension on that Wednesday evening."

This comforted me so much that I let him ease my head back against the pillows and re-adjust the ice-pack. I closed my eyes and he arranged the lamp so that it did

not shine on my face. I let him give me two pills which
the doctor had left, though I realised they were sleeping
pills and I especially didn't want to go to sleep just now
when I was on the verge of discovering all.

Iris, then, had suddenly recognised César. Good. But
. . . what had La Réserve got to do with it ? La
Réserve worked into it somewhere, that was obvious.

" On the way to Antibes," I yawned drowsily, " we
suddenly went through St. Isidore. There's a church or
something there which one ought to see. Only we didn't
stop to see it. Just before the road off to St. Isidore
there was an advertisement—*sa cave, ses spécialites, son
bar américain* one kilometre. I don't know whether I'm
putting this very clearly, but it's quite important, and
frankly, darling, I'm dreadfully sleepy all at once. Please
forgive me. Iris seemed to be avoiding La Réserve for
some reason. Unpleasant associations ? I *do* wish we
knew."

" César didn't drive Iris to the railway station that
night," Dagobert told me quietly. " He drove her out
to La Réserve."

For some reason this seemed entirely satisfactory. I
smiled at him and closed my eyes with the feeling that
everything was at last clear. It was very pleasant no
longer having to think. Even my headache had gone.
I felt my hand relax in Dagobert's and then I was
deliciously sound asleep. . . .

I had, in the middle of that night, what I thought at
the time was a dream. I had opened my eyes, felt
beside me for Dagobert and not found him. I knew it
was very late because there was no sound of traffic from
the Promenade des Anglais outside, only the quiet lapping
of waves.

A single light was on in the room, on the table over
by the window. It was heavily shaded with a coloured

silk handkerchief of Dagobert's so that it would not disturb me. Dagobert himself was sitting beside the open window leading on to the balcony. He had a stick or something in his hand, one end of which he was tucking under his right arm, while he rested the other end against the balcony ironwork. What interested me about the performance was that he was flinging his free arm—his left arm—around. With his left hand he seemed to be waving good-bye to someone who was invisible. It was a very peculiar spectacle.

I closed my eyes again, sorry that I hadn't the energy to go on watching it. Just as I went back to sleep I realised what the stick-like object was.

It was a rifle.

Chapter

30

" THE RIFLE ! " I EXCLAIMED SUDDENLY, SITTING BOLT
upright in bed.

The sun was blazing into the room; the windows
were wide open and the smell of sea air was mixed with
the smell of the carnations and syringa Dagobert and
Mrs. Camellini had put everywhere. Our battered but
generally accurate alarm clock said eleven-thirty. It had
taken a motor smash and two veronal tablets to do it,
but I had had the best night's sleep since our arrival in
Nice. Dagobert, in the arm-chair drawn up beside the
bed, looked up from Bertram de Born as though he were
glad to see me.

" The *rifle !* " I repeated. " And don't say, ' what
rifle ' ! "

" That's the trouble with living with a woman who
knows exactly what you're going to say," Dagobert
complained. " It takes the adventure out of conversation. How do you feel ? "

" Oh, no, you don't ! " I said. " I feel very well,
thank you. Where is it ? "

" In that case you'll want breakfast. I'll ring for it.
The doctor said you were to be kept very quiet."

" You know the best way to keep me quiet."

He sighed in resignation. " I took the rifle along to
a man I know. My ballistics are nearly as rusty as it was.
In fact I'm very vague about what ballistics means.
That's why . . ."

He shrugged, beginning to stammer slightly. He had stopped smiling and I saw that his face was drawn and tired. He had not, like me, slept for fifteen hours.

" That's why I thought p-perhaps the best thing would be to—to—you know . . ." He appealed to me. The crease in his high forehead was painfully pronounced. " To stop pretending that one is an amateur detective and—and, well, m-mind one's own business, as it were."

I sank back cautiously against the bolster. " Dagobert," I said, " you *know* who murdered Hugh Arkwright."

He lighted a cigarette ; his hands were shaking. The stammer became more pronounced. " Well, no, actually I don't. But one has theories, several theories as a matter of fact . . . some good ones that one doesn't much like, and some bad ones which one prefers. . . . I don't seem to be expressing myself very glibly this morning."

" No," I agreed thoughtfully.

Breakfast came. It included two perfectly boiled eggs and several times the normal butter ration. Dagobert poured out my coffee, insisting that I have it in bed, though in reality I had never felt—except for a tendency to shake slightly—fitter. Dagobert said, cheering up, or at least pretending to :

" It's probably like one of those situations where reader and detective have both been put in possession of the same facts. The detective knows who did it ; the reader pits his brains against the detective and tries to guess. Only in this case the reader has probably guessed the answer, while I haven't." He took a sip of my coffee. " There's a letter for us from your mother this morning. She trusts we're having better weather than they are at home and that we're getting enough to eat."

He read the letter out loud while I ate my boiled

eggs. We discussed the new tulips which were such a success and her continuing war to the death against snails. Finally he said :

" I suppose you want to know why the gun was rusty ? "

I nodded. " Was it the one stolen from Dompierre ? "

" Oddly enough, I forgot to ask him." He frowned. " It was rusty because César and I fished it out of the swamp behind La Réserve where Iris had thrown it on Wednesday night." He had risen and was pacing aimlessly around, kicking furniture. " Somebody ought to break that silly woman's neck. Perhaps Henry or Dompierre will some day. To steal a gun shortly after someone's been shot, put it in your suit-case, call a taxi, let the taxi-driver even handle the suit-case so he'd notice how heavy it was, drive to the station, change your mind half-way there and ask the driver to drive you out anywhere he can think of along the coast, have him stop at his own favourite bowling club, La Réserve, pretend you want your luggage to be brought in, then after dinner disappear into the darkness behind the place with a suit-case, chuck the gun into the rushes of the nearest swamp, return with the suit-case several pounds lighter, let the same driver not only handle the suit-case again, but also drive you back to the Pension Victoria late that evening, all the time looking as though you were frightened to death . . ." His voice continued to rise angrily. " And imagine you can get away with it ! "

I pointed out the wall which separated our room from the Makepeaces ; he said he'd be delighted if Iris knew exactly what he thought of her !

" She nearly did get away with it," I reminded him.

" That's true."

" Why wasn't César more suspicious ? " I asked curiously.

" He was. Only he thought . . ." Dagobert paused,

then hurried on, " he thought she'd had a still-born baby she was trying to dispose of without anybody knowing. César's mind works that way."

" If," I said, " Iris was clever enough to convey that impression she's not quite so silly as you assume."

" She must be," Dagobert grumbled. He added less roughly, " She's very pretty."

" Murderesses," I began, " often . . ."

I was interrupted by a knock on the door. It was Sophie, come to see how I was. She had brought me an immense box of chocolates, and Elinor followed with roses. I explained that I was receiving such lovely presents under false pretences and accepted them eagerly. Sophie said she just loved my bed jacket and Elinor promised to get her one like it. They wouldn't stay as that would tire me. I opened the chocolates and begged them to sit down. In the midst of this feminine chatter Dagobert escaped.

I got out of bed and we sat under the striped awning on the balcony. Glancing down, I saw Dagobert emerge from the building with a man I had never seen before. He was a brisk, rather tall man in the middle thirties in a chalk-striped flannel suit. He wore horn-rimmed spectacles, a grey felt hat and looked English.

I wondered idly who he was and how many other friends Dagobert had made in these last few days he hadn't told me about.

Elinor was saying : " As a matter of fact, Jane, you have a third visitor this morning — only he's too shy to come in."

" I'm sorry," I shook myself slightly, " I'd love to see him. Do ask him . . ."

I'd meant to add " some time " ; in fact still thinking of what Dagobert had just told me, I hadn't really meant anything except to make sociable sounds. Sophie immediately gulped down the chocolate she'd been nibbling

and ran to the door. Elinor gave me a " look." It
was half smile, half shrug.

" I think it's going to be all right," she murmured.
" In fact I know it is."

A moment later Sophie ushered Joe into the room.
If Joe was shy he only betrayed the fact by a slightly
heightened colour, caused less by my presence in négligé,
I imagine, than by that of Sophie and Elinor.

" Say, what's this I hear about you smashing up perfectly good Renaults ? " he greeted me. " You wanna
watch that."

He had brought along a bottle of Courvoisier V.S.O.P.,
which he told me was " Napoleon " brandy and just the
stuff when you had automobile accidents. He got it
wholesale.

I was touched. We decided against opening the bottle
immediately and compromised by finishing Sophie's chocolates, thus spoiling our luncheon. Joe had exciting news.
He had just done a deal. He had sold his interest in
the Brooklyn Bar to " another mug " at a very satisfactory profit and had become " a gentleman of leisure."
He wasn't quite sure what a gentleman of leisure did in
his leisure time but he was looking forward to standing
on the street corner with his hands in his pockets, whistling
at the girls. Sophie laughed happily at this kind of conversation, and Elinor, a little more hesitantly, managed
to join in. I began to admire Elinor.

They stayed for half an hour, insisted that I would
be mad to come down to luncheon and that they'd bring
it up themselves, with the new *Reader's Digest*, *Time*
and *Life*. Dagobert hadn't come back yet and I was
sorry to see them go. I realised I didn't want to be
left alone.

When Joe was at the door I suddenly said to him :
" Would you mind lingering for a moment ? "

He began to say something facetious, re-considered it

and came in again. He glanced at my face and then closed the door behind him.

" I don't know how to say this," I began, " for several reasons."

He grinned. " A favourite line is to start with : I'm old enough to be your sister."

" That kind of thing," I nodded. " You have already grasped the fact that I'm going to be impertinent. I hope you'll be very happy."

" Did—did Mrs. Duffield tell you ? "

" More or less."

He blushed, but looked pleased with himself. " The old lady, I guess, is okay at that," he said. " When you get used to her. Just figure it—me, marrying into the Duffield family. Maybe I'm a snob at that, thinking along these lines. But she's a good kid. Funny thing is, I love her. First time in my life it ever struck me like that. You wanta *protect* her."

" Yes," I agreed slowly. " I imagine you'll do that."

" You bet I will ! "

" I rather thought so. You know she had a sort of nervous breakdown before she came to Europe."

" Sure. She told me . . ." He stuck his hands into his pockets. " You know, they're a screwy pair in some ways," he said. " At first Sophie didn't want her ma to know anything about it. She wanted to run off and leave the old woman flat. Now she wants us to take her back to Buffalo to live with us. I said sure. But the old lady then takes me aside and advises me to *elope* with Sophie. It'd be more romantic, she figures. As for her, she'll drift around Europe for a while, looking at museums. ' You don't want to live with your mother-in-law, Joe ! ' she says . . ." He shrugged cheerfully. " It'll work out, I guess."

He removed his hands from his pockets, and thinking he was about to take his departure, I held out my own.

" Yes, I guess it will work out," I said.

I was aware that I was feeling slightly sentimental, though why I should be sentimental about people so admirably fitted to take care of themselves as Joe Orsini and the Duffields, I couldn't imagine. To part on a more practical note, I said :

" I haven't seen the paper this morning. Has the Brigade Mobile caught up with Juan Moro yet ? "

He shook his head. " Nope. I saw Don Diego this morning. According to Don Diego," he added, " *they never will*, either."

" That's a funny thing to say."

" Yeah," Joe drawled thoughtfully. " He said it in a funny way, too."

Chapter

31

IT WAS ABSURD KEEPING TO MY ROOM ALL DAY, EVEN with the armfuls of magazines people had brought me. At about five o'clock that afternoon, after Mrs. Camellini had brought my tea, I realised it was not only absurd, but impossible.

Dagobert believed I had taken the pills which, according to him, the doctor insisted I take. I hadn't, for I knew they were merely sleeping tablets, and I gradually became obsessed by the suspicion that Dagobert wanted me to sleep . . . until it was all over. Obviously this was the whim of an invalid, but it gained possession of me until I could think of nothing else.

I was being kept in the dark. I was being shielded. It was like a serious operation after which I was to wake up to be told with reassuring smiles that it was now all over—nothing more to worry about.

Though I was not an invalid, I was, by allowing myself to be treated like one, rapidly acquiring the invalid's morbid sensitiveness.

I decided suddenly that Dagobert was in mortal danger. Where had he been since luncheon ? Normally he came in about now.

I chain-smoked and took to haunting the balcony. The only person I recognised was Mrs. Camellini, emerging from the Pension with her shopping bag. It was nearly half-past five ; exactly one week ago at this hour Hugh Arkwright had been shot. Next door Iris and Henry were stirring. I could hear the murmur of their voices. Oddly enough, I thought I smelled burning paper, exactly as I had done before Arkwright's death. This, as it happens, was not a hallucination; I had tossed a half-extinguished cigarette in our own waste-paper basket.

At that moment Dompierre, on the floor below, began playing his piano, and I reached the climax of absurdity. He was playing the Bach-Brahms *chaconne*. My heart stopped beating; the depths of a diseased imagination are unfathomable.

I did the first sensible thing I'd done in hours. I put on my shoes and went out.

I went out in theory for that brisk walk which had done me so little good yesterday. Actually, of course, I was looking for Dagobert. I started vaguely in the direction of the Universal School, but changed my mind and walked up the Rue Ravel. The Brooklyn Bar was almost empty. Through the open doors I saw Suzette yawning over a glass of tomato juice at the bar. I paused to ask her if she'd seen Dagobert.

" It is against the rules of the establishment to answer questions like that," she shrugged, but noting the disappointment on my face added : " *Il était là, il y a dix minutes.*"

" *Là ?* " I repeated, wondering where " there " was.

" Here," she translated.

" Oh."

I sounded so bewildered that she laughed. " Not with a little girl ! He was talking with *ce salaud de Don Diègue*. They go, I think, to the Consulate."

" Thank you. It doesn't matter especially."

She laughed at me again ; I wasn't deceiving Suzette this afternoon. " I was one time in love, *moi aussi*," she said, shuddering at the memory. " It was a terrible thing. It was this Joe Orsini, but . . ." She shrugged with recovered equanimity and started to make up her mouth.

I began to go. She said, still rouging her lips :

" Do you think someone was poisoning Mrs. Andrioli with the *moules* ? "

I stared at her ; she continued with her lips, getting little streaks of red on her teeth. " No," I said. " The police say it was entirely accidental."

" I think maybe someone was trying to poison Don Diego," she suggested as though the thought was not entirely displeasing. "They were for him, the *moules*, no ?"

" Yes, but——"

" Maybe not," she sighed. " It is a very strange thing that two times now someone is maybe trying to kill Don Diego and both times someone else is getting killed instead."

" Don't say things like that ! " I muttered, starting up the street again.

I walked with restraint, aware that Suzette was watching me. When I reached the corner I turned it and increased my pace. I took the next side street through to the Boulevard Victor Hugo and turned left up the wide tree-lined street. It was a quiet, dignified part of Nice, with little traffic and, except for a few bookshops and music publishers, few business premises. From the first floor window ledge of a large building, once an hotel but now transformed into flats. I recognised the flag of Santa Rica, drooping on its flag pole. I walked past the entrance and read the brass plate : *Consulado de la Santa Rica, Premier Etage.* I walked on, crossed the street, and walked back again. From across the street I could see the windows of the Consulate and though it was actually impossible to distinguish anything behind them I fancied I saw the shadow of a man occasionally cross them. My imagination at once transformed this shadow into Dagobert.

I crossed the street again and repassed the door. There was no possible excuse I could think of for ringing the

bell. It was after six and I couldn't even pretend I
wanted to make some routine inquiry about Santa Rica.
I began to feel slightly foolish. I must have looked
foolish too ; for a woman with a child from some other
flat in the building came out of the door, glanced at me
curiously and asked if I was looking for any especial
address.

I said no, thank you, and pretended to study the window
of the music publishers next door. I remained engrossed
in the titles of sheet music until she had disappeared.
Then I walked past the Consulate again.

I hadn't consciously been taking in the sheet music
next door, but certain titles had impressed themselves as
it were on my retina. One of the titles was J. S. Bach—
Chaconne en Ré Mineur arranged by Johannes Brahms.
But there had been something more to it than that and
it was this something more which had set my heart
thumping again. I went back and stared. As I stared
my heart thumped faster than ever. I was remembering
in a distorted way how Dagobert had asked Dompierre
what arrangement of the *chaconne* he had played. Mixed
with this were those odd gestures of Dagobert's late last
night, when with his left hand he seemed to be waving
to someone while with his right he aimed the rifle.

The front door of the building was open and one
climbed wide, worn marble steps to the Consulate on the
first floor. I climbed them rapidly, knowing that I must
find Dagobert at once and tell him what I had just seen.

The Brahms arrangement of the Bach *chaconne* is
for left hand only.

Chapter

32

Don Diego opened the door himself. Beyond him in the dark, heavily furnished room, Dagobert was standing by the ugly marble chimney-piece. He looked blank and shocked by my sudden apparition, though he immediately disguised the fact.

Two glasses of whisky stood on the mantelpiece; Dagobert's, I noticed, was untouched. Don Diego recovered his manners before Dagobert did. He smiled pleasantly and bowed, though his pale face remained unnaturally flushed.

"This is indeed a charming surprise," he said, talking exactly like a suave villain in old-fashioned melodrama.

"Yes," Dagobert agreed shortly.

Don Diego looked quickly into the empty hall and closed the heavy door behind me. I sat down at his invitation and carefully avoided Dagobert's eyes. I knew without looking that they were angrily signalling me to get out.

"I hope I'm not disturbing you," I murmured.

"In a way," Dagobert admitted.

"On the contrary," Don Diego said smoothly. "I can offer you an excellent Tio Pepe or, if you prefer, a Dry Martini. Do you and your husband always work together? I should imagine that such a charming team-mate would be invaluable in his profession."

"What profession would that be?" I asked cautiously.

"We were just getting around to that when you

arrived," Dagobert said, finally resigned to the fact that I was here to stay.

Don Diego had poured out the Tio Pepe. " A polite description might be, er—' private investigator ', don't you think ? The sherry is not poisoned," he smiled, handing it to me, " like the mussels the other night."

" Since you put it so nicely, thank you," I said, accepting the glass. " What's he investigating ? "

" Up until now the movements of my servant Juan Moro. Personally I should have thought these were more the concern of the Securité Nationale, but it would seem no. I have shown him the route by which Juan escaped into the courtyard and the wall over which Juan climbed, but this leaves him unsatisfied. It satisfied Commissaire Morel, but not your husband."

He wandered around the room as he spoke, stroking his thin moustache and straightening an odd piece of bric-à-brac. There was no nervousness in his manner, but at times he would dart a glance at Dagobert or at me, as though trying to sum us up. I felt as though I were in a poker game in which I not only didn't know what cards the others held, but didn't even know those I held myself.

" It is for this reason," he continued, " that I ask myself if your husband is really a detective working for the police or whether he is not—how shall I put it ?—a ' business man ' working for himself."

" He means," Dagobert translated, " that I'm black-mailing him."

Don Diego clicked his teeth in reproof. " A word which has always distressed me," he said, getting suaver and suaver, " and a profession, I should imagine, not without its personal dangers. You tell me that the Colonel Arkwright was also in this profession."

" I keep telling people things they already know," Dagobert said.

" Ah yes, of course," Don Diego shrugged. " That stupid business of Juan and the chambermaid at the Pension Victoria. One forgets."

" Tell me about that, now that you've remembered," Dagobert suggested.

Don Diego went through the motions of thought. " These things, *vous savez*," he said, smiling apologetically towards me, "happen. There was a baby and as Juan was connected with the Consulate it seemed best that it should receive no publicity. Juan paid this blackmailer a few thousand francs for this reason. Naturally I repaid Juan this money because he only gets five thousand a week."

" *Got*," Dagobert corrected.

" Got . . . You will forgive my English, please."

" Your English," said Dagobert. " does honour to the Universal School where you learnt it . . . You only repaid Juan on this one occasion, I suppose ? "

This time Don Diego's frown of thoughtfulness was more convincing. He paused in his wanderings to refill his empty whisky glass. He took a sip and said : " I think it was only once. I don't remember very clearly. It was two or three years ago. The sum was unimportant. Why do you ask ? "

There was a large Dresden china clock on the chimney-piece. It said nine minutes to seven, and for the first time I heard its wheezy tick. Each time it ticked it sounded as though it were making a desperate effort which might be its last.

" Because," Dagobert said, " Juan went on paying Arkwright regularly up to the day of his death."

" No ! " Don Diego exclaimed in surprise. " I wish I had known this. Poor Juan—I could perhaps have helped him. It is a dreadful thing to be bled by a black-mailer," he added in a softer voice, staring at Dagobert. " And for such a little thing as this baby who may not have been Juan's after all."

" The really dreadful part of it," Dagobert said, lighting a cigarette, " is that Juan was paying Arkwright ten thousand francs a week—twice as much as he was earning ! "

" But—but how could this thing be ! " Don Diego spluttered, his English deteriorating.

" How, indeed ? "

" This you can have no way of knowing," he said at last. He turned to me. " This I think your husband is making up, yes ? "

" It seems a rather generous sum," I hedged.

" Exactly so ! It is a sum which makes nonsense ! For one baby . . ." He laughed. " Ha, ha, ha ! For one little baby. No, señor, this is nonsense."

" It had nothing to do with a baby," Dagobert said patiently. " Since you seem to know so little of your servant's activities, I'll enlighten you. Three years ago in Monte Carlo, Juan Moro killed a man. The man's name was Marcel de Poiligny and he was living in a suite at the Hotel de Paris with his wife, Paulette who had been a film actress and one of the prettiest young women in France. Paulette was also one of the most unfaithful young women in France and it was generally believed that Marcel de Poiligny committed suicide for this reason. He was found with a revolver—his own revolver, covered with his own fingerprints—one morning in the bathroom. You must remember the tragedy. It caused quite a stir at the time."

Don Diego nodded. His face was expressionless.

" But of course, I was forgetting," Dagobert continued, rising and fingering his untouched whisky glass, " you and Juan were also staying at the Hotel de Paris at the time."

" The verdict was suicide. Now that you mention it I remember perfectly."

" The verdict was suicide for a number of reasons. In

the first place, murder still causes more scandal than suicide. In the second place, Juan, as your servant, had a kind of diplomatic status. In the third place the police couldn't prove it wasn't suicide—in spite of the fact (unpublished) that Marcel de Poiligny was left-handed and the finger-prints on his revolver were those of his right hand. But Juan Moro killed him and somehow Arkwright found this out. Or guessed it. If he guessed it, it was a lucky guess. For it brought him in ten thousand francs a week—until the day of his own murder."

"None of this do I for one moment believe," Don Diego said slowly. "Though it would be interesting to me to know where you think you have learned all of these fanciful details. I think what you say is libellous and that if I telephoned for the police . . ."

He stopped suddenly and sat down. Though it was actually a little chilly in the room there were beads of sweat on his bald forehead. I wondered if he had suddenly thought the same thing I myself had suddenly thought : that it was from the police themselves that Dagobert had learned these details.

"It is a pity that Juan has escaped," he murmured, eyeing Dagobert speculatively. "Otherwise you might try to blackmail him as you say this Arkwright did."

"Yes . . ."

Again I heard the clock wheezing. This time it struck—seven—and all three of us jumped. Dagobert was clearly waiting for Don Diego to speak next, and it became a conflict of wills who should make the next verbal move. To be fair, both men were now sweating.

"In other words," Don Diego finally gave in, "you believe like Morel that it was after all Juan who fired the gun . . . But that he didn't fire it at me . . . That he fired it at Arkwright . . ."

" As you said at dinner the other night," Dagobert reminded him non-committally, " *Juan wouldn't have missed.*"

" No . . . I wish you'd have a drink. A cigarette perhaps." He turned to me, removed his gold cigarette case, snapped it open and then forgot what he'd meant to do.

" You understand," he said, " that if any of this were true . . . it would be awkward for me. Juan Moro was my servant . . . a member of the Consular staff. There are diplomatic reasons why . . . but all this you understand . . . I would be willing, in order to avoid . . . It is very difficult to say."

" You would be willing to pay me to forget all about it," Dagobert suggested.

" For Juan Moro's sake . . . for the sake, shall we say, of Santa Rica ? Within reason. You know that my salary has been cut recently. Of course Juan Moro is my responsibility only morally, but because of this . . ."

" Where is Juan Moro ? " Dagobert snapped suddenly.

" Where is he ? " The podgy, manicured hands which had grasped the arms of the chair tightened and relaxed. " But who knows . . . Italy ? Switzerland ? They have not, I understand, found him."

" Nor, I believe you remarked at the Brooklyn Bar, *will* they find him."

Dagobert was now prowling round the room and it was Don Diego who sat and watched. I saw Dagobert's hand brush the knob of a door which led into an inner room, move on and brush against another door-knob, like a blind man feeling his way to escape. He turned on Don Diego and said :

" You were Paulette de Poiligny's lover ! It was *you* whom Marcel de Poiligny had threatened to shoot, whom he would have shot had not Juan shot him first ! "

" Can I be responsible for the devotion of my servant ? "

Don Diego rose, and the corners of his mouth twitched. "Next," he continued with an irony which was handicapped by the sudden dryness of his throat. "next you will say that I ordered Juan to murder Arkwright!"

"*Did you?*"

"Now you become quite silly. A moment ago you are talking business. This I am willing to listen to, but not silliness. For the sake of Juan Moro's memory ..."

"*Where* is Juan Moro?"

I saw Dagobert's drawn face as he reiterated the question. It shone with sweat in the deepening shadows of the vast room. I saw his eyes and the intolerable fear in them, and I suddenly read his thoughts as clearly as if he had spoken them aloud. I think Don Diego did, too, for such fear communicates itself. He began to shake and supported himself against a mahogany stand which bore a fern in a vase. The vase toppled and fell with a thud to the thick carpet.

Dagobert believed he knew why the police had never caught Juan Moro. He believed it was because Juan Moro had never left this flat ...

And he believed that Juan Moro was dead.

I had started violently as the vase struck the floor and for a second I hadn't noticed that the door behind Dagobert was opening. I began to scream, shamelessly and at the top of my voice. I like to believe that this primitive behaviour served some useful purpose, though I think Dagobert had actually seen the man behind him in a wall mirror.

At any rate he ducked just as Juan Moro leapt for his back. Don Diego rushed forward and I caught a glimpse of Dagobert, looking happy for the first time during the interview, swinging a chair which crashed over the Vice-Consul's head.

Meanwhile, following my husband's instructions and not arguing, I was at last doing something useful. I was

scrambling down the worn marble stairs into the Boulevard Victor Hugo, shouting " Help ".   I almost fell into
the arms of the tall man with horn-rimmed spectacles
whom I had seen talking with Dagobert outside the
Pension Victoria this morning, and whom I had taken
for a typical Englishman.   He was Commissaire Morel.

Chapter

33

COMMISSAIRE MOREL'S ENGLISH WAS RATHER LIKE MY
French ; strictly speaking, we hadn't a language in
common, and it was his manner rather than what he said
which reassured me. He blew a little whistle and gendarmes materialised comfortingly from the tree-lined boulevard. He seemed to think there was nothing to worry
about at the Santa Rican Consulate and made me go
back with him in his small Peugeot to the Pension.

I, protesting, explained that Dagobert had found Juan
Moro for him. He seemed pleased, but not very excited.
I think he said that the de Poiligny murder would remain,
as it had always been, one of those things the police were
sure of but could never prove. It was one of the many
dark pages in Don Diego's past which the Commissiare
had been studying this last week.

I said a little wildly : " But Juan also murdered Arkwright under Don Diego's instructions ! " He obviously
didn't understand, for he smiled and said : " *Oui*, now
we go arrest *l'assassin* ! " I tried to explain that in
that case we were going in the wrong direction ; but by
the time I had made myself understood we had reached
the Pension.

In one respect Commissaire Morel's optimism was justified. Dagobert reached the Pension at the same moment
we did. His necktie was torn, his hair was all over the
place, he had a black eye and he was out of breath. But
he was still in one piece.

" I was wrong about the back wall," he murmured.

" You *can* climb over it. . . . What about the gun ? I mean . . . *est-ce le fusil ?* "

Morel nodded. " *C'est bien celui-là qui l'a tué.*"

" *Donc . . . allons-y ?* " Dagobert shrugged and gave it up. His face had fallen and he followed us into the lift in a resigned way.

" What about Don Diego ? " I insisted.

Dagobert looked unhappy. " He was one of my good ideas which didn't work out . . . though I daresay we'll have a new Santa Rican Vice-Consul in Nice shortly. Why aren't you in bed, by the way ? "

The lift had stopped at the third floor and we got out, Dagobert still lagging behind. The first person we saw was Iris, tripping up the corridor from Dompierre's room. Dompierre was following her reluctantly. Commissaire Morel looked much more like a new guest than a policeman, but at the sight of him Iris stopped dead in her tracks and seized Dompierre's hand. Dompierre tried to wrench himself away and continue towards the sitting-room. At a word from Morel he, too, stopped dead in his tracks.

I remembered suddenly that I hadn't said a word to Dagobert about the *chaconne* arrangement *for left hand only*. I realised with equal suddenness that Dagobert, of course, had known about this all along. It was another of his ideas. . . .

Commissaire Morel said something in French to Iris, at which she looked blank. He asked Dagobert to translate. When Dagobert is worried, it sometimes takes the form of bad temper, and it seemed to me that he felt better when he rounded angrily on Iris.

" When did you take Dompierre's gun from his room ? " he growled. " This is Commissaire Morel and he is investigating a murder."

Iris went scarlet, then white, but she made no effort to lie. " About six," she said.

" Go on."

" I saw it. The door was open. Pierre wasn't there."

" Yes," Dagobert nodded. " Dompierre went out for a drink at a quarter to six and came in an hour later—when you had your row together. Why did you take it ? "

This time Iris hesitated. " I—I don't know," she said.

" Don't lie. You thought Pierre had used it."

" No ! " she gasped.

" You realised he used his left hand only when playing that piece and you thought he'd used the other for murdering Major Arkwright. An extremely far-fetched idea, by the way. But from your viewpoint you were trying to protect a murderer ! "

" No ! "

" Whom you were in love with ? "

Iris began to cry. " I—I *had* a row with him," she whimpered, as though this fact completely justified her continuing to love a man she believed to have done murder. " I—I didn't *know* he was . . . I only . . ."

" You only thought he was ! "

Dagobert turned on his heel abruptly and left Iris where she was, tears streaming down her face. Commissaire Morel, who had followed this with difficulty, joined him. Morel led the way into the sitting-room. There were half a dozen people there, strangers except for Elinor, who was reading in one corner. She glanced up at our entrance. I've often wondered what she read in our faces, for she rose instantly and came towards us, keeping the place in her novel with her forefinger.

" You are Commissaire Morel, are you not ? " she said. " I've seen your picture in the newspapers."

Morel looked puzzled and Dagobert briefly translated.

" You speak a little French, don't you, Mrs. Duffield ? " he said anxiously. " I—I must—er—go and change."

" I read French rather poorly," she smiled, holding out the paper-backed novel she was carrying. " I'd much rather you acted as an interpreter, if the Commissaire does not speak English. There's no one in the writing-room, I believe."

She led the way, walking almost briskly. We followed her like three rather awkward guests she was herding into another room. She dropped her novel as she went and I stooped to pick it up. It fell open in the middle, and for some reason I found myself reading a line or two. I wanted something quite impersonal to think about. Dagobert, lingering beside me, pointed mutely to a word on the printed page and sighed. He had actually glanced at this novel previously. Its hero had the rather unusual name of Hippolyte.

" I'm so glad," Elinor was saying, " that I sent the children out to dinner to-night by themselves. . . . It is about Hugh, isn't it ? "

Dagobert nodded.

" You didn't quite believe me the other night when I told you that story about the swimming instructor and the night I spent in Room Six with him, did you ? " she said.

" The room was twelve, I suppose," Dagobert said wearily.

" Yes, of course," Elinor nodded.

" And," Dagobert continued, speaking more like an automaton who repeats meaningless sounds than a man who has something to say, " and the year was not 1927 —two years before Sophie was born, but . . ."

" But 1929," Elinor came to his rescue.

" The old records of the Negresco are still in existence," Dagobert nodded. " That was not to be expected. They do, as a matter of fact, mention a Miss Elinor Hickenfinkle in the spring of 1929. Why did you shoot Arkwright, Mrs. Duffield, why ? "

He said it almost pleadingly, as though even at this last moment she would deny it. She smiled faintly.

"But surely you understand why."

He nodded. "Yes, I think I do. But if you will tell Commissaire Morel. This is France, and French courts understand motives like yours."

She stiffened slightly. It was the first defence she had raised. "If the Commissaire wishes to know how I shot Hugh Arkwright, I am quite willing to tell him," she said coldly. "I was passing Monsieur Dompierre's room on my way to take a bath. His door was open and his back was turned. His rifle was leaning by the cupboard beside the door. I reached in and took it. It was loaded. I remembered suddenly that Hugh returned from school regularly at five-thirty, and this was just at five-thirty. In the bathroom, as you know, there is a window which overlooks the Rue Ravel and a part of the Promenade. I am a good shot and I shot him through the head. I then took a cold bath. Afterwards, finding Monsieur Dompierre's door still open and Monsieur Dompierre not there, I put the rifle back. I don't quite know why I did this, possibly a remnant of my habit of always returning things I borrow."

She had spoken coldly and precisely, almost as though she had rehearsed the speech. Even Commissaire Morel had followed most of it. She concluded in the same tone :

"That surely is all the Commissaire needs to know."

"*Mais sa raison ?*" Morel asked.

Elinor looked suddenly almost as tired as Dagobert. "If he needs a motive, tell him that I was a disappointed, jealous woman. I'd come back after twenty-one years to see a man I once loved. He didn't even recognise me ! Isn't that a motive ? "

"And he made love to others . . ."

"Yes. To my own daughter even. Surely that is a motive ! "

"I suppose so," Dagobert said.

He turned away, and I thought for a moment he was going to leave the room. He looked hopelessly at Morel, who was polishing his horn-rimmed spectacles and murmuring to himself : " *La jalousie . . . oui. Il y a toujours cela.*"

Dagobert turned back from the door and said :

" Mrs. Duffield, if you don't tell the Commissaire the *real* reason why you felt you had to shoot Arkwright, I will."

" He was attempting to seduce my daughter ! Isn't that enough ? "

" Not quite."

She slumped down against the writing desk and raised a hand to her forehead as though her head ached. But she seemed not to have the strength to complete the gesture. The edge had gone from her voice when she said :

" Sophie was strangely drawn to him. One night she even visited his room. How could I be sure that . . . But I *made* sure, didn't I ? Sophie was also *his* daughter . . . "

Chapter

34

Tourette-en-Provence, August, 195—

BAEDEKER, AFTER THE GRUDGING ADMISSION THAT
Tourette is " curious " and " picturesque," immediately
qualified by the *aspect sordide et misérable* crack, passes
on to the *Auberge de la Cigale*, where a simple " repas "
can be obtained for one franc, seventy-five centimes. Our
Baedeker was published in 1907 and Dagobert explained
that we'd have to expect a certain interim rise in price.

I don't know whether he had ever heard of the *Auberge
de la Cigale* or whether some blind instinct leads him to
such places. Actually the Guide Michelin gives the
Auberge de la Cigale its maximum two stars for cuisine
and the Club des Sans Club goes on for about two pages
about it. Last week they put up an A.A. sign.

We had dinner there the first night we arrived. We
had *Queues d'écrivisses à la Nantua, Chapon en pâte belle
aurore*, hearts of artichokes, flanked with asparagus tips,
and a *bombe* drenched in kirsch. I wrote my publishers
the next morning to beg for a small advance on my next
book, and have been writing *Corpse Diplomatique* furiously
ever since.

I have reached that point where I ought, I know, to
enter into detailed explanation. Personally, I can never
follow such explanations, but Dagobert feels I ought to
re-emphasise the fact that no one murdered Mrs. Andrioli.
Her death may, he says, have misled the reader, but it
also misled him—into redoubled and misapplied efforts

to bring the crime to Don Diego's door. He still feels it *ought* to have been Don Diego. Don Diego—through Juan —had been paying Arkwright nearly ten pounds a week for over three years, an income, incidentally, which Arkwright had managed to spend and still leave his wife with the impression that "his tastes were simple." Don Diego, we hear, has been recalled by the new president to Santa Rica and Dagobert feels we still may have at least an *ex*-diplomatic corpse to look forward to. But so far we've seen no reference to further Central American assassinations.

We had a post card the other day of the Buffalo Court-house from Sophia and Joe Orsini. They say "every-thing's swell" and hope they'll run into us when they come to Europe next April. They don't mention Elinor, but April next is the date when she will have regained her liberty. Radio Paris on the *Chaîne Nationale* played Dompierre's Symphonie in Ut mineur last week, but the wireless in the *Café des Sports* over which we have a room had broken down that night.

The most unexpected echo of our holiday in Nice was a long and bitter letter from Iris, who, "after having given up *everything* for the sake of her husband," went back to Streatham with him, "and now, my dear, he wants a divorce! To marry that little tart Mildred Hawkes, who I thought was my *best* friend!"

She goes on for pages, but Dagobert is hurrying me and insists that no one is interested in the fate of Iris Makepeace.

Actually he wants me to stop so that I can go with him to St. Etienne-en-Provence, a village about five kilometres away, up the mule-path. There is an ex-tremely important match to be played this afternoon between the Tourette and the St. Etienne *boules* teams, and as the blacksmith, our star player, is suffering from a liver "crisis," Dagobert has been chosen to play in his place.

THE END

THE PERENNIAL LIBRARY MYSTERY SERIES

Delano Ames

FOR OLD CRIME'S SAKE   P 629, $2.84

MURDER, MAESTRO, PLEASE   P 630, $2.84
"If there is a more engaging couple in modern fiction than Jane and
Dagobert Brown, we have not met them."   —*Scotsman*

E. C. Bentley

TRENT'S LAST CASE   P 440, $2.50
"One of the three best detective stories ever written."
                                    —Agatha Christie

TRENT'S OWN CASE   P 516, $2.25
"I won't waste time saying that the plot is sound and the detection
satisfying. Trent has not altered a scrap and reappears with all his old
humor and charm."   —Dorothy L. Sayers

Gavin Black

A DRAGON FOR CHRISTMAS   P 473, $1.95
"Potent excitement!"   —*New York Herald Tribune*

THE EYES AROUND ME   P 485, $1.95
"I stayed up until all hours last night reading *The Eyes Around Me,*
which is something I do not do very often, but I was so intrigued by the
ingeniousness of Mr. Black's plotting and the witty way in which he spins
his mystery. I can only say that I enjoyed the book enormously."
                                  —F. van Wyck Mason

YOU WANT TO DIE, JOHNNY?   P 472, $1.95
"Gavin Black doesn't just develop a pressure plot in suspense, he adds
uninfected wit, character, charm, and sharp knowledge of the Far East
to make rereading as keen as the first race-through."   —*Book Week*

Nicholas Blake

THE CORPSE IN THE SNOWMAN   P 427, $1.95
"If there is a distinction between the novel and the detective story (which
we do not admit), then this book deserves a high place in both catego-
ries."   —*The New York Times*

THE DREADFUL HOLLOW   P 493, $1.95
"Pace unhurried, characters excellent, reasoning solid."
                                              —*San Francisco Chronicle*

END OF CHAPTER   P 397, $1.95
". . . admirably solid . . . an adroit formal detective puzzle backed up
by firm characterization and a knowing picture of London publishing."
                                              —*The New York Times*

HEAD OF A TRAVELER   P 398, $2.25
"Another grade A detective story of the right old jigsaw persuasion."
                                    —*New York Herald Tribune Book Review*

MINUTE FOR MURDER   P 419, $1.95
"An outstanding mystery novel. Mr. Blake's writing is a delight in
itself."   —*The New York Times*

THE MORNING AFTER DEATH   P 520, $1.95
"One of Blake's best."   —Rex Warner

A PENKNIFE IN MY HEART   P 521, $2.25
"Style brilliant . . . and suspenseful."   —*San Francisco Chronicle*

THE PRIVATE WOUND   P 531, $2.25
[Blake's] best novel in a dozen years . . . . An intensely penetrating study
of sexual passion. . . . A powerful story of murder and its aftermath."
                                    —Anthony Boucher, *The New York Times*

A QUESTION OF PROOF   P 494, $1.95
"The characters in this story are unusually well drawn, and the suspense
is well sustained."   —*The New York Times*

THE SAD VARIETY   P 495, $2.25
"It is a stunner. I read it instead of eating, instead of sleeping."
                                              —Dorothy Salisbury Davis

THERE'S TROUBLE BREWING   P 569, $3.37
"Nigel Strangeways is a puzzling mixture of simplicity and penetration,
but all the more real for that."   —*The Times Literary Supplement*

THOU SHELL OF DEATH   P 428, $1.95
"It has all the virtues of culture, intelligence and sensibility that the most
exacting connoisseur could ask of detective fiction."
                                    —*The Times* [London] *Literary Supplement*

THE WIDOW'S CRUISE   P 399, $2.25

"A stirring suspense. . . . The thrilling tale leaves nothing to be desired."
                                       —*Springfield Republican*

THE WORM OF DEATH   P 400, $2.25

"It [The Worm of Death] is one of Blake's very best—and his best is better than almost anyone's."   —Louis Untermeyer

John & Emery Bonett

A BANNER FOR PEGASUS   P 554, $2.40

"A gem! Beautifully plotted and set. . . . Not only is the murder adroit and deserved, and the detection competent, but the love story is charming."   —Jacques Barzun and Wendell Hertig Taylor

DEAD LION   P 563, $2.40

"A clever plot, authentic background and interesting characters highly recommended this one."   —*New Republic*

Christianna Brand

GREEN FOR DANGER   P 551, $2.50

"You have to reach for the greatest of Great Names (Christie, Carr, Queen . . .) to find Brand's rivals in the devious subtleties of the trade."
                                    —Anthony Boucher

TOUR DE FORCE   P 572, $2.40

"Complete with traps for the over-ingenious, a double-reverse surprise ending and a key clue planted so fairly and obviously that you completely overlook it. If that's your idea of perfect entertainment, then seize at once upon *Tour de Force.*"   —Anthony Boucher, *The New York Times*

James Byrom

OR BE HE DEAD   P 585, $2.84

"A very original tale . . . Well written and steadily entertaining."
—Jacques Barzun & Wendell Hertig Taylor, *A Catalogue of Crime*

Marjorie Carleton

VANISHED   P 559, $2.40

"Exceptional . . . a minor triumph."
  —Jacques Barzun and Wendell Hertig Taylor, *A Catalogue of Crime*

George Harmon Coxe

MURDER WITH PICTURES   P 527, $2.25
"[Coxe] has hit the bull's-eye with his first shot."
                           —*The New York Times*

Edmund Crispin

BURIED FOR PLEASURE   P 506, $2.50
"Absolute and unalloyed delight."
              —Anthony Boucher, *The New York Times*

Lionel Davidson

THE MENORAH MEN   P 592, $2.84
"Of his fellow thriller writers, only John Le Carré shows the same
instinct for the viscera."   —*Chicago Tribune*

NIGHT OF WENCESLAS   P 595, $2.84
"A most ingenious thriller, so enriched with style, wit, and a sense of
serious comedy that it all but transcends its kind."
                           —*The New Yorker*

THE ROSE OF TIBET   P 593, $2.84
"I hadn't realized how much I missed the genuine Adventure story
. . . until I read *The Rose of Tibet*."   —Graham Greene

D. M. Devine

MY BROTHER'S KILLER   P 558, $2.40
"A most enjoyable crime story which I enjoyed reading down to the last
moment."   —Agatha Christie

Kenneth Fearing

THE BIG CLOCK   P 500, $1.95
"It will be some time before chill-hungry clients meet again so rare a
compound of irony, satire, and icy-fingered narrative. *The Big Clock* is
. . . a psychothriller you won't put down."   —*Weekly Book Review*

Andrew Garve

THE ASHES OF LODA   P 430, $1.50
"Garve . . . embellishes a fine fast adventure story with a more credible
picture of the U.S.S.R. than is offered in most thrillers."
                       —*The New York Times Book Review*

Andrew Garve *(cont'd)*

THE CUCKOO LINE AFFAIR P 451, $1.95

". . . an agreeable and ingenious piece of work." —*The New Yorker*

A HERO FOR LEANDA P 429, $1.50

"One can trust Mr. Garve to put a fresh twist to any situation, and the ending is really a lovely surprise." —*The Manchester Guardian*

MURDER THROUGH THE LOOKING GLASS P 449, $1.95

". . . refreshingly out-of-the-way and enjoyable . . . highly recommended to all comers." —*Saturday Review*

NO TEARS FOR HILDA P 441, $1.95

"It starts fine and finishes finer. I got behind on breathing watching Max get not only his man but his woman, too." —Rex Stout

THE RIDDLE OF SAMSON P 450, $1.95

"The story is an excellent one, the people are quite likable, and the writing is superior." —*Springfield Republican*

Michael Gilbert

BLOOD AND JUDGMENT P 446, $1.95

"Gilbert readers need scarcely be told that the characters all come alive at first sight, and that his surpassing talent for narration enhances any plot. . . . Don't miss." —*San Francisco Chronicle*

THE BODY OF A GIRL P 459, $1.95

"Does what a good mystery should do: open up into all kinds of ramifications, with untold menace behind the action. At the end, there is a bang-up climax, and it is a pleasure to see how skilfully Gilbert wraps everything up." —*The New York Times Book Review*

THE DANGER WITHIN P 448, $1.95

"Michael Gilbert has nicely combined some elements of the straight detective story with plenty of action, suspense, and adventure, to produce a superior thriller." —*Saturday Review*

FEAR TO TREAD P 458, $1.95

"Merits serious consideration as a work of art."

—*The New York Times*

Joe Gores

HAMMETT P 631, $2.84

"Joe Gores at his very best. Terse, powerful writing—with the master, Dashiell Hammett, as the protagonist in a novel I think he would have been proud to call his own." —Robert Ludlum

C. W. Grafton

BEYOND A REASONABLE DOUBT P 519, $1.95
"A very ingenious tale of murder . . . a brilliant and gripping narrative."
—Jacques Barzun and Wendell Hertig Taylor

Edward Grierson

THE SECOND MAN P 528, $2.25
"One of the best trial-testimony books to have come along in quite a
while." —*The New Yorker*

Cyril Hare

DEATH IS NO SPORTSMAN P 555, $2.40
"You will be thrilled because it succeeds in placing an ingenious story
in a new and refreshing setting. . . . The identity of the murderer is really
a surprise." —*Daily Mirror*

DEATH WALKS THE WOODS P 556, $2.40
"Here is a fine formal detective story, with a technically brilliant solution
demanding the attention of all connoisseurs of construction."
—Anthony Boucher, *The New York Times Book Review*

AN ENGLISH MURDER P 455, $2.50
"By a long shot, the best crime story I have read for a long time.
Everything is traditional, but originality does not suffer. The setting is
perfect. Full marks to Mr. Hare." —*Irish Press*

TENANT FOR DEATH P 570, $2.84
"The way in which an air of probability is combined both with clear,
terse narrative and with a good deal of subtle suburban atmosphere,
proves the extreme skill of the writer." —*The Spectator*

TRAGEDY AT LAW P 522, $2.25
"An extremely urbane and well-written detective story."
—*The New York Times*

UNTIMELY DEATH P 514, $2.25
"The English detective story at its quiet best, meticulously underplayed,
rich in perceivings of the droll human animal and ready at the last with
a neat surprise which has been there all the while had we but wits to see
it." —*New York Herald Tribune Book Review*

THE WIND BLOWS DEATH P 589, $2.84
"A plot compounded of musical knowledge, a Dickens allusion, and a
subtle point in law is related with delightfully unobtrusive wit, warmth,
and style." —*The New York Times*

Cyril Hare (cont'd)

WITH A BARE BODKIN   P 523, $2.25
"One of the best detective stories published for a long time."
                                        —*The Spectator*

Robert Harling

THE ENORMOUS SHADOW   P 545, $2.50
"In some ways the best spy story of the modern period. . . . The writing
is terse and vivid . . . the ending full of action . . . altogether first-rate."
—Jacques Barzun and Wendell Hertig Taylor, *A Catalogue of Crime*

Matthew Head

THE CABINDA AFFAIR   P 541, $2.25
"An absorbing whodunit and a distinguished novel of atmosphere."
                        —Anthony Boucher, *The New York Times*

THE CONGO VENUS   P 597, $2.84
"Terrific. The dialogue is just plain wonderful."
                                        —*The Boston Globe*

MURDER AT THE FLEA CLUB   P 542, $2.50
"The true delight is in Head's style, its limpid ease combined with humor
and an awesome precision of phrase."   —*San Francisco Chronicle*

M. V. Heberden

ENGAGED TO MURDER   P 533, $2.25
"Smooth plotting."   —*The New York Times*

James Hilton

WAS IT MURDER?   P 501, $1.95
"The story is well planned and well written."
                                        —*The New York Times*

P. M. Hubbard

HIGH TIDE   P 571, $2.40
"A smooth elaboration of mounting horror and danger."
                                        —*Library Journal*

Elspeth Huxley

THE AFRICAN POISON MURDERS   P 540, $2.25
"Obscure venom, manical mutilations, deadly bush fire, thrilling climax compose major opus.... Top-flight."

                 —Saturday Review of Literature

MURDER ON SAFARI   P 587, $2.84
"Right now we'd call Mrs. Huxley a dangerous rival to Agatha Christie."   *—Books*

Francis Iles

BEFORE THE FACT   P 517, $2.50
"Not many 'serious' novelists have produced character studies to compare with Iles's internally terrifying portrait of the murderer in *Before the Fact,* his masterpiece and a work truly deserving the appellation of unique and beyond price."   —Howard Haycraft

MALICE AFORETHOUGHT   P 532, $1.95
"It is a long time since I have read anything so good as *Malice Aforethought,* with its cynical humour, acute criminology, plausible detail and rapid movement. It makes you hug yourself with pleasure."

          —H. C. Harwood, *Saturday Review*

Michael Innes

DEATH BY WATER   P 574, $2.40
"The amount of ironic social criticism and deft characterization of scenes and people would serve another author for six books."

       —Jacques Barzun and Wendell Hertig Taylor

HARE SITTING UP   P 590, $2.84
"There is hardly anyone (in mysteries or mainstream) more exquisitely literate, allusive and Jamesian—and hardly anyone with a firmer sense of melodramatic plot or a more vigorous gift of storytelling."

       —Anthony Boucher, *The New York Times*

THE LONG FAREWELL   P 575, $2.40
"A model of the deft, classic detective story, told in the most wittily diverting prose."   *—The New York Times*

THE MAN FROM THE SEA   P 591, $2.84
"The pace is brisk, the adventures exciting and excitingly told, and above all he keeps to the very end the interesting ambiguity of the man from the sea."   *—New Statesman*

THE SECRET VANGUARD   P 584, $2.84
"Innes . . . has mastered the art of swift, exciting and well-organized narrative."   *—The New York Times*

Mary Kelly

THE SPOILT KILL   P 565, $2.40
"Mary Kelly is a new Dorothy Sayers. . . . [An] exciting new novel."
—Evening News

Lange Lewis

THE BIRTHDAY MURDER   P 518, $1.95
"Almost perfect in its playlike purity and delightful prose."
—Jacques Barzun and Wendell Hertig Taylor

Allan MacKinnon

HOUSE OF DARKNESS   P 582, $2.84
"His best . . . a perfect compendium."
—Jacques Barzun & Wendell Hertig Taylor, A Catalogue of Crime

Arthur Maling

LUCKY DEVIL   P 482, $1.95
"The plot unravels at a fast clip, the writing is breezy and Maling's approach is as fresh as today's stockmarket quotes."
—Louisville Courier Journal

RIPOFF   P 483, $1.95
"A swiftly paced story of today's big business is larded with intrigue as a Ralph Nader-type investigates an insurance scandal and is soon on the run from a hired gun and his brother. . . . Engrossing and credible."
—Booklist

SCHROEDER'S GAME   P 484, $1.95
"As the title indicates, this Schroeder is up to something, and the unravelling of his game is a diverting and sufficiently blood-soaked entertainment."   *—The New Yorker*

Austin Ripley

MINUTE MYSTERIES   P 387, $2.50
More than one hundred of the world's shortest detective stories. Only one possible solution to each case!

Henry Wade

THE DUKE OF YORK'S STEPS　　　　　　P 588, $2.84
"A classic of the golden age."
—Jacques Barzun & Wendell Hertig Taylor, *A Catalogue of Crime*

A DYING FALL　　　　　　　　　　　P 543, $2.50
"One of those expert British suspense jobs . . . it crackles with undercurrents of blackmail, violent passion and murder. Topnotch in its class."
—*Time*

THE HANGING CAPTAIN　　　　　　　P 548, $2.50
"This is a detective story for connoisseurs, for those who value clear thinking and good writing above mere ingenuity and easy thrills."
—*Times Literary Supplement*

Hillary Waugh

LAST SEEN WEARING . . .　　　　　　P 552, $2.40
"A brilliant tour de force."　　　　　　　—Julian Symons

THE MISSING MAN　　　　　　　　　P 553, $2.40
"The quiet detailed police work of Chief Fred C. Fellows, Stockford, Conn., is at its best in *The Missing Man* . . . one of the Chief's toughest cases and one of the best handled."
—Anthony Boucher, *The New York Times Book Review*

Henry Kitchell Webster

WHO IS THE NEXT?　　　　　　　　P 539, $2.25
"A double murder, private-plane piloting, a neat impersonation, and a delicate courtship are adroitly combined by a writer who knows how to use the language."　　—Jacques Barzun and Wendell Hertig Taylor

Anna Mary Wells

MURDERER'S CHOICE　　　　　　　P 534, $2.50
"Good writing, ample action, and excellent character work."
—*Saturday Review of Literature*

A TALENT FOR MURDER　　　　　　P 535, $2.25
"The discovery of the villain is a decided shock."　　—*Books*

Edward Young

THE FIFTH PASSENGER　　　　　　　P 544, $2.25
"Clever and adroit . . . excellent thriller . . ."　　—*Library Journal*

If you enjoyed this book you'll want to know about
THE PERENNIAL LIBRARY MYSTERY SERIES
Buy them at your local bookstore or use this coupon for ordering:

Qty	P number	Price

postage and handling charge $1.00
_____ book(s) @ $0.25

TOTAL

Prices contained in this coupon are Harper & Row invoice prices only. They are subject to change without notice, and in no way reflect the prices at which these books may be sold by other suppliers.

HARPER & ROW, Mail Order Dept. #PMS, 10 East 53rd St., New York, N.Y. 10022.

Please send me the books I have checked above. I am enclosing $_____ which includes a postage and handling charge of $1.00 for the first book and 25¢ for each additional book. Send check or money order. No cash or C.O.D.s please

Name_____

Address_____

City_____ State_____ Zip_____

Please allow 4 weeks for delivery. USA only. This offer expires 1 1/30/83. Please add applicable sales tax.